D0249804

Six Weeks to Toxic

A Novel

Louisa McCormack

KEY PORTER BOOKS

Copyright © 2006 by Louisa McCormack

All rights reserved. No part of this work covered by the copyrights hereon may be reproduced or used in any form or by any means—graphic, electronic or mechanical, including photocopying, recording, taping or information storage and retrieval systems—without the prior written permission of the publisher, or, in case of photocopying or other reprographic copying, a licence from Access Copyright, the Canadian Copyright Licensing Agency, One Yonge Street, Suite 1900, Toronto, Ontario, M6B 3A9.

Library and Archives Canada Cataloguing in Publication

McCormack, Louisa
Six weeks to toxic / Louisa McCormack.

ISBN-10: 1-55263-885-5, ISBN-13: 978-1-55263-885-9

I. Title.

PS8625.C675S59 2007 C813'.6 C2007-901724-X

The publisher gratefully acknowledges the support of the Canada Council for the Arts and the Ontario Arts Council for its publishing program. We acknowledge the support of the Government of Ontario through the Ontario Media Development Corporation's Ontario Book Initiative.

We acknowledge the financial support of the Government of Canada through the Book Publishing Industry Development Program (BPIDP) for our publishing activities.

Key Porter Books Limited
Six Adelaide Street East, Tenth Floor
Toronto, Ontario
Canada M5C 1H6

www.keyporter.com

Text design: Marijke Friesen
Electronic formatting: Jean Lightfoot Peters

Printed and bound in Canada

07 08 09 10 11 5 4 3 2

Praise for *Six Weeks to Toxic*

"A clear-eyed, fast-paced depiction of ambition and female friendship, *Six Weeks to Toxic* begins with a hangover and ends with the loss of a best friend. In between, Louisa McCormack reminds us that we sometimes have to lose what we have in order to win what we need."

DAVID LAYTON, AUTHOR OF *THE BIRD FACTORY*

"*Six Weeks to Toxic* is delicious! Rich in character, smart and sassy, it's a highly enjoyable read, and one that I'm sure most of us, especially as women, can relate to."

TANYA KIM, HOST OF *eTALK DAILY*

"*Six Weeks to Toxic* has the hyper-quick, no-nonsense dialogue of *Gilmour Girls*, the consistently surreal discussions of kinky sex, penis size and designer clothing of *Sex and the City*, and the sneaky, conniving, shallow, but compelling women of *Desperate Housewives*. . . . *Six Weeks to Toxic* is a new breed. The thinking girl's chick-lit. . . . McCormack is a quick and deft writer. Witty, concise, controlled. . . . It's fun, sassy, sexy, wild and . . . it's self-indulgent."

THE GLOBE AND MAIL

"Louisa McCormack has written the perfect guilty-pleasure novel. . . . It's a fast-paced, honest account of two hetero gal pals nearing their mid-30s and treating each other badly in the name of best friends forever. . . . Funny and entertaining."

NOW MAGAZINE

"Louisa McCormack pushes chick-lit in a new direction."

ELLE CANADA

"*Six Weeks to Toxic* is a sharp, sexy and witty read that delves into the female psyche."

WEEKLY SCOOP

"Tales of relationship dilemmas, awkward parental visits and botched dinner parties are peppered with laugh-out-loud moments. Just right for a lazy afternoon."

WISH MAGAZINE

"Toronto author Louisa McCormack has more interesting things to talk, think and write about than boys. . . . On the surface, it looks as though [Maxine and Bess are] torn apart when they meet guys they'd actually like to commit to, but there's more to it than that. McCormack's plot touches on issues of family pressure to conform, class and money as dating issues and being a single woman in a world that fetishizes youth."

TORONTO STAR

"Breezy and compelling."

FLARE

"A treatise on the complex character of female friendship. . . . The writing, to be sure, is smart."

VANCOUVER SUN

"A hogtown version of *Sex and the City*."

WINNIPEG FREE PRESS

"[McCormack] writes with verve and originality."

BOOKS IN CANADA

Friendship can exist only between the good.

—Cicero, *De Amicitia*

Maxine Bishop and I had been best friends for sixteen years as of December 31, 1999. Y2K turned out to be a big anticlimax, publicly. There was no computer malfunction, no lining up for water, no Messiah outraged by warfare and thongs. Personally, however, I was losing it. Despite what tweedy old Simone and Jean Paul would have made of such a landmark event, I was thinking I'd prefer oblivion. It was like a milestone birthday, only worse—adding up what I had done, subtracting that from what I'd always expected to have done, then trying not to feel like a zero. Basically, the new millennium was a chance for Maxine and me to remind ourselves that we were going on thirty-five years old and that the last of our youth now lay draped over the bitter end of a former century. I thought maybe we would finally stop living like teenage boys: endlessly antsy, pining for toys and obsessed with sex. Unless immaturity was the new wisdom? Maxine was leaning more toward maturity. Or at least she favoured the trappings.

Maxi: my life's great accomplice. I cherished her catalytic ways.

Little did I know that I'd soon be doing everything without her—for good. Maxi dumped me, as friends can do. And there's no protocol for dealing with that, no institutionalizing of it, no easy way to relieve your disgrace. When guys do the breaking up you can comfortably fling blame their way, or others will do that for you; righteous indignation is a very popular hobby. But losing a best friend is eerie and disquieting at first. What's even sadder is when it starts to come as a relief. My heart would flood if I caught sight of Maxi now, making it tough to stage a fight or a flight. I doubt Maxi would react much if she saw me, not in any way she'd want to share.

No more taking liberties, no more hitting the spot, no more confidences high and low—we're definitely over. So much for my second nature.

Week One Mould

I snapped awake late the morning of January 1, 2000, and mangled my sheets for an hour or two before admitting to myself that I was conscious. My hangover symptoms are sinister. I'm not lucky enough to puke, tremble or clutch at a migraine. Instead I get very, very low. The foundations of my life crumble and I'm left to crawl in the rubble. My personality strikes me as inhabitable. My nature feels unnatural. I am haunted by beasts that patrol my psyche like grouchy supply teachers. They abandon me for as long as it takes to top up the world supply of malevolence, only to sneak back into my headspace like union scabs at some dark satanic mill. Plato's essence of hangover, you might say. Maxi and I call this "The Nothingness." I thought I might as well get out of bed and face the requiem.

I had a lot of daze to process. The mass of frothing suitcases, unplugged appliances and stacked boxes I was calling an apartment didn't help. Maxi had officially moved into her very own house so I had just snatched up her lease on the Maxi Pad: a one-bedroom apartment with soaring windows above Antonetta Ladies Clothing on College Street. Maxi had always been somewhat embarrassed by Antonetta's stolid emporium but I loved having cardigans, overshoes and girdles on display. I hoped Antonetta would never get ousted by a bistro or a record store. Moving on December 31 had been Maxi's doing. She'd closed the deal on her new house imperiously swiftly. Maxi had a domineering way with service personnel. I'd have reminded her we all become our mothers but I wanted to stay friends.

It was one of those days when I needed to brush my teeth four times over in order to make peace with my tongue. Bright orange corkscrew curls—yes mine, unfortunately—were sprouting even more hysterically than usual from my head. I'm a fairly sober person but my hair is on LSD. Incidentally, all my hair is orange: eyebrows, eyelashes, forearms, etcetera. Whatever charming freckles I should have had on my nose ended up on my shoulders. I have dusty blue eyes, skim-milk skin, and prim, pink baby's lips. I sound very china doll but I'm more like a cheap sixties doll; I either look wide awake or dead asleep. Maxi got to be this strapping, sleek chestnut beauty while I look like someone who'd get stuck in a Benetton ad. We could have been in one together, actually: the rough juxtaposed with the smooth, ragamuffin and damsel, commuter-town escapee and chick to the manor born.

It was hard to figure out how much of Maxi's body image was clinical dysmorphia versus run-of-the-mill false modesty.

I thought she was fortunate to display such a consistently feminine hip-to-waist ratio. Maxi's hair was Breck-Girl thick but she kept it trimmed to a very executive shoulder length. And she was highlighted instead of outright blond. There were blemishes once in a while but Maxi's cosmetic skills would have been the envy of a Pentagon logistician. She might have big bones but she's got the big eyes, definitive eyebrows and wide mouth to go with them; her features are downright plentiful. Maxi always looked to me just like Lauren Bacall from the "Just put your lips together and blow" era. It's the tall, creamy beauty of the corn fed.

My cheeks were still corduroyed from the bedspread. My leftover makeup made me look Cubist-Picasso-mistress, the way it went skidding around my planes and sockets. I filled my palm with a glob of cleanser and got busy.

The bathroom mirror was still displaying little below my chin. Maxi had hung it Amazon-high to suit herself, and I knew if I didn't fix it right away that I probably never would. I kept meaning to find out my height in metric in case it sounded taller. Five-two. Sixty-two inches. Maxi is five-nine, which sounds perfect. I also envied her the A cups because D cups look ridiculous on little people.

I scanned the regiment of lotions that Maxi had left behind on the bathroom shelf. She preferred to move with full bottles. I'd long become used to Maxi's hand-me-downs. If there was one thing I'd found, it was the courage of my gratitude.

The phone rang. I tripped over a box.

Mom.

She wanted to remind me what a good person I was. Dad had helped me move the day before and no doubt reported on my tears. There had been a homeless guy in my new stairwell. My father had given him five bucks and asked him please to move on. We would have banged him with armchair legs if he hadn't. He lumbered away unsteadily, clutching the fiver, his gin-blossom nose a beacon of his afflictions. It was one of those situations when vulnerability and hopelessness suddenly seem to pinball everywhere. I was probably feeling extra woebegone about being back in the city after Christmas week. I'd stayed put at my parents' place out in Burlington, eating Toblerones and fruitcake and watching the Grinch cartoon yet again. My brother, Eddie, was spending his first married Yuletide with his in-laws in Saskatoon, so it had been all up to me—the shortbread consumption, the stocking joy, the requests for seconds with gravy. My mom really does wear an apron and my dad really does smoke a pipe. It's hard to rebel against tranquility. That was likely why I'd extended my extended adolescence.

"And may I just say one more time how much your father and I love our gifts. I haven't managed to hypnotize him yet but he has the 'Yield' sign up in the den and I've put together the yogourt-maker and we're getting just such a laugh out of the six-foot back-scratcher. You always find the perfect thing. Great powers of observation—all your teachers said so. What a bright spark you are."

"Ma, please stop counting my blessings. You sound born again, for Chrissakes."

"Oops, must go. I don't want to overcook the roast again. You know your father's barbaric tastes. He's just come in from the daily saunter. Do you want a word?"

"No. Tell him thanks again for yesterday. Love and bye!"

My father always took ten minutes to stomp the snow off his galoshes and relocate his slippers, and I thought the delay might finally drive me insane on a day of such appalling aimlessness. But it was nice of Mom to call. She's a very warm woman, a retired kindergarten teacher who trails a benign legend behind her. Her former school superintendent is my dad. They live in an older part of Burlington where the houses are detached and the lawns need sprinklers but the pools are few. My parents were probably keen to get a Rummoli game going in any case. They play for quarters, and winner donates all to unfashionable causes that only my parents seem to know about, like rusting World War Two battleships or obscure forms of arthritis. Neither of them has orange hair but I'm promised there has never been a milkman.

Tea. Now I definitely needed tea. In the Brown Betty for sure. But where the hell was that? Time to haul stuff out of boxes with a coal miner's doggedness. It was like Christmas all over again, only with newsprint for wrap and my same old plates, pans and tumblers as gifts. My counters were piled with china, cutlery and the collection of salt and pepper shakers that I was thinking my sensibilities might have outpaced but no; decoratively, I was still more a cabinet of curiosities type than serenely Zen. The teapot was hot and full. Genius Mom had sent me downtown with a bag of 2 percent and a large box of Red Rose from which she'd thoughtfully removed the cellophane since I was notorious in my family for never being able to find a way in.

The phone rang again.

"Babe! Guess what? A little get-together! Tonight!"

Maxi's enthusiasm was not as contagious as she would have liked.

"Oh yeah?"

"Tom just called. A good friend of his, Marcus, is having a do. He's disappointed that all the Y2K hype was for nothing so he wants to create his own disaster. All the food is going to be genetically modified and the music will be techno, and he wants people to dress in artificial fibres. Sounds fun! You don't have to work tomorrow, do you?"

Maxi is a freelance writer who sets her own schedule. I'm a foley artist for the movies. Every cinematic sound that isn't dialogue, music or from the effects library is up to us. We're named after pioneering sound man Jack Foley, who simulated the footsteps of three people with his two feet and a cane for thirty-three years at Universal Studios. He saved the day on *Spartacus* with a key chain when the Roman army needed armour that clinked. You hear someone walk down a street, open a door or wrestle a gator: that's foley. Very little sound that's recorded live is usable so we simulate most of it in a dark studio with props and tricks, layer upon layer, mimicking the action up on screen with timing that's by necessity precise. Post-production is where it's at if you ask me. As a little kid I had a thing for cabooses. Foley people are renowned for their quirkiness, nimble ways and attention to detail. As soon as I heard about foley, it sounded like me. I was still climbing the learning curve but I'd worked on some pretty big features. Thanks to our wallowing dollar and competitive tax breaks, Toronto was a runaway production centre. We film types didn't give ourselves much time off.

"Hollywood North stops for no one, Maxi."

"But will you come? Tom said to bring you."

Tom Babinski had showed up at the New Year's Eve party as if on cue. He was one of Maxi's flames from university days. As the lead in a satirical cabaret she'd worked on halfway through second year, he'd been cast more for his alpha-male looks than his comic chops. But Tom was the kind of guy who could actually sing. He opened up his mouth and booming notes came out on key. The show had been a rousing success; then the cast party introduced Maxi to single-malt scotch and Tom's groaning residence bed. They dated out the school year, after which he transferred to McGill, taking his fanfare with him. Now Tom was back, with clipped Roman emperor hair, superior fitness levels and a law partnership. A guy with plans. A guy with enough dough to take you out to dinner without a second thought. A guy who'd never show up in fat-man jeans and pilly fleece. A guy to make Maxi beam and Nietzsche weep at the way supermen had been reconstituted for a video-game-playing population. I had never really been all that fond of Tom but I didn't mind knowing him. It seemed like some kind of credential.

"What the hell," I said.

With Maxi's voice pitched that high, I had no choice. Favour point, advantage me. My thoughts flickered a little bit at the thought of the friend. Then I extinguished the glow, fast. That way if anything nice happened I'd have the added pleasure of surprise. Besides, I liked having my slate clean. Usually my slate was dusty with residue.

"I'm so glad Tom called already. Now I can relax and resize my sisal mats, do my bathrooms over again and Easy-Off the oven."

"Your oven is brand new."

"True, but you never know."

Growing up, Maxi had spent more time with an international series of housekeepers than with her parents, learning to wax, knead, iron and scour precociously young. I suspected the kitchen had remained a welcome sanctuary from her mother, as had sex and cigarettes.

"So is destiny making dreamy sense? Am I losing you to true love? Will you ever have anything else to do with me now that there's a man in your life who looks like he belongs in an ad for high-thread-count sheets?"

"Don't jinx me, Bess, you know better than that."

"Sorry, bad case of The Nothingness. Remember how we used to get that together?"

"I'm thinking of buying a car," Maxi said, as she spritzed and rubbed, Windex and a window likely. She hated the way I'd always breathed on them. Her new telephone headset kept her infuriatingly mobile.

"First a house, now a car? Slow down for fuck sakes."

"Relax, it'll be good for both of us. Help me pick a colour."

"This is no good. You're way too rosy and I've got the blues. We're going to end up purple."

"Write something for *Modern Gash*, Babe. That always perks you up."

"Maybe. Thanks."

Maxi was referring to our private magazine, written by just Maxi and me, subscribed to by just us, read by strictly no one but us. Maxi pasted all my *Modern Gash* contributions into a scrapbook; I collected all hers in a shoebox. I promised soon I'd get my own computer; meanwhile Hotmail kept voiding my address. We were up to maybe a hundred articles between us since we'd started years before, back when Maxi was a psych major and I was still choosing between English lit and communications. We both lived in a crumbling edifice on Bathurst Street. I was in the sloped ceiling attic, and Maxi was the cool-looking girl on the second floor who wore espadrilles and listened to Echo and the Bunnymen. She befriended me in the laundry room by scolding me for tinting my whites mauve, then hauled me up to her place to loan me the latest *Mademoiselle*.

My latest *Gashitorial* had examined the implications and complications of doggy style. We weren't always so vulgar—especially not Maxi—but to be nice she wrote a companion piece on pussy farts. When she wanted to, the girl could let it rip. *Modern Gash* was our sly antidote to the poisonous hectoring of *Vogue* and its wicked sisters. We'd long been addicted to pretty well every major woman's magazine. We needed to know how everyone else was getting instructed regarding skirt lengths, Pap smears, art collecting and relationship building. I guess *Modern Gash* gave us our chance to slither under the bulk of all that advice and upend it a little bit. We pushed ourselves as far as we could. Parody was getting hard to carry off without brutality.

Maxi was right, coming up with some new *Gash* was just the therapy I needed. With another cup of tea down me, from my *Porky's II* mug, I had enough vitality to Allen-key the legs back onto my kitchen table. Dad had made me tape the key to the underside. This demonstration of know-how was encouraging. I set the table upright in its spot by the wall. The empty surface was a treat. My office supply box wasn't hard to find and I had a fresh legal pad good to go plus felt tips. I could slip the results to Maxi during the dinner party.

GASH FLASH

Your Ass Shape and You

By Bess Grover

Scientists at the University of Pittsburgh have recently documented a long-suspected biological truth—the shape of your bottom is a direct clue to your personality! Thanks to a questionnaire distributed to 941 female participants that was then cross-referenced with Polaroid photographs, doctors have determined that a circular and protuberant posterior is a sign of an optimistic temperament. "Better rounded in every way!" cracks Dr. Robert Hind, the professor of nutritional psychology who spearheaded the study. The flatter your butt, the flatter your hopes, apparently, as those with poorly demarcated buttocks reacted less positively to photographs of kite flying, piano tuning and cake baking. Heart-shaped bottoms are brandished by those with the hottest tempers, statistically. An oblong or droopy shape indicates a more easy-going, versatile nature. Dimpled bottoms are associated with mania and compulsions.

The scientists are now embarking on a similar study of men's butts and are in the process of correlating the data with that of the women's. No significant patterns have been detected as yet regarding the potential for the owners of differing ass shapes to attract each other and mate. "You wouldn't think there's as much variety in men's rears but the study is shaping up nicely," says Hind. As long as the photographers remember to bring their combs and brushes!

~

Maxi's new home really was something else. I was getting another look at it on the way to Tom's friend's party, from the window of an idling cab with a back seat so huge I felt like I needed a bicycle to get from one side to the other. She was three blocks from the Maxi Pad, around the corner on Crawford Street. The house to her left was peeling yellow and the one to the right was vinyl-sided with concrete lions posted at the gate. Little Italy wasn't very Italian anymore but it was still half Portuguese. Maxi's house was a gentrified special: a freshly sandblasted, red-brick Victorian with black trim and shutters, steep gables, one stained-glass window and a porch where she wanted to set out Muskoka chairs in the summer and serve up the season's cocktail.

Snow was falling on Maxi's patch of freeze-dried grass, the kind of purposeful, chubby flakes that snow globes aim for. Soon we'd be saying "But the wind chill is minus 23," cursing hockey management, pulling our toques down past our ears and resorting to all the other habits of the frigid. I'd been thinking it was demoralizing to be citizens of a nation that's branded as sexless no matter how many rockers or runway models we churn out and about. I'd toyed with the notion of Maxi and me visiting New York and London with a posse of our hottest friends, dispensing expert BJs and mind-blowing sex and leaving little Canadian flags planted around afterward. Maxi thought it was a perverted suggestion with a soupçon of nobility. I said in any case, I was hung up on the execution. I'd been feeling beleaguered. Like I'd need to take mountaineering gear along to my next date. Like I wanted to attend my own funeral and give points for sobs. Like I could have followed Charlie Brown to see Lucy for some five-cent therapy. I'd been fighting the impulse to just once, once in my life, scream aloud my name. Where do you do that? Is that why people invest in country houses?

Maxi responded to the third toot. I tossed open the cab door when I saw her coming.

"I LOVE YOUR PANTS!" I yelled.

"Thanks. Olivier Theyskens." They were tweed hiphuggers with a kicky flare and flecks of Lurex. The designer probably had both Katherine Hepburn and Keith Richards up on the inspiration board. "Boxing Day." Half-price sales were Maxi's favourite part of Christmas. "Scootch over, Babe. I'm smushed."

"How did Belgium get to be sexier than Canada?"

"Don't ask me. Are those the new boots? Good work."

I'd visited Burlington Mall for old time's sake and scored a pair of black pointy ankle boots that looked like they had the courage I didn't to hold a grudge and lash out. I knew they were going to pinch but I figured it was time to get acquainted. They went well with my navy velvet bodysuit, the one that helpfully allowed me to double up on underwire. I'd never have time to see a shrink what with how busy I was finding enough support for my tits.

"I've decided shoes don't count as a shopping victory. They're too easy to pick."

"Bess, you know I'll help you find a skirt that isn't denim."

I was wearing my shredded old denim mini with new black tights.

"As long as it isn't size zero. Whoever invented size zero has an evil mind, if you ask me. For five years of elementary school I was stuck in fucking 6X and now I feel like I've matured into invisibility."

"I hope those jeans I got you fit."

"As soon as I get them hemmed they will. Thanks again. I love them."

Maxi had given me low slung, hand-whiskered, stretchy Earl jeans for Christmas. For New Year's, actually, by the time we exchanged gifts. The only truly chaotic aspect of the new millennium so far seemed to be the soaring cost of denim: jeans had gone designer again. Evidently our culture had become so bored of collarbones that we were now pulling down our pants; the fly on my new Earls was mutantly short. I'd given Maxi an antique lamp I'd found after weeks of fretful shopping. I'd hoped it was always going to welcome her home to her kitchen with a generous farmhouse glow. Then it turned out she had hired a professional *lighting consultant* for her new place. Who knew?

"Tom's friend is in film. Maybe you've heard of him? Marcus Crockett?"

"Nope."

"He's just moved back from LA. He's directed a lot of commercials. Now he wants to do a feature."

"Surprise, surprise."

"He's finishing off the screenplay."

"I wonder how he'll manage without Budweiser production values?"

"You can ask him soon enough. Just please, please, please, Bess, don't be a snark. I'm thinking hair of the dog for you, and fast."

"I wouldn't have come if I had plans to snark out."

"Well, save it for my mother."

Maxi tended to chuck me at her mother like a T-bone tossed to a surly guard dog. As the owner of an established PR company, Josephine Bishop regularly contributed chunky sums to the Liberal party, dined with chairpeople and governors, and wore New York sportswear head to toe. She had met Maxi's father at McGill University, where she was majoring in domestic science, dirndl skirts and ball breaking. Maxi's commerce-major father was now an exclusive chartered accountant, with clients who remained fat despite their spa visits and winters in Bermuda. Maxi's parents were still together but people never guessed that when she first described them; likely she was conveying too much of her mother's centrifugal force and too little of her father's powers of endurance. Her dad wore two-toned shirts and Gieves & Hawkes suits, drank dirty double gin martinis and had kept all his hair—grey since his early twenties.

"Are you having your parents over to see the house soon?"

"God, don't remind me. I wouldn't mind if it was only Daddy, but I know how much my mother loves the fact that I still need help while totally pretending to resent it."

Josephine and Bernard had "loaned" their only child the money for her down payment and more. They should probably just have set up a trust fund and had done with it. Maxi worked hard, but not at anything that paid for truffle oil, European undershirts and custom drapes.

"She's quite the dame, your ma. She reconstitutes the breed."

"It's just so, I don't know, hampering. I suppose you talked to yours today? Thank God for call display. I upgraded. Now I can see who's on call waiting as well."

"Next time Josephine and Bernard come donating, tell them to get a wing in their name instead."

"No more, that's it. Not until I'm engaged. Or preggers."

"I love your mother."

"Oh, fuck off!"

Maxi was in a good mood. She swore only when she was in high spirits. She took advice columnists to heart and there were more of them around lately. Updated ones who talked you through one-night stands and cat fights. Some new Miss Manners had sworn Maxi off the F-word and now she used it only when sex flitted merrily on the horizon.

"This is date number two," I said.

"Really?"

"You kissed last night, right? And it's not like you two have never done it."

"You're right, you know. Goody."

We couldn't believe some people waited until date number three for sex. We thought it was a Moral Majority myth. It hardly seemed wise now that we'd been introduced to the dangers of male performance anxiety. Guys our age still missed the halcyon pre-condom/post-Pill era; dicks are nostalgic that way. Maxi and I didn't mind condoms, the way they made things so slithery at first and somehow kept you at a useful distance. In fact, condoms had unleashed our deepest phase of promiscuity. I could now slap one on anyone with the showy dexterity that chefs reserve for cracking eggs.

"Tom seems like the kind of guy who'd have a nice dick."

"Nice and unremarkable, from what I can remember."

"That's what you firmly want in a dick."

Maxi giggled. She had every reason to be in a good mood. I was just wondering if there would be any left over for me.

The cabbie was yapping away on a cellphone, contributing to what would no doubt be the vast incidence of cab driver brain cancer in 2025. We were keeping our floozy murmurs safely tucked well behind his Arabic chatter in case he was a proponent of *shariah* law and wanted us sluts stoned to death. Sometimes I thought Maxi and I simply lived to be the diametric opposite of two females in the Saudi hinterland. No shocker that we weren't adamantly discussing the power of our vote, or new ways to raise charitable funds, or the role of institutions in a time of moral relativism. It was our post-feminist privilege to go boy-crazy instead. Maxi called it "exercising our sexuality."

"Maxi, I wonder if we could spot the guys we've been with in a police lineup from a purely penile ID? I honestly don't think I could do it. Could you?"

"I doubt it. It took me years to take a real look."

"Not that chicks don't have differences. Apparently skinny girls can be real empty caverns. More flesh equals more suction, maybe? I'm going to have to ask."

"Just remember your resolution please, Babe. Especially tonight."

Maxi loved resolution season. She had self-improvement projects on the go all year round, but at New Year's they were easier for her to admit to. I always let her make mine, too, but I cut her off at one per year. For 2000 I had pledged to be less *alienating*, to men particularly. Apparently, I'd been building up a *self-defensive attitude*. I had to start showing the fellows my *sweet side*.

"Okay, Maxi. Fine. I get it."

"I'm just saying, Babe. Trust me."

We subsided into quiet as the cab ploughed in fits and starts through the snow. The streetlights wiped my expression blank while Maxi scowled at her compact and blotted. We penetrated the murky heart of Parkdale. Women were patrolling the sidewalks in miniskirts with thigh-high boots and bleached split ends. Whiskery guys stumbled along with their jackets unzipped. Teens hung out in smoking, hooting clumps. I was glad Maxi was good with directions. It wasn't the kind of route you wanted to take in error. Toronto was never very scary but it could get bleak. Hopefully the party would be worth it.

For a time Maxi and I were famous for our own parties. They swarmed from her apartment up to mine, with manic themes that sent everyone scurrying for fishnets and wigs. They always filled up with strangers. Jewellery and knick-knacks usually went missing; once Maxi's colander went AWOL and my Niagara Falls toothbrush mug mysteriously disappeared. We progressed over the years from chips and dip to wine and cheese to full-blown dinner parties. We were both freelancing by then. I was working as a PA on rock videos and Maxi had quit her mother's PR firm due to having slapped a client. Ms. Bishop Sr. was none too impressed; she expected Maxi to emasculate clients more subtly than that.

We went halves on expenses but Maxi usually wrested control of the guest list, she being the one with the dining room and table. The first time it happened, I ended up crying right before all the invitees arrived to devour the choicest groceries I'd ever bought. The guests were Maxi's latest attempts at power networking—her power, her network. Maxi kept hissing apologies at me all night—while hanging up coats, in between dessert and coffee, when I cracked in two the old platter my mom had loaned us as I washed up after the tiramisu. Maxi didn't cry. She never cried. She didn't find it useful.

"We haven't had a bash for ages," I said, as the cab drove past Patty Nation, my favourite roti shop, and I had my hundredth pang of longing for pyjamas and takeout.

"Don't blame me. I wanted to do something at Thanksgiving, remember?"

"I had to go out to Burlington. Besides, I haven't been reading enough shelter porn. I don't know what people are doing for napkins to go with the new appetizer. It's papyrus and herring roulades for all I know."

"Down this alley, I think." Maxi squinted at a scrap of paper. "He lives in a converted egg-packaging plant. Don't worry, he's had it architected."

"I don't care if he lives in a dry-cleaning plant, as long as you put some Merlot in a sippy cup."

I wasn't planning on having that much to drink, but the tomboy in me liked to feign party spirit. Not so Maxi. She was always claiming she was going to teetotal and then getting trashed. She insisted on paying for the cab.

"I'll get us on the way home," I said, knowing I'd probably be alone.

We spied a massive steel door and made our way toward it. I hugged the bananas I'd brought—bright yellow, freakishly huge ones that I trusted had been injected with growth hormones. Plus a box of instant shrimp-chip mix: add water and fry. Maxi had Chilean wine because she'd heard it contained the most pesticides, individually wrapped string cheese and strawberries so chubby and red that they looked like a caricature of themselves. Hopefully these all qualified as fruits of doom. Having once been the kinds of assholes who put on theme parties, we did our best to respect the impulse in others. The slush was making my ankles ache until the big door opened and we slid inside.

Marcus, our host, was seven feet tall. Six-three, actually, but I couldn't tell for the clouds. I suspected he was another one of those guys for whom a loft functions as a significant other. Industrial cosy, that was my first thought. Enormous antique surgical lights clamped to beams and pillars cast a warm glow. The art collection specialized in graffiti and found objects. The shelving was chrome, filled with equal parts books and videos. The dining-cum-picnic table was a nice touch.

"Très ski shack," I said, dumping my fruit.

"It's from Finland," said Tom. "It's a one-of-a-kind item from this avant garde atelier. The guy chops down the trees himself." It was weird to see Tom unequivocally admiring anyone's taste besides his own.

"Fabulous," said Maxi.

"Down, boy," Marcus said.

What people saw in pitbulls, Rottweilers and mastiffs I really needed to know. This dog was an ungodly combination of all three. Its head was a ham-charred black, its tongue dripped gallons and its claws had chattered toward me across the poured concrete floor until it had taken a final lunging bound and launched its bulk right at my hose. The thing was trying to climb me and snog. Never had I gazed into eyes containing such passion.

"Rocks, I said *down*."

The hound shambled over to its massive doggy bed, patchy shoulders sagging. It sat, groaned and gave everything up for lost, dumping that huge head on its paws. Down for the count, I prayed. What the fuck? Maxi had surely been glad of the chance to grab Tom's hand at the scent of danger. Lately I was becoming the centre of attention in such unwelcome ways. I wasn't ready to check the skin of my knee for damage.

"Sorry about that. Welcome, friend of friend of friend. I'm Marcus. I see you've met Rocks."

The guy extended a foot-long hand. He had black mad-scientist hair springing from his skull every which way—a midnight Raggedy Andy. He had on a bowling shirt that said *Ray*, scuffed motorcycle boots and teal sharkskin-suit pants. He was lanky, but in a way that allowed for shoulders. His skin was olive, his stubble was tended. His black eyes seemed dozy but I could tell his face was going to keep filling up with his next remark. I figured from his drawl that he was the kind of guy who said *duly noted*, *I hear you* and *it shall be done*. I'd have to figure out a way to congratulate him on irritating me so effortlessly. There was no one else at the party. Maxi had already insinuated herself between Tom and the stainless steel stove. I thought I could be out of there in an hour and a half if I faked my first migraine.

"I'm Bess," I said. Somehow we managed to shake on it, although my hand in his hand looked like a Save the Children poster.

"Thanks for coming, Bess. I think I scared off everyone else with my square tomatoes."

"I brought seedless watermelon and hydroponic lettuce," bragged Tom.

"Cheers?" Maxi asked me carefully as she handed me a glass.

"Cheers," I agreed. "To a cowardly new world, everyone."

To which Marcus whooped, "HEE HAW!"

Luckily everyone was into eating right away. Marcus was very much at home, especially at his kitchen island. He and Maxi started preparing the hodgepodge of foodstuffs and piling them on the picnic table where Tom and I sat and snacked, in my case on a corn dog. Maxi must have whispered something to Tom, because he was refilling my wine glass like a busboy hired on a trial basis only.

"Yo, Bess, remember the time you howled like an ape all around the men's residence lawn?" Tom asked. "Jesus, that was funny."

I once made the huge mistake of perfecting a gorilla imitation. That was back in my punk days when femininity still felt like a bit of a trap. Maxi used to dare me into it, the fink. But alcohol is never a good excuse for anything.

"That's how I would unwind after a show," I whispered.

Back in the neon era, late mid-eighties, the year before graduation, I was the lead singer of a band called The Revolted. Until our bass player got mono and we disbanded once and for all, we played the dingiest places on the circuit: basement clubs with warped linoleum and old-man taverns with crusty carpeting and Knights of Columbus halls whored out to the highest bidder. Maxi didn't miss a single Toronto gig. She'd wear one of her paradoxical combinations of fun fur—zebra, leopard and bathroom carpet. She found me go-go boots in Kensington Market, a perfectly preserved pair, white, pointy, with zips up the back that were pulled by little leather tassels. The Revolted had one quasi-hit, "I Suck," that got played on FM 102.1 for years afterward: "You're out of luck/you lousy shmuck/I won't satisfy you/because I SUCK!" I finally stopped singing it, no matter how hammered I was or how much I'd been goaded.

"She'd only do that when she was blotto," Maxi called over.

"Drink up, Bess," Marcus said. Then he threw me a banana.

"Where are you living these days, Tom?" I asked. I already knew from Maxi it was a condominium loft on King Street West that would be less than ten bucks away from her place by cab. I congratulated him on the bachelor palace even though he'd decided against the fireplace option.

"Are you positive you don't want to rent my basement, Babe?" Maxi then saw fit to ask. "I could fix it up for you. I don't think there's anything I can do about the ceilings, though."

"You're short, right?" said Marcus.

"Your ghost and I are getting along just fine at your old place, Maxi, thanks."

"Equity, man, you don't want to go without it," said Tom. "And I'm getting some sweet deductions come tax time."

I guessed the time had come in my life when I'd have to get used to proliferating home owners and their swaggering concerns. I'd certainly been priced out of my own neighbourhood. I would likely never own a furnace. That was okay; I thought it would be kind of like having a troll.

"I'm so glad I finally bought. Now I feel properly represented, domestically. Once I refurbish, that is." Of course,

Maxi would have been officious in an outhouse. That was a large part of her charm. She was so good at the details she kept God's nose right out of them. I figured I could relate a lot better to Maxi's commandments than the Lord's.

"Rocks pays me rent," said Marcus. "I told him it wasn't necessary but he insisted and then his damn cheque bounced." I gathered Marcus and Rocks were some kind of lapsed ventriloquist act. And who had ever really liked ventriloquists? Back in the subverted mid-twentieth century, they might have served well as truth tellers, but now we had *Vanity Fair* columnists for that.

"So where did you guys meet?" I asked, pointing my second corn dog back and forth between Tom and Marcus.

"We met at law school," said Tom. "Marcus dropped out right before bar exams."

"I didn't think it was fair to anyone else," Marcus said. "I love tests!"

"He made a documentary about bar exams instead," Tom explained. "It was hilarious. No shit. It was on the Comedy Channel and toured at all these short film festivals."

"I'll be screening that later tonight," Marcus said. Then he popped a shrimp chip in *my* mouth.

I was betting Marcus felt all debonair with a dishtowel tossed over his shoulder, talking the walk and cocking the talk. I grimaced at Maxi as she set down a popcorn-chicken Caesar salad on the table, along with a shaker of vegetarian bacon bits. She just grinned and shrugged. Maxi could sometimes go Stepford on me when there was enough testosterone in the air. Marcus brought over some Dijonnaise and a platter of curly fries. Rocks followed, nose aloft.

"What's the story on the dog?" I asked. "Can I call it a dog?"

"I got him from this crackhead couple who were hanging outside the 7/11 last summer. They always seemed to be stoned, and Rocks here kept getting skinnier. I felt guilty in a way for giving them a hundred bucks but I really wanted this guy. So I got him."

Marcus and Rocks gazed at each other with a devotion that would have put Ronnie and Nancy to shame. Unfortunately for the rest of us, Marcus had learned how to scratch behind Rocks's ears with his feet.

"How adorable," said Maxi.

"I know he's grotesque," said Marcus, swivelling to sit beside me properly at the table. "But he's got a good heart. He's like one of those friendly meathead guys in a weight room who chats about the weather in between reps."

"At least he doesn't have a mullet," I allowed.

"Or ask to get spotted," Marcus said.

I turned to take another look at Rocks and he laid his head down on my knee. He discovered the patch of grunge he'd created and licked it.

"He likes you," said Marcus.

Evidently no one was going to apologize for the mangling.

"Great," I said.

Rocks' ears snapped to attention. His puddle eyes searched mine for meaning. His nose quivered like it hardly dared confirm the truths he had detected. I was hoping Marcus didn't have the thing trained to sniff out party malaise. I still had a ways to go before I could leave without Maxi discrediting my big favour. Since I was unwilling to say anything further about the dog there was a serious party pause. Morcheeba and

Massive Attack had been crooning in alternation on the sound system, formerly in the background, suddenly now in the foreground.

"Our generation's Muzak," I eventually said.

"Nailed," said Marcus. He strung out his arms Jesus-style.

In my haste to look away I knocked over my wine, but Marcus said not to sweat it and before I could clean up, Rocks slurped it. Marcus jumped up to dim the lights. I guessed he couldn't take too many more pointed remarks from a pointy chin like me and had to bathe us all in softness. Or he wanted to show off his finely tuned rheostat. Or he wanted to aid and abet Maxi and Tom's seduction of each other.

"Now that Rocks has a drink in him he'll be wanting mood lighting," Marcus said.

"You men, always suiting yourselves," I said.

"My mother is Muslim. I was raised entitled."

"Marcus's mother is an architect," Tom piped up. "She specializes in libraries."

Was this how I acted around Maxi, a one-person cheerleading squad? If so, it was really annoying.

"Neat," said Maxi.

"And my dad is a biologist," added Marcus. "So I'm very well taken care of."

How nice for Marcus that we should all spend the first night of the new millennium taking in The Marcus Show. I preferred to tuck into the last piece of string cheese pizza. Before I knew it the others were contesting issues of alimony. Maxi said she refused to sign a pre-nup, that it was a bad sign from the start. Tom told her she was a fool and that her parents wouldn't let her get away with it. Maxi's face shut down in alarm as she busied herself figuring out what that meant. I said it was a moot point as far as I was concerned. Marcus wanted to know if I was marrying a Mr. Moot.

"What's for dessert?" I asked.

Marcus strolled over to a kitchen closet. Actually, a polished beech installation that coasted outward, suavely revealing plentiful shelves and wire baskets. He had obviously learned a lot from art directors; his space was so well designed that subtle things were bound to happen there.

"Leftover Halloween candy. For some reason no one trick-or-treated me. Take your pick—Eat-Mores, Oh Henrys! or Aeros."

I didn't mind if I did. Maxi was in best behaviour mode so she took a mint Aero and nibbled it instead of asking if she could smoke.

The action switched over to Marcus's two big orange bean-bag chairs. Tom and Maxi got cosy in one and Marcus took over the other so I was stuck on a lime suede ottoman feeling like an elf on a toadstool. With Marcus nodding off and Tom and Maxi rubbing up against each other, the banter was running dry. I was getting too weary to add to things. I fought off the case of potential Tourette's syndrome that afflicts me when I'm socially destitute like this. I definitely didn't want to be jumping up and screaming, *We're just a bunch of fucking asshole posers with petty, shitty little survival strategies and goddamn zilch to contribute to our world!* or Maxi would die from a rush of blood to the face. I'd once read an article by a woman who had the disease. She'd look lasciviously at strange men in the subway and scream the N word aloud in bank lineups without wanting to at all.

"So what's this screenplay of yours about, then?" I said to Marcus, with Captain Highliner cheer.

"Nothing much—" He stopped to yawn. "Sorry. Chocolate makes me sleepy. Nothing I'd dare to reveal in the bright light of night anyway."

"Crazy, man," said Tom. "I think I just heard Marcus say he was sorry."

"I used to apologize for things, years ago," said Marcus. "That was before law school."

"Art get the better of you?" I asked.

"No. Nothing's ever done that."

"Bess is in film," Maxi thought to mention.

"I see," said Marcus. His lizard eyes bobbed low. He really was drowsy. I admired the lack of host nerves. Either that or we ladies were a total non-event. Tom was comfortable, too. He was caressing Maxi's nape. It was making his fly bulge.

"Look at the time," I said. "That late!"

Why on earth I had worn my new boots in such weather I did not know. Tom's car was a sloppy block away. I trailed the lovebirds, hopping snowdrifts. Tom had cowboy ways at the wheel, being conceited, balding and pushing forty. I slid my latest *Modern Gash* into Maxi's pocket while she was hugging me goodbye. She played that down nicely. It was probably the same kind of discretion her father used to slip her hundred-dollar bills. I had trouble with the Maxi Pad lock since I hadn't learned the tricky jiggle yet, but at the very last moment it gave.

"Sleep well," Maxi said.

Maxi wasn't supposed to tell me that because it's advice an insomniac is obliged to take depressingly literally. I found sleeping really hard to do. As a rule I saw Maxi's splitting headaches and raised her calamitous sleeplessness. Any headaches Maxi had that night were likely to be ignored. I could tell from the way she jumped back into Tom's idling Jeep that her every last corpuscle was soaked in relief. He'd been waiting for her curb-side; Maxi had been waiting for him for years. I waved goodbye but they were off in a burst of speed that didn't call for backward glances.

Consciousness seemed like a cruel place, swarming with wasps, forested by bayonets, ventilated with chlorofluorocarbon. As was typical after a big chow down the night before, I was even hungrier than usual upon awaking. I made English muffins with a thick load of cream cheese and my mom's cherry jam on top—poor lady's cheesecake. The only plan I had for the day was to put my own finishing touches on the Maxi Pad. I couldn't stand the thought of hammering; Maxi's nails in the wall would have to do.

I went to the living room to sort through my shrink-wrapped posters—a Matisse, a Manet, an Irving Penn and a couple of cool Polish advertisements. With a lurch of affection I spied my Stability Ball, abusively deflated in the corner. I found the pump cowering at the bottom of the household tool/office supplies/extension-cord box, which I could now give myself credit for unpacking. I left the ball a bit squishy because it would have been too big for me fully inflated. I was so grateful to it for giving calisthenics a welcome, light-hearted circus touch. I did some crunches, feet up against the wall, navel sucked to spine, levering with a precise attention to form that I deserted by rep four. Push-ups made it easier to pretend I was a Green Beret. I'd bought the ball to make up for cancelling my gym membership. I could no longer deal with the cloying bonhomie of the ladies' locker room, and there had been something way too Reverend Sun Myung Moon about step class. I'd left all that for Maxi to dominate. Maxi had a heart-rate monitor on a wristband. My own trips to Boost Zone had only ever been an adult equivalent of recess. Eighteen, nineteen, twenty push-ups and I had indeed worked up a little Marine sweat: *If you like your pussy tight, stomp your left and drag your right*.

It was time to say howdy-do to the TV. I was maintaining Maxi's cable account and had bought her old television because the time had come in my life to spring for specialty channels and the remote to go with them. There was extreme snowboarding. There was *Pretty in Pink*. There was open kneecap surgery. That would do for now. If I wasn't careful I'd start shuffling through states of mind and landing on them as aimlessly as Food, Vision, Life, Discovery, Bravo. I feared the five-hundred-mood universe. Maybe I should have been at church hearing a sermon after all. Maybe I should have been giving a sermon: Gather Ye Wisecracks While Ye May Because God's the Only Joker in Heaven.

I assembled a living room I thought I stood a chance of inhabiting. Then I took another look at the bathroom mirror. I decided it wasn't a day to fix the mirror; it was a day to practise makeup. When Maxi and I first met I was unfamiliar with the aesthetics of eyeshadow and the proper width of belts but after we shared cramped hotel rooms in Manhattan, Cancun and Barcelona, I learned about the difference between face and neck moisturizer, about nether waxing, about eyelash curlers, about the peripheral uses for concealer. All those things you ignore when you read *Vogue* unless you're Maxi. I tried to remember her latest eyeliner instructions, a pencil poised at my eyeball. If I'd been a really depressed chick in a French movie I could have just speared my eye and then crashed my Peugeot, thereby ripping my tight skirt so someone called Thierry could fall in love with me and quote me Camus in bed. *Hélas, non*. My eyes did not look *highlighted and opened up*; they looked sad. Caught unexpectedly in shop windows, kettles and side mirrors, I always looked so sad. What a brave person I was to go through life without downing Clorox cocktails.

Definitely, I was sinking into the kind of funk that only Maxi could drag me out of. There was no calling her, though. Definitely no dropping by. Not with such a male glamourpuss lolling around at her place. I could only guess what fashion-forward antics the two of them were getting up to. Maxi and I were used to each other hooking up, but Tom seemed more monumental than that. I knew better than to take a look at a monument up close.

I didn't think I had clinical issues. It was more of a non-health-threatening disenchantment that Milton, Lady Brett and Stanley Kubrick could have related to. I shuffled into the front room and tugged on the venetian blinds with the vim of a last-place regatta contestant hoisting a ripped spinnaker. I wanted to fill my eyes with enough photo electricity to reset my body clock. But the sky was low and mushy. I stood on tiptoe with my nose squashed against the window pane to get a look at the street. The curbsides overflowed with slush puddles the colour of coffee made with skim milk. An empty streetcar trundled past in distress; the tracks twisted a bit right outside the front windows so the wheels were always letting out woe-is-me shrieks. Dads dragged tubby kids along behind them; the neighbourhood liked its five-year-olds to waddle. One more day of holidays for the more traditionally employed. I kept my forehead pressed against the cool glass until I felt an ache starting.

The phone rang like shrapnel on the wing. I lunged for it, in keeping with trench warfare.

"Brunch," said Maxi. "You, me and Tom."

"Oh fuck, Maxi. I don't know."

"Come on, Babe. It'll be fun. I'll order you a grilled cheese."

"Where?"

"At Googoogaga. We're in line for a table now."

"Are you sure you don't want to be alone with Lover Boy?"

"No!"

"Okay then. See you soon."

I dropped the phone back in its cradle. I laid my face down on my knees. I clawed at my curls. I shook my head no, no, no. I groaned in a way that ought to be reserved for hospitals and battlefields. But it was too late. I'd capitulated. Now I had to act. I dashed into the bedroom, flapped my quilt into place, tugged open some dresser drawers, snapped on the closet light, wrangled out of my pyjamas and into jeans and a sailor top. Then I got out of the top, into a bra, back into the top and put on some Nikes with treads so technological they counted as platform shoes. Then came the *pièce de resistance*: the cherry red, snap-happy, puffy, 100-percent down jacket that I'd bought before Christmas with money I'd known was coming and wrapped up for my parents to give me. It was going to lend me consolation when winter went cruel. Likewise a pink, crocheted hat I'd bought from a sweet-hearted Queen Street vendor with no front teeth. I jogged to brunch, leaping puddles, unzipping my nifty new vents as I got warm. My mood was way too dodgy for public transport; I knew enough to dilute it outside, although my tits were killing me more with each bounce. Day Fourteen: soon they'd be getting even bigger.

By the time I got to Googoogaga, Maxi, Tom—and Marcus—already had a table. I sat down beside Stretch Oddball. Now I could see the lovebirds in the flesh, plus Marcus and me in a rusty mirror. I'd forgotten to bring a Kleenex for the spigot in the middle of my face. I'd forgotten to check my wallet to make sure I had a twenty. I'd forgotten to get surgery on the armpit vein that once snipped could prohibit chronic blushing.

"Where's Rocks?" I asked. A head laid itself down on my foot.

"They let dogs in here as long as they're well-behaved," said Tom.

"Gee gang, I sure hope *I* can stay."

How lame could I get? Self-deprecating humour was a no-fly zone—the new era was calling for playful arrogance instead. The kind that these three had mastered. I needed to duck fast, I was vermilion. Rocks was there waiting for me.

"Hiya, Rocksie," I cooed. "How's my buddy?"

Rocks's grin jacked open and glowed in the gloom. The odour of grub had turned on his saliva ducts full stream. He rolled over and bared his muscle-man torso so I was morally stuck patting him. Meanwhile Marcus's mega legs were a sight. Divorced from his upper body, they were *très* Paul Bunyan. Was it possible I was the same height as Marcus's legs? Perhaps he and I weren't the same species. No wonder Rocks had been so excited to meet me—he'd sensed a fellow creature.

"You love that dog," Marcus said when I re-emerged. He had ordered a stein of latte and was sipping it hot. I could tell the ding-dong was purposefully trying to get foam to stick to his upper lip.

"No I don't." Rocks yawned with a little yelp at the end. "Well, maybe a bit. He's rolling around in boot slush."

"This water is delicious!" Maxi seemed glad for any excuse to swivel her face toward Tom. Tom seemed glad to have his arm stretched along Maxi's shoulders. His watch strap was made of links so gleaming it looked like poured mercury. "San Pel rules," Tom let us know. "I don't like anything too bubbly."

"I do," said Marcus.

Maxi took another cold swig and shivered in her plum sweater with the nice long sleeves and the nice short waist and the beautifully swooping neckline. Usually, she liked ordering shots of espresso as if she was a real Italian, but around Tom she wouldn't risk coffee breath. I needed a water glass. Either that or a three-fruit smoothie with echinacea and spirulina.

The eggs arrived. Everyone else's eggs and my sandwich. I've never been able to stomach eggs. I think it's because they quiver, although I love the thought of eating something *sunny side up*. Maxi always ordered hers that way and usually ended up using them as an ashtray. Tom was having a chive and pancetta omelette. Marcus's Grand Slam came with pancakes.

"Blueberry," he specified, offering me a speared and dripping parallelogram.

"No. No, thanks."

I offered Marcus a spear of my pickle and the bastard took it. On went brunch. I did my best to partake, gamely deciding what era I would most liked to have lived in (screw Shakespeare, give me Voltaire), my favourite beach (Brackley, PEI, a childhood haunt, and then everyone else at the table went sexy hideaway), where I was keenest to dine (Toto), and what body parts to improve.

"Lip augmentation," I volunteered. Marcus looked at my mouth. This necessitated some immediate action. Unfortunately it was goofy kissy lips in his direction with a raspberry to follow, something better done in the privacy of a photo booth. Luckily, I still had some sandwich to turn to. I took a huge bite that absolved me of conversational responsibility. I was in my electron mood—denied access to a nucleus, incessantly peripheral, lone and stray and tiny. The smell of toast mixed with the smell of Rocks and the smell of the sheepskin item with toggles that Marcus was calling a coat. I stared at my crusts.

"Want to, Bess?" asked Maxi.

"Huh?"

"Do you want to come see *Magnolia*?"

"Oh."

"Tom Cruise is supposed to be fabulous in it."

"We have a bet going," said Tom. "She owes me if it sucks."

"Sure, why not." It seemed like the move of a dud to break

up another get-together. I had nothing against Tom Cruise completing me for a couple of hours.

We extricated ourselves from the table while waiters with ER energy attacked it with rags and fresh settings. It turned out that Marcus had treated, and he wasn't coming to the movie.

"Oh," I said.

My social duty to slump my way through a matinee now seemed less imposing. Afternoon movies always made me feel frighteningly indolent.

"Rocks just isn't into Tom Cruise," Marcus explained. "They're too much alike."

"Right."

"Bess!" Maxi was yelling at me from Tom's Jeep.

"See ya," said Marcus.

"Okay," I said. "Sure."

I hopped in the back for my front-row view of the live-action courtship ritual. Maxi reached behind her and grabbed one of my hands to kiss it, probably for Tom's benefit in some way that was farther beyond me the more that I thought about it.

"Pocket Venus," she said proudly.

Maxi was very fond of my fingers. She said they should have their own cartoon show. I saw that she had manicured professionally again. Gone, I guessed, were the days when we'd swap polish and go through two large bags of Smartfood, trying not to eat it until our nails were dry. My hand was unruly with hangnails and cuticles. I sneaked it back.

"You didn't tell me Marcus was coming to brunch." We sped past dollar stores and Chinese restaurants on our way uptown.

"We spotted him from the lineup. He'd already had breakfast but he said he could always eat again."

"Nice of him to pay. I wouldn't have had the large smoothie if I'd known."

"Bess eats like a horse," Maxi said.

Tom's gaze flickered at me in the rear-view mirror for a moment. *I don't know where she puts it*, I said to myself.

"I don't know where she puts it," said Tom.

"In my mouth."

Maxi merrily chuckled. Tom had stayed over; I could smell a double dose of Maxi's high-end conditioner. While nothing had as yet been set in stone, I figured their bond was becoming quite the eleventh commandment: *Thine bushes shall burn*. Usefully, Maxi and I were never attracted to the same guys. The only exception had been Bogdan, the writer-in-residence during our last year of university whom we actually befriended, whom we drank liqueur with and endured weepy recitations from. Poor Bogdan was a PEN placement from somewhere formerly Yugoslavian. He looked and acted like a bison—massive, shaggy and stoic about not having a neck, among other losses. I never did him, I just really needed help on my "Chiaroscuro in Milton" paper. Maxi thought I had, though, so she did. She said it was no big deal; Bogdan had been ripped, tearful and overly grateful. He had a cute thing. It looked like it was wearing a World War Two helmet. Maxi encouraged me to take a look if I wanted to but I declined. Now I understood why he'd sent the roses. Yellow ones with flecks of red. Maxi had hated them and given them to me; she thought they'd looked like open sores.

When the movie was over—Cruise in his underpants taking on a respectably corrupt persona—we creaked to our feet and trooped back up the aisle like churchgoers with agnostic secrets. Tom had parked at the Four Seasons. He and Maxi were distinct hotel-bar types. Maxi for one thought martinis tasted better at eighteen dollars.

I was adamant about preferring to walk home. Now that the stores were closed, Bloor Street's three-block imitation of Madison Avenue seemed liable to soothe in the gloaming. The day had continued mild, and the worst of the puddles were dried up. In a tactical frenzy, Maxi decided to come with me.

"I had a *great* weekend," she assured Tom on the sidewalk outside Tiffany's, swinging her hands in his, tossing her hair to and fro, loading up a couple of kisses and firing away without mercy.

I felt like I was in the shadow of two monoliths. I felt like the movie was still going on, that lifestyle was eligible for awards and one should never be happy simply to get nominated. Mostly, I was sick with worry that I wasn't going to dredge up enough happiness on Maxi's behalf to last the whole walk home. Admittedly, I also felt like I would never be in love again myself. Even in its embryonic stages, love seemed too capacious for me.

"I'll call you," Tom told Maxi, scouring her face like it was a legal document. He tossed a captainly salute my way, rested his glance on Maxi for one more moment, then took off. He needn't have worried about his bum looking good.

"Tom's amazing," I said quickly. "You are *so* lucky. I am *so* happy for you."

My sarcasm alarm was starting to buzz but Maxi looked pleased.

"He is, isn't he?! Thanks." Maxi was doing her happy walk, the one studded with skips that made me caper like a munchkin to keep up. "Wow! Check out these shoes!"

A crazy pair of copper-and-gold intergalactic Mary-Janes gleamed in a honey-lit vitrine. They would punctuate Maxi's wardrobe just right. No doubt she would be back to get them. I made a mental note to attempt some impracticality of my own; my look was getting less frivolous by the month. Great, now I was worrying more about worrying less. It's hard not to fret when you inhabit the tundra. Northerners have saved their skin over the eons by cultivating the kind of pessimism that performs well during blizzards. The Belgians probably took every advantage of their proximity to the Scandinavians. In protest, I resolved never to read Tintin again. Maxi stopped outside another store with spotlighted Italian accessories.

"So did you have fun?" I asked, tearing my glance away from a hideous pink-fringed bolero. It might have been because we were down the street from the museum but I thought Maxi's profile was possibly Etruscan, her nose is that straight. It's a face that would actually work on a coin. She veered her gaze into mine.

"Absolutely!"

"You *like* him? He makes you happy?"

"Why wouldn't he? He's cute, he's nice to my friends, he's got great style, he's good in bed, he's got money of his own. And he doesn't completely mind me smoking. It's like, bingo!"

"I knew a man he had a dog and Bingo was his name-O—"

"Be quiet, you. And doesn't that make Marcus bingo?"

"Um, no. Definitely not."

"Well, don't blame me next time you get lonely."

I surprise attacked with a bra-strap snap; Maxi was still zipped low for Tom's benefit. I ran fast because I knew exactly how she would retaliate. I didn't make it. Hat head on me is a defiance of Newtonian physics; my hair doesn't so much flatten as gain propulsion. Maxi never failed to be amused. I snatched my hat back from this sadist I was calling a friend. Maxi skipped over to a bag lady rooting around a trash can and handed over her leftover movie popcorn. The thunderously huge old woman in layers of rayon and Orlon, split shoes, a shower cap and ear muffs looked up in wonderment. Maxi blew her a kiss and waved goodbye as cheerfully as one would to a cranky toddler.

"That was nice of you."

"I didn't want to carry it any more. Look, there's Chanel."

I was pretty sure Maxi's had been a weekend much like an expensive bouquet, delivered on Friday and smelling wonderful for a good ten days afterward. I just wanted to make sure.

"C'mon, Maxi, tell me all. Did you guys reconsummate?"

"Not at this time of the month. I know you think it helps with the lubrication but I'm sorry, Babe, I just don't think it presents well."

"I'm with you this time. Tom isn't exactly the kind of guy you can send in search of dark towels. Not right away at least. But he better be, eventually, if he's The One."

"I thought you didn't believe in The One?"

"I don't. I think the whole idea is vain to the point of retarded. It's a myth designed to sell facelifts and aftershave. It's faith gone askew. But you do."

"I've worked hard. I think I deserve The One."

"I'm just glad you didn't sprain your tongue."

I knew Maxi would have been priming Tom with the kind of high-quality fellatio that would leave him sacked out on her altar for weeks. Maxi enjoyed staying in charge of a man's urges without necessarily stirring her own. Orgasms were one thing I had reliably over Maxi. The poor girl couldn't even get herself off.

"Tom seemed to appreciate my new techniques, I'll put it that way. I tried humming and it does totally cut down on the time factor. As long as you pick the right song. Don't go Elton John."

"Maxi, I have a feeling your blow jobs get kind of argumentative."

"Bess, that is one of the worst things you've ever said to me!"

"Be proud. I lack the rhetoric. So are you seeing him again soon?"

"Who?"

"Fred Flintstone! Who do you think?"

"Touch wood."

"Of course you are."

"Once he catches up on his holiday backlog. Lordy, look at Prada's resort wear. All those iridescents, I love it! Why am I not surprised the woman has a PhD? I should get Tom to go to the Caribbean this winter. No package deals, though. One of the good islands."

"Sounds like Stage Two to me: 'Romantic Acquaintanceship.'"

"So help me God, Babe, I am determined to make it to Stage Three this time."

"The much heralded 'Combination of Assets.'"

"One of us has to grow up and live with a man, don't you think? Properly, I mean."

The summer before Maxi moved out of Bathurst Street, I was missing her a lot because she was spending it with this guy called Logan up at his parents' cottage. They were both supposed to be working on novels but ended up writing their names on each other's backs in suntan lotion.

Meanwhile, this guy called Rick Dexter had been staying with me. We were both staying at Maxi's place, actually, while Rick apartment hunted for himself. He had ulterior motives to shack up long term that I fortunately nixed by the time Maxi needed her apartment back. Rick eventually went on to make a fortune from a motivational speaking business complete with videos, pamphlets and *Say It Like It Should Be* mugs, stickers and T-shirts. I'd hated having to worry about what mood I was in. I'd hated having to hear television noises before sundown. I'd hated having to compile our dirty laundry into one bag. Why is it the good-looking ones can never be bothered to wipe properly, or have I just answered my own question?

Maxi and I had strolled beyond the flashier stretch of Bloor Street and entered the granola domain. The shop windows were now crammed full of batiks, turquoise jewellery, cotton totes and incense kits. We lapsed into one of those silences that people idealize so much as comfortable between old friends, but they're comfortable only if you're distracted. I was. I was contemplating how natural it was that Maxi and I should be exiting this prolonged phase in our lives. Our man-as-infotainment era. The sister power epoch. The abounding, tiresome pop-culture fetish for oversexed, overripe girl gangs should have been our first clue that the *modus vivendi* we'd rigged up for ourselves was fast expiring. I hated being fodder for zeitgeist editorialists and trendy novelists and Maxi pretended to hate it, too. A high-octane, best-friendship like ours was bound to sputter eventually; I'd always known that. Now I saw how it would likely give way to Maxi's marriage to Tom (Here's Your Blood Diamond) Babinski. And my old-maidhood. Hopefully, Maxi would come by with her brood for fleeting visits, bring me cold cream and tea bags, and tuck my afghan under my dentures.

"Maxi." I came to a full sudden halt outside Ali's Babba's Eat In and Take-out. "I am very, truly happy for you. About the house and Tom and everything."

"Oh, Babe." Maxi hugged me without dangling me, which was nice of her.

"I'm sorry, is it just me or do falafels smell like BO?" I whispered in her ear.

Maxi held me out at arm's length. "You're a really good friend, Bess."

"That's good, because I want to be."

We kept walking. The breeze was as mild as a pat on the cheek. It was probably our last such stroll of the winter. Maxi was humming the way she did when she liked her plans.

"I'm sorry I made a face when Tom was going on about how only babies vote Left. For sure he didn't see."

"I was just glad you thanked him for the movie. I was scared you were going to forget."

"Nah, I was bolting for the popcorn line. I knew he really wanted buttered, by the way. Everyone always does. People should just relinquish themselves."

"Thanks for sharing yours, Babe. I know how much you hate that."

With the jazzed energy of the smitten, Maxi walked me right to my door. She didn't want to come in because she needed some "alone time." That sounded to me like something you get punished with at nursery school but I didn't say anything. I still missed the days when Maxi and I lived under one roof. It had made for reassurance that was often instant. And some serious Tequila Sunrise consumption. The first time, I was sick in Maxi's toilet. She chased me in there with a can of Lysol spray. I actually laughed while I puked. Nothing before had ever felt quite so much like friendship. Not even sitting beside Sherry Foster all the way through Grades One to Eight of French immersion.

I had to chill out myself or the workweek would lunge like a cobra. The dark helped, and sitting quietly. Then I had to laugh at myself when I realized my shoulders had sunk to the point of comic-strip condor. Somehow, my reverie had inspired a quickie *Gash*, the gift Maxi and I kept on giving. Or at least that I kept on giving. She was understandably getting too busy with real articles to come up with gag ones, but for sure she'd get a kick out of this.

MODERN GASH'S
Top Ten Tips for Coping with Romantic Destitution

By Bess Grover

1. Do not, under any circumstances, buy any pet from the mammal, rodent, tortoise or fish family. You may, however, buy a horse.

2. Avoid masturbation festivals. Yeast and/or bladder infections will leave you feeling only lonelier.
3. Read back issues of your diary to remind yourself that you have always been lonely.
4. Subscribe to *Divorce Lawyers Monthly*.
5. Contemplate Cher.
6. Divest your life of pilly sweaters, shaggy toothbrushes and worn-out socks: the purge that refreshes.
7. Practise casual anorexia or eat plenty of starch.
8. Be rude to your mother: the guilt will distract you.
9. Seek out bitchy gossip columns.
10. Pray, pray, pray that your best friend's wonderful new boyfriend will stop calling her.

Week Two Blight

My phone wasn't ringing much in the new millennium. It took me a while to get to it because I knocked myself out with a mixing bowl full of mashed potatoes and the front section of the newspaper. I'd been trying to read it, not just skim. I knew very little of the Middle East, East Timor, Kashmir and Nigeria and I didn't think much of myself as a citizen. Famine, purdah, clitoridectomies—nothing had been yanking me from my perch.

"Hellooooo," I said very knowingly into the phone, thinking Maxi was reporting on another Tom call. I had plenty of time to listen to her in my void. He'd booked her in for senior-partner social duty Friday night at a cocktail party in Hazelton Lanes. The partner hosting the party was from Venezuela, and a sort of Yorkville version of Ricardo Montalban. Better Maxi than me. I always double-dipped and never traded notes on *West Wing* episodes.

"Good news!" she began.

"Great, what's up?"

"I got assigned that story I wanted. A Tara Dickens profile."

Tara Dickens was a stupendously nubile and symmetrical Canadian who had made it in LA, or made it enough to get her photo snapped at a Malibu Starbucks for the paparazzi pages of *People*.

"Way to go, Maxi. That's fantastic."

"For *Toronto Magazine*. I got the cover."

Graphics included, *Toronto Magazine* was one of the least bashful parts of Toronto. A few years before, it had introduced the city to acid green and liberally borrowed its fonts from high-end restaurant menus.

"Jackpot!"

"Sue says to bring my edge but not all of it. That's good, right?"

"You better believe it."

"I'm thinking the questions we never got to ask Marilyn."

"I love it. Way to go."

"This could make me, Bess. Really make me."

"Right on, Maxi. This is wonderful."

"Things are falling into place. God, I needed this. I can hardly wait to tell my mother. Wait, maybe I shouldn't even tell her, let her find out from someone else. That would serve her right. I still can't believe she got so mad at me for giving her a shawl. They aren't for old ladies. Not pashminas, anyhow. She was the one who got me jeans that were much too small. 'Don't blame me for those hips, miss, you got those from Grandmother Bishop.' Honestly, whatever!"

The first time I met Josephine and Bernard was the first Christmas I knew Maxi. She wanted me to serve as a demonstration that she was capable of making a good friend after all. Josephine was in the study, reading *The Times*, airmail edition, wearing captain-of-industry bifocals on a nose that was a lot bonier than her daughter's. She didn't so much compliment me on being tiny as point out that I made Maxi look like an ox. Bernard quickly passed around the sherry. Bernard Bishop sometimes appeared to teeter but he was never more rock solid than when he had a drinks tray in his hands. I hoped it was Maxi's first sip of Christmas spirit, a moment that was finally, vaguely, holiday. But before she knew it her mother and I had loaded up our laps with old photo albums. Josephine loved baby Maxine, the one who cried for her sometimes. I couldn't help but delve eagerly into these early versions of Maxi, too—Maxines who were finally shorter than me. Josephine let me pick almost all the Chinese food that the four of us ate in the drafty Bishop dining room. And made a fuss over my chopstick skills although Maxi's far outdid mine. Thankfully, her father distracted us by spilling plum sauce on his tie. Bernard Bishop's mishaps absorbed so much tension it was hard to believe he didn't plan them. Something told me Maxi would never forget that night's fortune, so ghastly it made her eat the cookie: *You must look further than a mirror to see who you are.*

"Tell your dad about the article anyhow, Maxi, and he can tell your mom. They'll both be so proud. *I'm* so proud. You're going to end up writing *The New Yorker* letter from Canada."

"Is there such thing?"

"No but they'll start one just for you."

"Well, Tom thinks it's great."

"You told Tom already?"

"Absolutely, when I had such a good excuse to call. You're right, Babe. I'll try Daddy's line. Toodles."

Maxi's good news was good news. Absolutely, we were each allowed to get promoted, fall in love or fit the last size of something on sale. Ours was not a friendship oiled by distress and calamity. I insisted on that. There was no weird binary system at work that said yes to one of us while saying no to the other. I was sincerely happy for Maxi; that was my accomplishment.

Marisa Carmody, the stupendous woman who was my boss, is an internationally revered foley artist with a tidy grey ponytail and the world's best collection of turtlenecks. Marisa always seemed serene. Not just compared to Maxi and me. It also had to do with the way her steel-grey hair didn't get wispy, the way her shoulders never seemed to get knots and the way she never appeared to wear an expression she wasn't feeling. It was like I was working for Jane Goodall; on my better days I felt like a research assistant, on my worst a chimp in situ. Marisa has conferred on me a treasure trove of foley skills: high-heel clacking, back patting, water churning, sword swiping and all the other stray sounds that are liable to pepper a sound track. I was blessed to have been her assistant for many years, first as her apprentice, then as her deputy. Marisa is that rare woman who looks good without lipstick, who pronounces every consonant, who never idles long enough to worry about the usual.

Marisa was busy, shopping for a property in Aurora, Uxbridge or Caledon, where pretty acres beckoned. She had a horse named Zeus the colour of cinnamon that she wanted nearby once and for all. Marisa was my own personal goddess. Her rare spite was reserved for stupid producers, bad directors and corrupt local politicians. She wrote many letters to the editor, about the lakefront and nursing shortages chiefly, although she also weighed in on daycare, food banks and public transport. Marisa had been adopted as a toddler by a British-doctor couple and brought up to contribute. Sixpence a week had been for comics and sweets, sixpence for her piggy bank and a shilling to give away to others. I once told Marisa about the time that I stole a quarter from the collection plate at church. I lived in fear of Satan's sudden scarlet, glistening appearance for months after—in my Grade Two classroom, in my bedroom during homework, in the kitchen while the Pillsbury rolls were baking. How would I explain him away—all lobster red with that rude tail and deafening laugh—to Mom or Mrs. Shaver? Marisa informed me that the devil is a Christian invention, borrowing heavily from some pretty well-intended pagan traditions. Apparently, he's not such a bad guy after all. The kind of guy I wouldn't mind taking as a date to a Christmas party or sitting beside at a wedding. Anyway, it was thanks to Marisa that I not only had the makings of a career but also a serious tea habit. And an escape hatch from the solipsism that was starting to bug me in others.

"It's a pharmaceutical thriller, shot in Toronto and set in Boston," Marisa explained. "Starring Tara Dickens. Largely malarkey from the looks of things but pretty straightforward from our point of view. Nothing you can't handle, Bess. I'm going to get you started today, then for the most part it will be all yours."

"Seriously?"

"You can call me if you need me but I doubt you will. Hank will be here."

"Do or die, kiddo," said Hank. "But don't die on my time. Too messy."

"Hank, please, show me some respect. I'm contending."

Hank Glatt, a kvetchy sound mixer with a walrus moustache, the entire Old Spice collection and a tendency to cause hullabaloos typically joined us in the vampire-dark studio. Films were projected on a screen up against one wall, and car doors, windows for smashing and gates with latches were piled up against the others. Foley studios notoriously resemble an exploded garage sale. For the next few weeks the two of us were going to be in there seeing a lot of Tara Dickens—her marble midriff and her bangs that worked.

Now I understood why Marisa had allocated the better part of four weeks to one movie. In the nicest way, I was being tested. It wasn't anything to boast about yet but I hoped it soon would be. Maxi would help interpret my new advantages. She'd love it if I could start getting us into more film festival parties.

Our foley team didn't generally listen to dialogue at a discernible volume, but it's rarely hard to follow the story. Tara/Jessica's tale began with her hard at work late at night in her research laboratory. That was easy: we had tons of glassware on hand for the pipettes and beakers. And paper clips taped to gloves worked for rat claws. Jessica's arrival home was a matter of light switches and coat doffing and wicker laundry basket creaks. I was excited to see Jessica put on her slippers. I have a knack for slippers. My foley pair were fuzzy, screaming yellow, Tweety Bird ones that no one else besides me fit into. In fact I had an identical secret pair at home. I pointed a microphone at a square of linoleum squeezed between some hardwood flooring and a piece of shag carpet. I scowled up at Tara/Jessica and counted her footfalls. Mine had to be exactly in sync. I analyzed the scamper-pause-scamper as Tara spotted her evil benefactor's limo out the kitchen window and scooted up her condo stairs to lock herself in the bathroom. I was ready for the first take. I flubbed it.

"This is going to be quite some millennium," Hank hollered. He was leaning back in his chair patting his belly. The more proud Hank was of the point he had to make, the further back he tipped. "That Tara Dickens is a CUTIE!"

It was true. Tara was a miraculous cross between Gwyneth and Winona but without any of Gwyneth's prep school airs or Winona's druggy look in the eyes. She was rumoured to have dated both Matt and Ben and to have quit the boys when she quit smoking.

"It's easy to be cute when you're that young and rich," I said. Big mistake.

"Bess's biological clock is ticking!"

Hank thought it was hilarious when I turned thirty. Making it to forty would qualify me for a freak show as far as he was concerned. Marisa wagged a finger.

"Leave Bess alone."

"Yeah, you old fatty."

"Try it again, please, Bess. More scuffle this time," Marisa said.

Foley has taught me so much about second, third and—worst-case scenario—fourth, fifth and sixth takes. Eventually I nailed it and on we went. My work is like church in that it comes supplied with reasons. One requirement after another distracted me from doubt and brought on evening like a blanket. On the way home I bought a big soft avocado, vine-ripened tomatoes, boutique cream cheese and a loaf of warm multigrain. Plus caramel yogourt. I was doing a lot of menu planning around calcium because I was damned if I was going to lose a single millimetre to stooping. Unfortunately I also had lonely-girl food in my basket—virulently green coleslaw, double-filling Oreos and Molly McButter. Marcello, the head bartender from Antico, the College Street venue to which Maxi and I continued to give the most credit, was behind me in line. He had Frosted Flakes, devilled ham and a jar of Yum-Yums, but bartending at Antico was a lot like being mayor so Marcello's dignity was fairly foolproof.

Mercifully, there was going to be a gritty BBC detective series on the Buffalo PBS station that night, a brand new one full of gore, hollering and moody camera angles that was debuting with a two-hour special.

Once I got home I called Maxi first thing. Her land line didn't answer and then her cell didn't either. I left chirpy messages at both numbers. Halfway through my dinner she called back and I was able to tell her about my slight promotion.

"Bess, that's amazing!"

"As long as I can carry it off, it will be."

"I mean the coincidence—that Tara Dickens is starring."

"In all her glory. She's cellulite free. I made Hank freeze-frame to check. What a freak. I bet she also has penetration-only orgasms and her best friend is probably her mother."

"What else have you got for me, inside scoop?"

"Let's see. Tara—Jessica, I should say—is this bio-tech research fellow who was put through medical school by an evil benefactor who takes horrible advantage of her sexually. Hank's doing the mix with me. He predicts that by the end there'll be a courtroom scene with a black woman judge and La Dickens on the witness stand in a tight little suit. I hear she was late getting back to town for reshoots, five pounds lighter and hooked on meditation."

"What are they calling it?"

"*Love Is a Drug*. That's the working title anyway."

"So the Svengali man is financing her studies?"

"Yes. But the drug she's so painstakingly developing is going to further his fortune, not world health. It's got hallucinogenic properties. He wants the earliest possible version sold in the street, with himself as world emperor of supply. Once he has no more need of Jessica, he'll cut her funding, then he'll cut her throat. She's calling the product Evoke. She's part Norwegian, part noble savage. The shamans of her grandmother's tribe harvest this drug from a local wildflower. They believe it brings back memories from the minds of their ancestors. Jessica's theory is that the stuff might one day cure Alzheimer's, which her granny is beginning to show some signs of. And that's as much as I know right now."

"Well, keep me posted."

"Okay. Congrats again on the cover story, Maxi. That's truly amazing."

"My mother wasn't too impressed."

"What's Josephine's problem?"

"She's in crisis mode over some oil spill. Some conglomerate she represents is donating cleaning supplies for the dirty birds so she's all in a tizzy over that. When I told her it was Tara Dickens I was writing about of course she had to have some connection there herself. She's going to go after an endorsement deal for her jewellery clients and do a big, high-end advertorial, so she says."

"You were smart to quit working for your mother, Maxi. I'll always say that."

"Hopefully *she'll* get Alzheimer's one day and we can both just forget about each other. I have something for you, by the way."

"*Gash*?"

"No, but thanks for yours. I found you a new disorder. Vaginismus."

"What the hell?"

"It's this syndrome whereby a vagina seizes up, even when it's aroused, so tight that no man can get a thing in there. A complete and utter clamp-down."

"Talk about *it's not you, it's me*. You'd have to go on every date prepared with soothing pamphlets."

"I came across it today while I was online. Lordy, a full-length profile. I'm going to feel like a stalker."

"If we'd lived in Olduvai Gorge we could have just kidnapped the chick, dragged her to our berry patch and made her dance around the fire for us."

"Babe, I was wondering, do you think our fates would be the same without each other around?"

"You're asking if fate is one-size-fits-all?"

"I just hope we're not fate co-dependent."

"Someone's been watching Oprah."

Since Maxi worked at home she couldn't really be blamed if Oprah regularly drew her over. Maxi succumbed to Oprah on her yoga mat, absorbing panel discussions while performing the sun salutation, and the postures were probably making her extra susceptible to the therapy-speak. "The guest experts raise some really good points. I should drag my mother on the show somehow. Oprah would have a field day."

"Your mother doesn't mean to hog all the ambition to herself, Maxi. She's just scared to do anything but work. She really does love you, in her own crazy way."

"When it flatters her, yes." Maxi hiccupped.

I could tell it was red wine hiccups. Tom was safely tucked away in Air Canada business class, heading westward to defend a litigious Silicon Valley dot-com. Maxi told me she'd let me know if he called from the road. I told her I wanted to hear all about it. Presumably, Tom hadn't called that night. I knew Maxi was busy trolling Tara Dickens Web sites for muck and shiny objects, and when she wasn't working on her article she was making barking comparison calls to electricians and closet design specialists. Or StairMastering at Boost Zone. Then exploring her South African vintages some more. Maxi and I usually talked at least once a day but there were no rules that said that we had to. When I was getting ready for bed later that evening, I walked by the front door to make sure it was locked. There was a surprise waiting for me, posted through the Maxi Pad mail slot. Maxi had come through with some *Gash* after all, one of her "Fucking Life" columns, my favourites, that she'd sweated out as if she'd signed a contract for it. I was grateful for the thought, definitely.

THE FUCKING LIFE

January 2000: Bearded Ladies

by Maxine Bishop

What is the big deal about a little fellatio? All you scaredy-cats out there, tuck in and give the knob a good gobble. There's a lot to be said for taking the bull by the horn. Power, first of all. Aren't you used to that, or the pleasure of a job well done? Admittedly, this isn't dignity for beginners. No one said you'd have to recreationally rewire your jaw, for instance. And here's another useful dictum: knock it off when your gag reflex kicks in, twits.

Quite frankly, men have a lot to learn here, too. Fellows—when we're composing for the woody wind section (tromboner, skin flute and prickello) we likely have an overture in mind rather than an entire symphony. Evolution has decreed that our mouths can open penis-wide just about as long as it takes to chomp down a couple of ripe bananas. Risking asphyxiation by swallowing your sword for half an hour is no way to get to know you. Correct, there is a contingent among us—a small cadre of ladies with erogenous tonsils—who like it when your Spamsicle takes an hour to reach melting point. My guess is about one or two of these gals per province, but maybe I overestimate.

Hints for those who need them: hum. The vibrations speed things along nicely; on trips abroad I opt for *O Canada* when homesick. Keep things moving. Drool. Don't—yucky, yucky, yucky—swallow. I never said I swallowed: what am I, a masochist? This is one occasion when I prefer to make a mess.

I'd rather give a blow job than do many things. I'd rather give a blow job than sit through *Nell*. I'd rather give a blow job than sew on a button, attend a bridal shower or shop for a bra. I'd rather fellate than get nudged into a 69er, which always makes me feel like I've been given a Fisher-Price Activity Centre to play with that's geared beyond my age group. Furthermore, BJs are one instance when bigger isn't better, a special way to appreciate the slimmer Jim you may be dating. And let's face it, none of us are getting any younger—you might have to lick it so he can kick it.

They say it's more blessed to give than to receive. Blessings be damned: it's shrewd to take the initiative. It's fun to put on a show, take a bow and unwind. It's exciting to take up a hobby, refine it to a craft and elevate it to an art. Get ahead by giving good head. Put your man in a good mood and urge others to follow—make the world a better place, why don't you? Unless of course you don't have a man. I do apologize if this has been too much of a tongue-lashing. I guess I'm just argumentative.

When I got home from work on Wednesday there were five messages waiting for me. That was exciting. I considered taking off my coat before listening to them, maybe even putting on the kettle and composing myself. Basically, treating my messages to the respect the French show lunch. Screw that. Hang-up, hang-up, hang-up, hang-up, hang-up. Maxi was obviously having a meltdown. She'd had her first meeting with Tara Dickens that day, on set in Tara's trailer. I guessed it hadn't gone well but I was too tired to call and ask right away.

Then the phone rang again. I didn't have the heart to feign absence.

"Hello," I rasped.

"Bess, how marvellous, hello there."

"Josephine?" Josephine? This was a first.

"Yes, sorry, is this not a good time?"

"It's okay. How are you?"

"Fine, fine, fine! How are you, Bess?"

"Fine."

"I was wondering if you'd like to meet for lunch some time? Soon."

"Maxi didn't mention anything."

"Not with Max, actually."

"Oh."

"I'm just a bit worried about her, Bess. I was hoping maybe you could put my mind at rest."

"I don't know—"

"I'll be very discreet. She needn't know. Please, Bess. I know this must seem strange to you. Call it mother's intuition."

"Um, uh . . ." I couldn't help but sigh in the positive.

"After work if that suits you. I could bump into you. At the Park Plaza bar. Let's say tomorrow at six."

If I lived a nice life I could conceivably head uptown first to the Roots flagship store nearby for cosy accessories; winter had decided to get nasty again and take swipes. The martinis at the Plaza were the size of bird baths. Josephine and I could numb our way through whatever this was going to be.

"I'll be dressed for the studio."

"*Entendu*. See you there, Bess. Thank you very much."

By the time I got off the phone with Josephine beads of sweat were trickling down my rib cage inside my layers. I was almost too tired to get undressed. But I knew what I needed: a Maxi-style bath. They were good for the soul, she said. She'd left behind some of her exclusive powdered flowers. I let the taps fly and the lilacs waft as I shucked off everything then got out a slobby track pants–sweatshirt combo and laid it ready on the bed. Back in the bathroom, water churned fast and deep. I stepped into the tub. I sprang back out like a bullied squirrel. I turned off the hot and let a lot more cold circulate. Eventually, I slipped back in up to my neck and bobbed adrift. No woman is an island. The bubbles were lavish and crackly and a total boon since my boobs were disguised by suds and my bush wasn't around to taunt me with Clairol's lack of pubic options.

My bath was bliss, but my phone was bawling like a baby. I abandoned whatever choice I had not to answer. My wet towel grabbed at my hips like a lecher. The ends of my curls were a hundred little rivulets. Across College Street, the tenant above the hardware store had an unimpeded view of my telephone table and my tits. I did a quick laundry-in-the-Ganges squat.

"Oh my God, Babe. Guess what?!"

I was constantly amazing Maxi with my ability to guess things correctly but when the news was mighty she couldn't bear to give me thinking time.

"What's up?"

"Tara is a genius! A bloody genius! I am so excited, Bess. This is going to be one amazing article. She's a pugilist, but in this amazingly friendly way. She was a cheerleader but she also did Model UN. She got stoned before reading Huxley. She Eurorailed around eastern Europe."

"How very paradoxical of her. Careful, Maxi, you'll end up making friends."

"So what? She says she's going to set aside as much time as possible for us to hang out. She'll love what I'm going to do. I want to reveal her subtle, sustained cultural disruption, you know?"

"Someone's been jotting down notes."

"Tara says as long as Danielle—that's her personal assistant, I want one of those—as long as Danielle doesn't get in trouble for letting her run off at the mouth, she's fine with whatever. She likes my work! She subscribes to magazines from home out in LA. She remembered from one of my contributor profiles how much I love Michael Ignatieff, and frozen grapes, and so does she! She's reading this month's *Harpers*. You haven't even read that yet, Babe."

"Wow, *Harpers*. And this from a girl who doesn't have pores."

"How did I put it? Wait just a sec, here it is . . . A starlet as clean and inviting as a Hockney swimming pool, beguiling bathers, refracting impressions—"

"And chemically treated for purity."

"Nice, Babe, thanks! Let me just add that in. You don't mind, do you? I almost forgot the best part. Do you remember Charlie Dickens?"

"That guy you met at the Kraftwerk concert and that you dated for a few weeks in third year? The geek?"

"Make that a rich geek living in Haight-Ashbury with a geek wife and two geek children. He's Tara's older brother!

She remembers me from Easter dinner. She says I introduced Agincourt to leather pants. Talk about a head start. I'm not going to tell Sue. I want her to think I cracked my way in without any help at all."

"So we like Tara?"

"I love her! She was wearing head-to-toe winter white today and it totally worked. Her hair is long, but good long. The perfect blond, need I add."

"As boldfaced in the salon's press kit."

"I am so going to borrow her aura to blow away Tom."

"Right, power by association. Trust me, it works wonders."

"Tara calls me 'Journalista!' She calls Daniellc 'Bunny.' Danielle has got this twitchy little nose. And a PalmPilot. I want a PalmPilot."

"You have such a buzz on, Maxi. I haven't heard you like this in ages."

"Well, it's partly sugar. Danielle made me coffee and I could tell asking for Sweet'N Low wasn't on. I just know this article is going to be my breakthrough, Bess. I feel clear, I feel sharp. Tara has the best 34B's ever. They're these perfect, I don't know . . ."

"Orbs?"

"Yes! But not fake. She says if I get her drunk she's going to let me squeeze them. She's hilarious! She wasn't really late for the reshoot, she was petitioning the studio for rewrites. I noticed a ring on her engagement finger while she was in makeup but later it was gone. One-carat cushion cut, I'd say. I wonder what that's about? Can you find out for me?"

"I don't think Hank will know. It's just the two of us in the studio right now. I think I mentioned that."

"Well, maybe you can call someone in the production office? Oops, I have to dash to Boost Zone. It's Spin'n Abs at seven. I'm still saving the weekend for Tom, by the way. I hope you understand, Babe. I had a hang-up that I'm sure was him."

"I understand. Go, go burn rubber."

No bath was going to relax me after two calls in a row that reminded me of Grade Thirteen geometry in their wearisome tour of obtuse and acute angles. I drained the tub although I had hardly soaked and there were bubbles left. I'd realized with a familiar rush of relief that I was PMS'd to the gills. Hormones were to blame for my poor spirits rather than anything truly wrong with my life. Although there might also have been something wrong with my life. What on earth was I doing feeling threatened by Tara Dickens? One wasn't supposed to feel personally intimidated by Tara Dickens because Tara Dickens was supposed to stay safely put in La-la Land. Maxi wasn't really going to make friends with her. They were just going to use each other in the necessary ways and move on. And if Maxi did make friends with her, then maybe I would, too? I didn't want to make friends with Tara Dickens. I needed only Maxi. I needed Maxi to need me. Maxi had always exercised more power but I was the one who really understood it. Without Maxi around to elucidate to, I wondered how well I'd understand things myself. This was deep vein symbiosis we had going on. Losing Maxi might not rip out my heart but it would mess horribly with my arteries and capillaries. If only the girl spent more time with her mother, then I wouldn't have to. I had poor hopes for my busybody skills but I'd do my best to massage the sprained mother-daughter relations. Hopefully, Josephine wouldn't pinch all my secrets.

I was thinking the term "happy hour" had never been more of a misnomer. Josephine was waiting for me at the bar in her new fur. A jaunty, urban, hip-length number, handy for trips to the Starbucks or the organic market. Josephine had forced Maxi into a soccer league for ten years in her youth and watched from the sidelines draped in minks and otters. Soccer was one of the few things Maxi was actually grateful to her mother for—early muscle tone. Josephine didn't come to that many practices, however. Maxi had had a soccer maid more than a soccer mom.

"Bess, welcome, I took the liberty of ordering you a little something."

Josephine had remembered I wasn't much for gin. Unfortunately the result was a lychee martini. These were everywhere nowadays, even in this sector of crystal and mahogany, and they never failed to make my teeth ache.

"Thank you. Cheers."

"Let me get straight to the point, Bess. Does Max seem happy to you? Because she doesn't seem happy to me. I hoped the house might help, might make her feel a little less lost. But it doesn't seem to be doing the trick. She won't let her father and me come to see her. I guess I could just barge over there but that hardly seems useful. What do you think, Bess? I think she's struggling, I just don't understand why that would be, with all of her advantages. Did I bring her up to want more, more, more, is that it? I only wanted to install a sense of ambition. Lord, this isn't easy. Sorry, Bess, I do apologize. I'm at my wits' end."

Josephine paused for another gulp. Obviously, she had been stuck in one too many airport lounges with nothing but the Wellness section of the newspaper to entertain her. Maxi had given up having a shrink when Josephine had picked up the habit. I could see why it would be a lot less fun for her to discuss her mother when her mother was so busy discussing her.

"Spoiled, a spoiled child, just what is that supposed to mean, spoiled? The mother's fault is what it means. I tried hard not to spoil my child. It wasn't as if her father and I weren't going to share our comforts with her. Why else have we worked our fingers to the bone? But I tried to make my daughter aware of her benefits. For her sake I tried not to spoil her while I provided for her, provided very well I might add. She's supposed to be the happier for it by now. But when is she going to be happy enough to forgive me, Bess? Don't I merit some acceptance by now? When is she going to learn to relate to me?" Josephine pinched her nose between her eyebrows; Maxi's migraines were inherited.

"Maxi seems okay to me. Maybe a little stressed out. By the renovations mostly."

"Her father and I discussed that at length. It didn't seem wise to just, poof, give her a house. We wanted to make it a project. It will improve her sense of direction if she has to contribute in some way, don't you think? It's not like she's had to finance a thing, lucky girl. Of course, you and Max are as thick as thieves. She has no conflict with you, Bess. She saves that for her mother. That's our comfort zone, unfortunately. Not my doing, not that I'm aware of, but there you go. Well, there you don't go, Bess. There I go. I've tried many times to do something about it but I confess I'm about stumped. I hoped some of your magic might rub off on me, Bess. You seem to have just the right touch. Better you than me, I suppose. What Max needs is a good friend."

The lychee garnish floated in my drink like a ghastly, flaking eyeball. I had an awful feeling any moment a couple of pinstriped grey-hairs two bar stools over were going to hit on Josephine and me. I had thought I looked too Grade Nine for that. I felt pretty ungainly, belly-up to the fancy bar beside powerhouse Josephine, with my jacket stuffed underneath my bum, my sweater thick and zippered up, my jeans unredeemed by any heels. I felt like a hit man checking in with the mob boss. None of this was fair on anyone.

"Maybe it was just Christmas, do you think, Bess? Christmas depresses everybody."

Josephine reached into her snakeskin baguette, popped the cap off a vial of pills and downed one. It was the size of a jumbo olive. I thought maybe she should have plopped it in her drink.

"Maxi tends to idealize things," I said. "That can make it hard to live up to her expectations, hard for anyone. Maxi is as ambitious as you but it's harder for her, in a way. She got a big head start, sure, but that can make it more pressure to run the race. Maxi does love you, in her own crazy way."

Josephine blinked. I had never seen her do that before. I felt like I'd taunted a bull with a blue cape.

"Thank you, Bess. Thank you so much for that. I promise I won't let on anything to Max. This has been unfair of me as it is. I do apologize."

"I know you're trying to do the right thing. Listen to her carefully and she'll give you the clues."

I could have also told Josephine that Maxi had an unbounded ability to soak up compliments, and this came in handy in a crunch. But I had to fly. Maxi would kill me if I was spotted in a hotel lobby without her, let alone with her mother. Josephine held out a creamed, be-ringed hand; Mr. Bishop had brought maximum arsenal to bear for the engagement and added to it over the years. They were the same hands as Maxi's, hefty and enveloping and manly in their energy and grip, manicure notwithstanding. I waved goodbye with one of my moist little ones as I backed out past the polished tables, framed caricatures and elderly unionized waiters. Outside it had really started to blow.

Maxi was trying hard to persuade me that Tara was brilliant but I still didn't think much of Jessica. At the foley studio I was busy with Jessica busying herself in her laboratory again. Obviously, that powdery compound she'd developed was akin to pulverized Holy Grail. Then came a heartwarming scene of her petting her favourite lab rat farewell for the night. As for her subsequent stroll through dark, wet, downtown streets: Marisa could nuance a difference between happy footsteps and sad footsteps, male and female, old and young, hearty and cowering, cool and uncool, and I too wanted to cram Jessica full of character by tread alone. Then came a montage over which Hank and I got to fast-forward, thanks to some pop song that would cover the scene. Something to do with Jessica spying her sugar poppa in a restaurant window with company that looked a lot less savoury than the fare. Of course, you could see it plainly dawning on Jessica's face, how cruelty was an elaborate system, with cogs, pulleys and tipping points. Off she went to snoop through her evil benefactor's apartment while he was slurping his *linguine al vongole*. Behind an oil painting—a storm-tossed galleon—was indeed a wall safe, in keeping with the kitsch golden rule. Jessica made an improbably lucky guess on the combination after a bitten plump lower lip. All I cared about was the click and kachoink of the lock mechanism, an effect I managed with a steel comb and vice grips. Stashed inside the safe were mini-surveillance tapes that Jessica popped into the matching recorder—we had one of those, too—and listened to with a brow so furrowed she looked almost thirty. I finished her darting back out into the damp streets and then we were done.

Now that Marisa was away, Maxi called me at work. I suspected Maxi was secretly terrified of Marisa. Her effortlessness always made Maxi work twice as hard, and since she generally worked too hard as it was, the result was invariably a kerfuffle. She'd talk to Marisa a little too in depth about what it was like to be adopted, or she'd question a little too intently why Marisa had never moved to LA, or she'd chat for a little too long about how dangerous horseback riding could be.

I was doing my best to be nice to Maxi. Tom was giving her the runaround. He'd left one message from the road, then reduced their calls to phone tag. Now it turned out she was ragingly keen for her and me to get together.

"So is Wonder Boy busy?"

"That's not it! I haven't been seeing enough of you lately, Babe, that's the issue."

"So he's busy?"

"Yes, he's busy. Client dinners, tomorrow definitely and probably tonight. But he wants to meet for squash on Sunday morning."

"Hang tight, by the time he's middle-aged he'll be delegating."

"In any case I can't stand Saturday nights out on the town any longer. Too much hoo-ha. How about a girls' night at my place? We can watch *Breakfast at Tiffany's* and do home facials. Tom will think it's so cute."

"You hate Audrey Hepburn. Her accent always makes you jealous. And drugstore face packs give you zits."

"Fine. It was just a thought. Honestly, I don't know what I can do to make this house more inviting. Evidently some of us have homes that people like to drop in on and some of us don't. If there's some special formula—"

"I'd love to come over, Maxi. We don't care what we do, Aunt Flo and me, as long as there's Midol involved."

"No wonder you're so prickly!"

"Sorry."

"Can you cope with a Tara Dickens retrospective? I need your input, Babe. No one critiques like you do. This article is such a big deal for me. I promise to fast-forward if you're bored."

"Better stock up on Smartfood."

"Bess, you're the best!"

It was one of our good old plans, the kind that filled Saturday nights with consolation and sanity. Plus now I could relax and spend Friday evening alone at home without worrying that I was a hermit. I'd picked up the January *Harpers* after all, cover story: *The Unfinished Twentieth Century*. Then I could turn to Alice. Reading Alice Munro was like filling a syringe with maturity and injecting some. But the hit never lasted long enough. Before I knew it I was back to my own wobbly first person singular with no omniscience to my credit.

By the time I got home, snow flurries were holding up everyone metropolis-wide. There was no point hitting the books without a big dinner to keep me going. Just as I was settling into three tofu dogs with *Who Do You Think You Are?* propped up behind them, I heard hollering out on the street and a pinging against my front windows. My name was being called and I heard a pining kind of whine. I looked out the front window to see Marcus and Rocks gazing up at me with their little faces. Even their big mugs looked tiny from on high. I clomped down and let them in, not exactly loving the parade back up the stairs. Marcus eyed my three stuffed buns, oozing carnival red and yellow.

"What do you know, you were expecting us. Rocks loves ketchup."

"No, not really."

"I assure you he does. Rocks loves all condiments. He takes his Alpo with mango chutney, right, buddy?"

Rocks was so enticed he was having trouble breathing. But he was more polite about it than Marcus. Rocks's gaze held a lot of entreaty; meanwhile, Marcus tucked in.

"I'll get you guys some plates," I said. "Anyone for a beer?"

"As long as you don't mind us farting," said Marcus.

I had some Red Stripes on hand. I was trying to maintain a steady supply of Caribbean beer. It was like having a poem in the fridge about sun and sand. "Bottoms up," I told the lads. I poured Rocks a little splash on his empty plate—an emptiness he couldn't quite seem to grasp, having basically inhaled his wiener.

"Irie, mon," Marcus said. I didn't bother to cringe but I would have in the right company.

"Have you ever been to Jamaica?" I asked.

"Yup." Unlike Tom, Marcus did not tend to elaborate.

"When was that?"

"Oh, about two years ago. I went down there to shoot a diet root beer ad."

"Wicked."

"If you think bossing around a bunch of freakishly pretty young things for five days straight under the burning sun for the sake of a sickly sweet beverage is *wicked*, I guess you're right."

"I do. I was not speaking ironically."

"Excellent. I love agreeing with you."

"Do you miss LA?"

"No. Ask me if I miss the money."

"Do you miss the money?"

"Sometimes. I paid some dues. Now it's time to see whether I was really slumming like I hoped."

"Or whether all you're good for is cameos for commerce."

"Time will tell. Actually, a fuck of a lot of work will tell."

"But you got out before you bought a Porsche?"

"Yeah, well."

Marcus took a bite of dog and a sudden interest in my ceiling. I discovered cobwebs up there, but I knew the chat had got stuck on something else.

"You have a Porsche?"

"Guilty, your Honour."

"Where is it?"

"Sitting in a garage, waiting to get sold. I'll live off that for a year when the time comes."

"I see. Wow."

"You kind of had to have one if you were doing what I was doing. Porsches are like suits out there. Especially if you dress for shit, like me."

Now that he had taken off the decrepit hide, I saw Marcus had on droopy 501s and a Motorhead T-shirt. Rocks had a nice new collar, red leather with grommets.

"Rocks is lookin' good." I tugged a fuzzy black ear, thick as quadrupled felt. Rocks's eyelids drooped closed as his pleasure grew. What is it with guys and ears? When Rocks woofed in appreciation I gave him the last of my bun. His tail thumped against the floorboards. Rocks had no time for ambiguity.

"Sure he's looking good. That's because he'd do anything for you. I had to stop him from bringing over his collected e.e. cummings. He wanted to read you the one about how nobody, not even the rain, has such small hands."

"Rocks better watch the unconditionality. Dangerous stuff."

"Unconditional, my ass. Don't try reading him any Anne Sexton. Anyhow, he keeps whining your name. When he smells *my* crotch his tail stops wagging. I can't get him to sit through Bergman movies any more."

"Life's a struggle, Rocksie."

Rocks barked again, thrilled that the conversation had taken this turn in his direction. He shifted his weight from paw to paw and looked back and forth at us with glistening attachment. I could tell he wanted to woof once more but gentlemanliness prevented him.

"We were on our way to the starts-with-a-*p*-ends-with-a-*k*-with-a-lot-of-poop-in-between," said Marcus. "Rocks is thinking tobogganing and, quite frankly, I don't blame him. Want to come?"

Actually, I did.

The flurries had tapered off, leaving a fluffy layer of white that had gone blue in the relative dark of the park. I felt hypocritical. Many was the time I'd cursed the irritating dog club that congregates there, owners yapping to each other with leashes dangling from their pockets while their huskies and pugs maraud. I had no idea what I was doing besides answering Marcus's challenge to my idiosyncrasy quotient. It was like if I didn't keep up with him that night I'd never be the proud owner of a quirk again. Rocks barrelled around like a little bull in a great mood for the arena. He pretended to snack on my mitts then got distracted by his shadow, potentially yet another friend. He stopped twirling for a moment to yodel his joy to me, Marcus and the moon.

Marcus had on a black knit hat that said "Fly" and mitts that looked like makeshift boxing gloves. "Let's hit Rocks with snowballs," he said. "He loves it."

Rocks had a Nureyev side to him that was actually nice to see. We kept trying to shush his yelping, which wasn't easy: Rocks was on a natural high. He seemed thoroughly glad to see me, dumb dog. Whatever Marcus did was incidental, whereas I was Her Majesty. Marcus had a pocket full of dog biscuits and a thermos of spiked cocoa.

"I thought chocolate made you sleepy," I said.

"It does. But cognac wakes me up."

Sliding down the park hills in cardboard boxes we'd grabbed on the way there was a laugh. We had races, which I won easily because Marcus's carton burst to bits.

"I think outside the box," he said.

I felt my clothes grow hot and damp beneath my jacket and my breath rush harsh through my lungs in a way I hadn't since my snow-fort days. Marcus was even taller when I was in snow boots. The conditions were poor for snow angels but I lay down anyhow.

"Funny," I said, "how when you get older you don't notice the sky. I used to stargaze and cloud watch all the time when I was young."

"I'm always so disappointed when I get constellations pointed out to me. They seem like too much of a stretch. I really want there to be horses up there. And lions, and crabs, and seven twinkly sisters."

"I've got to get going. My inner layers are starting to freeze."

We crunched through the park and back toward College Street without a lot more to say.

"How's your millennium going by the way?" I asked at my door. "Apocalyptic enough for you?"

"Still working on my script. Lots to iron out."

"No offence, but you don't look like the ironing type."

"You are so wrong. I iron my tighty-whities."

I watched the boys set off, very Mutt and Jeff. I guessed with me along we had looked like Mutt and two Jeffs. Marcus's knit hat turned out to be a balaclava. He unfolded it down over his face before pecking me a woolly goodbye. He was so tall that when he leaned over I wanted to yell "Timber." A nasty white patch started to grow around his mouth hole. And I'd wondered why Canada wasn't sexier. Well, I'd had fun, I guessed. And no one had seen us. Thanks to the boys, I slept instantaneously and deeply, no brawling with my pillows.

I ate leftover toasted hotdog buns with butter and marmalade for breakfast. That gave me strength to tackle the Saturday morning papers, anvils that they are around my neck, rubbing my nose in my world before the weekend can even get going. Maxi would be happy to see the professional Toronto gossips abuzz to have Tara back in town, happy and provoked into a *Fountainhead* frenzy. Back in our university days I could never get Maxi to step away from the Ayn Rand; she'd been dating too many frat boys for that, and stewing in their competitive juices. Me, I was provoked to finally fix the bathroom mirror. When in doubt—power drill.

Definitely, I thought about telling Maxi how Marcus, Rocks and I had enjoyed a nocturnal adventure. It was going to be hard not to, all cosy over at her place with umpteen girly hours at our disposal. But I decided against it, no matter how well it fit the bill. Maxi would be delighted I had man action of my own to relay, with gangly, weirdo Marcus. With me keeping him busy, he'd be lot less likely to hook up with someone who might outshine her on a double date. Also, a mere trickle of my own data would crank Maxi's floodgates wide open. Torrential, drenching volumes of Tom info would come sluicing out, and soon I'd be soaked flat and senseless. Knowing Maxi, for the last two weeks she'd been fine-honing her estimations of Tom until she could have exhibited him at the Smithsonian as an exemplar of his species: *Bachelorus supereligibilis*. I don't know why I ever presumed Maxi's ultimate man and I would have anything in common. I had little elegance with which to bully people. I didn't expect to be reckoned with. I loved a bargain. Maxi had always excused me for all that, but I wondered if she would find it as easy to do with a fellow paragon by her side. I wasn't going to feel very attractive hanging around as court jester.

First off, I got in trouble for banging the chomping lion door knocker. Maxi was flushed with hospitality excitement and up for an old-fashioned front-hall fuss.

"Babe, you're walk-right-in status! You know I always unlock for you."

"But your door knocker is so much fun. You should use it yourself. Wow, I feel like an Indian widow."

There were candles every which way. I'd almost ignited my elbow taking off my jacket. A fight to the finish was going on between vanilla columns and imported lily-of-the-valley jars. Josephine had given Maxi an entire crate of Diptyques when she'd said that was all she wanted for Christmas. Maxi was in grace-note overdrive. Her bouquets had obviously been fluffed. She'd got out her Balinese wooden bowl collection and laid in a junk food smorgasbord: Smartfood, pretzels, jujubes and wine gums, Smarties, licorice pipes and a large bar of her favourite 70 percent cacao stripped to the foil. I knew I was supposed to fall completely in love with Maxi's house that night so that forevermore I'd always come over when requested. I knew she had a splendid vision of Crawford Street as my haven, too, herself as a highly urban mother superior with cocktails up her bell sleeves and a keen ear for sex stories. Basically, Maxi was laying the groundwork for an asylum now in case no men ever worked out later. I did appreciate it, this shelter from our combined potential disappointments.

"Maxi, look at all this. You're such a humanitarian. Someone should rustle you up some UN clout. I bet you could turn the whole refugee-camp thing around if you wanted to."

"Come to the kitchen, there's more."

Tara was taped to Maxi's fridge now, gleaming away. There were six Coronas waiting for me plus lime wedges. Maxi was already sipping from a flagon of Chianti. I didn't have the heart to tell her she had a red wine moustache. Right away, Maxi was keen to show me around her upgrades. I tossed my beer cap in her new nifty, chrome, foot-pedal kitchen garbage.

"Don't!"

"Don't what?"

"Don't tidy up after yourself like that. Not so uptightly, I mean. I almost feel like you're making fun of me."

"Um, okay."

"Just relax, Bess. Please. It's not that much to ask, right? Ow!"

"Shit, did I get you? I'm sorry."

It was partly Maxi's fault. She had cut the limes really chunky and the citrus was juicy. Maxi had high-end produce delivered twice a week.

"Oh God, ow, bloody hell. Pass me a dishtowel, they're in the drawer there, no, a plain white one. That's better. I'm fine, Babe, no big deal. Okay, follow me!"

Maxi's new bed had the potential to be a significant destination; I made sure to let her know that. Apparently, the latest in mattresses cut down on intra-partner reverberations. We tested that out for a moment, but a fast one. Maxi was keen for me to give her new Aeron chair a twirl. Dutifully, I then ogled her heated bath towel holder.

"Nice rack."

"Thanks. It's the sort of thing that counts when you're pitching *House & Home*."

"Is that why you traded in all the appliances?" We were heading back down to the kitchen so Maxi could grab a refill.

"Black was just so eighties. I wanted a matte finish."

"These ones look like they belong to artsies in Belgium."

"What is it with you and Belgium lately?"

"Nothing much. I always have a nemesis, this time I picked a whole country."

"Have another beer, here, I insist, but let me do the lime this time. Wait, here's an opener, don't use your teeth. I hate that, Bess, and so do other people."

I could have mentioned how some people hate the sound of back cracks, too; power yoga had got Maxi's spine sounding like popcorn on high heat, but I bit my tongue. I literally bit my tongue. That was what I got for eating jujubes and popcorn in the same mouthful. A Tara Dickens filmography was lined up atop Maxi's VCR all ready to roll. Tara would be appearing that evening as Tammy, Tracy, Zara and Anemone. *Danger Beach* was the first up—Tammy was a perky lifeguard who helped her detective dad solve suspicious drowning cases. I arranged the candy bowls for optimum snack rotation. Maxi settled into the couch beside me. She had no shortage of pillows. We heaped them behind us and between us, then Maxi leaned over to take a good sniff of me, her nose brushing my neck. I knew what she was up to. She wanted to get in close. She swore it kept her cycle regular to take a good smell of me now and then. Gone were our days of complete synchronicity; too much took place over the phone for that now. Of course, I had always gone on for a few days longer and needed reminding to take my iron supplements.

"NB, I keep to one spritz of Happy now, as per your instructions."

"Good. I hope you don't mind but I just had to say something. If not me then who? You just don't have the surface area for two, Babe. Do you want the last of my Shalimar? I think it's lost its oomph."

Maxi once read that the average woman owns six perfumes and alternates between two. She herself stocked as many classic couture scents from the thirties as possible and was very sensitive to shelf life.

"I'm good with just the one, thanks."

"God, this wine is smooth. Are you sure you don't want some? My nerves keep absorbing my buzz lately. Funny how we've never been druggies, isn't it? I could never get away with the pot thing. The munchies would do me in."

"I say we're better off with controlled substances. At least that way we have a vague idea where we're headed."

Maxi and I had had an ecstasy phase—a very, very brief one in the early nineties. I wasn't that interested but Maxi wanted to see what everybody else was raving about. Our friend Nunci did the honours; she was dating the deejay at 1,2,3 Go. The results were fairly Roman orgy. Somehow Maxi and I got squeezed into a washroom cubicle with several other semi-clad clubbers while Crystal Waters throbbed over the sound system, "She's homeless, she's homeless." The repetitiousness was exquisite to me. As was the feel of skin, half velvet, half silk, anyone's and everyone's. I got stuck at the bottom of that particular heap. I went home with a wad of green gum in my hair. Maxi couldn't stop laughing when she snipped it out at dawn. Then she gave me the green Armani top her mother had given her that she swore suited me better. Maxi's colour wheel revolved a lot more smoothly than mine. She never let me dye my hair. "Anne got Gilbert in the end, Babe," she always reminded me. Maxi was my saint and I hoped I was hers, too. That night I'd slept with the green top on my bed so I'd see it first thing in the morning.

"Maxi, remember that green top you gave me? Thanks again. I always loved that top."

"No problem, Babe, it was too high cut for me anyway. Thanks again for coming over tonight. I really looked forward to it."

I knew that too many mental previews dulled the Technicolor of Maxi's events when they actually occurred, but fortunately this one appeared to be unfolding as she'd envisioned. She seemed happy enough, but that could have been the Chianti. She had a pad and pen poised for notes. I took a closer look at Tammy. Tara Dickens had been a very fulsome eighteen, looking twenty-five before her time, and now she was going to look twenty-five for twenty-five years straight. There was something inherently heroic about her, I had to admit.

I put down the wine gums. "Sorry, I'm feeling kind of mild this evening."

"Well don't. You're here to nitpick."

"I suppose Tammy's crush on the jock is kind of stupid. It's obvious the nerd is going to be really cute when he ditches the Dilton Doily glasses."

"Even I got that much."

"Okay, not meaning to get too Mr. Weatherbee on you, but if you think about it, Tara is half Betty, half Veronica. It's what we all want but it's very rare. Speaking Betty to Veronica here. The chick is genius at combinations."

"The next ones will be even better. Tracy was switched at birth. Zara is an extraterrestrial. Anemone has hippy parents."

"I know. Duped by a nefarious chemical company into leasing out their sheep meadows. It actually got pretty good reviews. I'll say this much about Tara, she doesn't have an edge exactly but she has a twist." I helped myself to some Smarties. Maxi had somehow found out how to buy only red ones.

"Go on."

"She's predictable in her slight unpredictability. Here, pause this shot, see how she knows to keep her lips soft while she hardens everything else to a sneer. In short, the chick *knows*."

"This is more like it, let me get that down."

"While you do that I'm visiting your facilities."

"Feel free to use the guest soap, it's already broken in."

"No thanks, I'm trying to cut down on my handwashing. All I need now is an obsessive-compulsive disorder. I'd rather spread bacteria." Alone together, Maxi and I weren't completely closed-door types. "You must love having a powder room. There sure isn't one of these in the Maxi Pad."

"Bess, please stop calling my old apartment by that ridiculous name. It's embarrassing."

I washed my hands after all.

We forged ahead, movie after movie. Maxi put up with my credit watching; I'm religious about that. It turned out she was more interested in fast-forwarding through Tara's artistic development than I was. By the time we got halfway through the third video she was lobbing candy at the screen. We'd just triple-checked but Tara Dickens simply didn't have cellulite.

"I don't know why you're so upset about it, Babe. You don't have any either."

"Yeah, but I'm a dwarf. We all have our price to pay."

"You and your metabolism. That's one thing we'll never have in common. Look how much you had to eat tonight."

"Sorry. Your hunger for success always just makes me want to pig out."

Maxi hauled herself to her feet to load the last movie and retrieve a green jujube that had narrowly missed a Tiffany-framed portrait of her mother from her sorority-sister phase. Not even hilarious cat's-eye glasses could hide the suspicion that had always brimmed from Josephine's gaze.

"I think I'll open up another bottle-ee-o of vino, why bloody not?"

"Go ahead. But you are eating properly, right?"

"Bess, please! Eating disorders are so passé. We decided that ten years ago, remember?"

"Fair enough."

By the time we were done Maxi seemed pleased to have two of me sitting beside her on her couch, where we'd made two warm, deep dents. It was just too bad Maxi's tongue had gone adipose. I got her to weave me to her door. She was due to meet Tom in a squash court in seven hours, ponytail hiked for action. I hoped for her sake her bangs wouldn't clump. We'd blown out all her candles, one by one together, which had felt like casting a spell. Wind was hooting outside Maxi's windows with *Wuthering Heights* flair. It suited her—the mythic maiden on the moor thing. Though maybe not right at that moment.

"I'm shupposed to do lunch again with Tara on Monday."

"Way to go."

Maxi was helping me with my coat, which was burning up every calorie I'd eaten. She seemed to have forgotten what sleeves were. Unfortunately, I then got help with the snaps.

"Here'sh to our friendship, Bess. C'mon, cheersh, Babe. c'mon, come back in, Cheersh."

"Maxi, get back here. I've got to go. I'm vanquished."

"Shtay over!"

"Nah, no need. We never have The Nothingness when it's just us two."

"I have to conshentrate Tara down to her esshence. Right? Right?!"

Maxi was out on her porch, hopping from sock foot to sock foot, making sure I didn't leave her behind with any dangling questions.

"Then you will."

"I'm going to treat her as ironically as she treatsh hershelf. She will get it, oh yeah she will sooooo get it. We'll be partners in her shuperb, delinquen—, delinquensch . . ."

"Why don't you just tell everyone what they want to hear, Maxi, which is that Tara Dickens is a cute bitch?"

"She ISN'T! She ish not. She jusht uses cuteness and bitchiness as SIGNIFIERS."

"This is for general interest, don't forget. Not *Semiotics Monthly*."

"To teach AND delight, Bessh. To delight AND teach. Have shome goals why dontcha?"

"Maxi, shush, your neighbours are going to turn against you. They're not used to tarts."

"Tom misshed me tonight? Right?"

"Of course."

"I have to give this little housh some SEX. It'll love it. It'll love me even more than it already doesh, for reshcuing it from tasteless people."

"Absolutely. Now go inside."

Maxi knew when she needed to slop on some Crème de la Mer and crash. She said it was one of her wisest investments since women who buy top-quality face cream are statistically proven to feel better about their whole body. She'd also read that one's adult body image is profoundly determined by the appearances of one's siblings during adolescence, but no one had ever explained to her what that meant to an only child.

Walking home that night, I made a mental note to myself—a living-in-the-moment kind of thing that is never quite as potent an experience as one strives for—to be grateful for time spent together, just Maxi and me. I was wondering how many more Saturday nights like that there were left to us. A few dozen, maybe, our whole lives long. It was a strange feeling, to count something down to its demise. It was kind of disruptive. Ever since New Year's it had felt like there was this cataclysmically loud marching band closing in tighter and tighter around Maxi and me, the tubas honking out portents, the snare drums jittering in apprehension, the trumpets squealing concern. Maxi had heard the new tunes first, I could tell; she always noticed things before I did. And she was always the one whom people noticed first. Maxi was the shot, I was the chaser.

I decided to head out to Burlington and get my first Sunday visit of the year over with. It would be a doozy. My brother, Eddie, and his wife, Elaine, had flown in out of the blue from Manitoba because they had a "family announcement" to make. I'd been warning everyone that I might not be able to make it, but for my own good I didn't keep up the ruse. I knew I'd feel too sick with guilt holed up downtown with the phone turned off, missing all the gossip, the pork chops and applesauce, the pound cake with lemon cream. Besides, Eddie had offered to come and pick me up at the train station so I wouldn't have to put up with Mom's speed demonry. I told him I'd call Sunday morning to confirm my train.

"The three-thirty," I told him at noon.

"Did you sleep last night?" Eddie asked.

"Yeah. A bit."

"Oh no."

"I did sleep but not last night. I slept a lot this morning."

"Try to sleep on the train, okay?"

"The train's the fun part!"

"Elaine's looking forward to seeing you. She has a special announcement to make."

Eddie hung up on my baby cry; I do even better infants than apes.

I took some Alice Munro on the train with me. *Friend of My Youth* lay like a talisman on my lap while I gazed out at the grey lake slapping and rebounding off the windows to the south and the bewilderingly uniform subdivisions to the north. During station stops my attention got dragged back inside the carriage to survey any hustle and bustle. When I was younger I'd people watch with nary an agenda but lately I studied families more critically. I rated kids on a spoiledness scale and tallied barbs and kindnesses between spouses. Sitting across from me was an East Indian family. The wife looked supremely elegant in a magenta silk sari with almost matching pumps and a thinning camel hair coat over top. The father wore pilgrim shoes, a tired trench and a part as perfect as a barber's diagram. They had a skinny little boy of kindergarten age, with a head that jerked this way and that along with his short-fuse curiosity. The mother held him between her legs as he kept his balance with one little hand poised on each of her plump knees. I saw with a pang that his jeans had an elasticized waistband. I felt overwhelmed by this family picture. I wished I were Bess Gates, Guggenheim or Soros. I wanted to offer them a Toyota sedan, warmer coats and a year's supply of Levis. I wanted them to attend buffet dinners and walk on plush carpets. I wanted to ask the father if he had a doctorate in gravitational physics that he was having trouble applying to the Toronto economy. I wanted to ask the mother if she'd teach me the secrets of a good curry and how to dance with bells. I wanted to ask the little boy if he'd like a PlayStation with every available accessory. But I stayed quiet, needless to say. I was curious who they were meeting at Port Credit, but the train left the station before anyone had pulled up to the curb, where they waited patiently in formation like half the family von Trapp.

Eddie was punctual in meeting me at the station, being an engineer whose life success was founded on notions of precision.

"So how are you?" Eddie always craned before making a turn.

"Shitty."

"How's Maxine?"

"Great."

I thought Eddie had always secretly carried a torch for Maxi, which was ungainly of him. It's the younger sister's friend who's supposed to get the crush, not the older brother. I felt gypped that Maxi was an only child with no princely heir for me to fling myself at. Just because Maxi and I weren't gay didn't mean we couldn't fall for male versions of each other. Not that Eddie and I corresponded in any evident way. We were as unalike as chalk and cheese. Compared to Eddie's chalk, I was Muenster.

"When we get home, do me a favour and help Mom. She's really outdoing herself. They're not as young as they used to be, you know."

"Why isn't Elaine helping?"

Elaine is also an engineer whose professional skills find untold domestic applications. She buys my mom kitchen tools on every occasion. The previous Mother's Day I'd informed Elaine that a life in which the twisting of a hand-held can opener was held to be too labour intensive was not my opinion of a life worth living. She just laughed. As I gazed out the car window at the ragged unfurling of a fast-food strip, I surprised myself by remembering the family from the train. I wondered if they had an electric can opener. I should have asked them if they had friends I could drop in on in Mumbai. Maybe I had to get out of absolutely everyone's hair and try out a new continent.

"Elaine gets tired easily these days."

"I'm thinking of going to India," I told Eddie.

"Don't drink the water," he cracked.

Eddie had never taken me very seriously. Once, this had been a misery. Now I'd be horrified if he did. Showing neither of us much mercy, Eddie drove past Burlington Collegiate. I still wasn't sure if I'd ever recover from the pep rallies; it was my dream to invite a bunch of French post-structuralists to my alma mater and have them deconstruct it to bits. Maxi, however, harboured thwarted cheerleader ambitions. She would have revelled in the tidiness of a squad: the pleats, white socks and syncopation. Instead she'd gone to a girl's school in Forest Hill where she wore a tie and a kilt for fourteen years and excelled at playing lacrosse, debating with the boys' schools and smoking behind large oak trees.

"I still can't believe you were school treasurer," I said.

"You're surprised I got elected?"

"Not at all. I just can't believe you bothered."

Soon enough 142 Farthingale Crescent poked itself into the windshield and filled it. A house that could not have been more normal if it tried. White siding, yellow brick, a two-car thrust-garage with one Volvo and one Civic, a clique of birch trees out front and a pool cover flapping in the wind out back. Eddie and I had both lived here from day one. Dad must have been in a good mood because Herb Alpert and the Tijuana Brass weren't taking no for an answer. I'd been right about the pound cake. Mom had trouble hugging me with a wooden spoon dripping from one hand but Elaine was quick on the draw with the paper towels. I tried not to scope out Elaine's boobs too obviously but at a glance they looked bigger. I hadn't thought that was possible. I recalled reading in *Allure* that women retain three times more sperm from an illicit lover than they do from a steady partner. Of course, Elaine was a living, breathing refutation of the all recent theories that females had only ever pretended to be monogamous and were programmed deep down to be sleazes.

"So," I said. "What gives?"

"We were waiting until you got here," Elaine simpered. Imminent motherhood had already wilted her around the edges. "Seven weeks!" she howled. "We want to keep it quiet for a while longer but we just had to tell all of you!"

I gave the woman a hug, even before Mom did. "I'm thrilled," I said.

I was. I was hoping I could lure the little tyke over to my side as an ally. There were too few of us cool people in the family fold. In fact, there was only me. Elaine and Eddie ate three square meals a day, my mom said "Jeepers" and when my father had emerged from his study I noticed that there were actual suede patches on his sweater elbows. The bunch of them belonged in a low-budget TV ad for insurance. It made for a relaxing Sunday for me. I swanned around like Cleopatra on her barge, waiting to be fed, entertained and transported. No one objected when I watched *Family Feud*. I helped out Mom by whipping the cream; licking the beaters was as hard on the tongue as ever. After dinner I was cheered for clearing the table with a flashy demonstration of my busgirl skills.

"No more waitressing for Bess," I heard my mother say. "She got a promotion."

"Kind of!" I hollered from the kitchen. I was taking extra care with the barn-shaped butter dish my brother had a thing for even though I had bought it myself a few years before at a church jumble sale.

"I can't believe you didn't say anything," Eddie said.

"No big deal. You're the one with the big news. And it's not as if it's more money, not yet. Marisa had to take a loss on this one so I could use it as a learning experience."

"Now, now, Bessie, you know the dollar isn't almighty," my dad said.

"No, carbs are almighty. I think I'm on a serotonin high right now, you guys. Can I take some cake home with me just to make sure?"

"Oh the pain when she doesn't call my home her home," my mother moaned.

"You take the cake, Bessie," said my father.

"I've gained five pounds already. No morning sickness at all!"

We never begrudged Elaine her chance to say something, no matter how off her rhythm, conversationally. I hoped she was going to take my parents up on their offer to fly out and help with the baby when the time came. It was the perfect adventure for them: 75 percent altruistic, 20 percent patriotic, 5 percent out of the ordinary.

Eddie drove me back to the station in time for the eight-twenty.

"Congratulations." I unbuckled. "The dynasty continues, thanks to you."

"It's a big change," Eddie said.

"No more raising hell at the curling bonspiel?"

"It's a new responsibility that I'm very much looking forward to assuming, is all."

"Do you want to know another way to spell responsibility? D-I-A-P-E-R-S."

I cackled and fell out of the car. It would have been cruel of me to defy expectation and not be snide at such a moment. I thought fatherhood would suit Eddie. He'd be stable and discreet and no doubt give rise to the same mixed brood as our own dad: one clone and one freak. Medium-height, medium-smart Eddie with hair the colour of Wonder Bread crusts.

"Have a girl, they potty-train faster," I poked my head back into the car to say, blew Eddie a kiss, then shut the door and hurried to the waiting room.

There were no pleasant families to scrutinize in the train on the way home. Lumbering teenagers in shiny bomber jackets instead, who hooted and fought over CDs that they played in jacked-up Discmans that sounded like tinned bees. I decided to get out at Union Station and start walking, one step ahead of the cold. I was scared to approach bedtime after a day of such indolence. The grandeur of the downtown business towers was so precise as to be antiseptic. My reflection walked alongside, all warbled in the windows. I stopped to consider myself and had one of those surreal moments, when you wonder how it is that you are this person, living inside this life and this mind, with this face, and this expression, and how it is that you have that mother, father, brother, friend. Sometimes, familiarity breeds too much contempt, but how many of us would ever trade ourselves in, given the weird chance?

Maxi got us to dress up and play the part of Bay Street power babes once, just to see if we could. I was too chicken to pretend to be anyone but her deputy. Maxi's method acting was a revelation; I was convinced myself she analyzed South American agribusiness. Maxi liked the clipped brokerage talk and collecting business cards. I liked the wasabi peas. She said we didn't have to feel guilty for not calling anyone back. With her investment mistress persona she scored a cab instantaneously. As usual, Maxi promised she owed me. As usual, she knew she didn't. She said we could stop for a bowl of pho on the way home but my pumps were killing me and I was freezing since I didn't own a convincing shoulder-season coat.

When I got home from my bracing walk, there were no messages to pick up so I had time to call home.

"Thanks, Mom, for the delicious dinner."

"Why, it was my pleasure. Did you get back safely?"

"No, but they're all in jail and I only needed fifty stitches."

"Funny one."

In any other family, next I would have said "I love you" but mine was so normal I didn't have to.

"'Night, Ma."

"Good night, Elizabeth. Don't let the bedbugs bite."

I didn't.

Late as it was, I came up with some *Gash* before bed, just to thank Maxi for Saturday night—and apologize one last time for my PMS, which had been undetectable to anyone else on earth I was sure, but who was I to question Maxi's sensitivities? I was in fact grateful for registering with her to the degree that I did. If there was one thing that Maxi implied over and over, it was that I was a real experience.

GASH FLASH

Super-Charged Tampons Mystify NASA

By Bess Grover

A bizarre discovery has physicists, biologists, paranormalists and female victims reeling. The story begins at a disused hydroelectric power station twenty miles outside Flubbed Lip, North Dakota. Night-shift security guard Doris Ames says her job was "weird enough in the first place." For over ten years, Ames drove to the abandoned plant five times a week to patrol the deserted premises between 6 p.m. and 6 a.m. "It's lonely as hell out there and those generators are creepy. But I can watch TV and it sure beats nursing, know what I mean?" Ames is currently on medical disability leave.

Ames kept few personal effects in her desk drawer. "Just the basics," she has told police and academic investigators. "Spare keys, gum and mints, the odd *People* Magazine and," here Ames pauses to laugh nervously, "my feminine products." Both science and the law have failed to come up with an explanation as to how Doris Ames's econo pack of super-absorbency tampons became super-charged.

"I prefer o.b. brand as a rule," Ames explains. "Some women don't, they hate the fiddling, but I have what you call a tipped uterus, so I favour something I can adjust. Mother forgets. She bought me the Tampax, you see. She put 'em in my Christmas stocking a few years back. I guess I had them sitting in that drawer down there at the station absorbing who knows what for quite some time." Eventually, Ames, 37, was forced to make use of the products.

"I noticed a tingling," Ames admits. "It kinda grew and grew, into more of a buzz. Before I knew it I was flat on my back. I must have had about fifty orgasms, minimum, before I managed to pull that thing out and calm down." With some trepidation, Ames opted to insert another of the tampons. Again, a multi-orgasmic result.

Eventually, Ames wadded up some toilet paper as a stopgap measure and called her mother, who denied having tampered in any way with the feminine hygiene products. "It's just not Mother's style," said Ames. "Besides, everything was all still sealed up when I cracked it open, the box and the plugs."

Ames revealed the strange powers of the super tampons to her close friend, Gert Roy, mother of three, who volunteered to test out another of the cotton/rayon/cardboard items. Ames gave her two for good measure. "I tried one and, oh yeah, it worked," says Roy. "It wasn't just something Doris got into her head."

Word spread throughout the small community of Flubbed Lip, and beyond. Ironically, Ames the security guard was robbed from her home while at work. The culprits got away with all thirty-six remaining tampons. "I wish I wouldn't have saved them for special occasions," Ames states. Roy relinquished her other (unused) tampon to North Dakota authorities, who then shipped it by armed guard to NASA headquarters. Dr. Penelope Wooster, research fellow in Neuro-Eroto-Physiology, may soon be recruited to test out the effect of the super tampon in a closely monitored clinical environment.

Meanwhile, rumour has it that the mystery-powered tampons are selling on the black market for upward of $500 each, with the price climbing as supply dwindles. "This is the crack of sex toys," claims one anonymous source. "If men knew what was good for them, they'd destroy them for all eternity."

Modern Gash will keep you posted.

Look for us on your newsstands, every month, that time of the month [Ed].

Week Three **Miasma**

Monday evening Maxi called. The squash date had lasted twenty-two hours. Tom had won the game exuberantly. We hoped he kept a lid on his victory glee when he played his clients and colleagues. Maxi had almost cracked his extra racquet in half. She wished she had; she wanted to have made it into his weekend highlights. They'd gone to Empire for a late brunch once the lineup had died down; Toronto was gaga for the lobster chunks in the Hollandaise. Tom was cranky until he ate but then he'd hugged Maxi on the sidewalk outside afterward, as showcasey as a Moscow businessman from the sounds of things. Then they'd gone to the Sunday pay-what-you-can at Theatre Ixnay, a multiply-awarded remount of strippers putting themselves through grad school who debate the meaning of life in the dressing room. Maxi thought it was so-so but Tom loved it. He wheedled another BJ when they got back to his place. I asked Maxi if she was feeling like Sisyphus. Tom left for work some time between the dead of night and dawn. Maxi could snoop with audacity that dumbfounded me but she hadn't that morning. She wanted to focus on her meeting with Tara, who had now taken to calling her "Keyboard Fingers" and had invited her back to her trailer for another tête-à-tête in between reshoots.

"You gave me so much practice at being a good friend, Babe. It's great, now I can reapply it. I think Tara's eyes get more blue the more excited she gets. I wonder if that's her secret?"

"I know movie stars tend to have huge heads."

"Tara has a huge laugh. She had to get strung up in a harness because they were doing a green-screen scene. The one where she takes some Evoke to inspire her?"

"And ends up with rainbows and eagles and psychedelic lightning flapping around her head? It's a mega epiphany."

"So she comes hobbling over at one point, she always gives me her chair when I'm there, and asks how on earth women ever put up with menstrual belts!"

"Oh no, Maxi, you didn't?"

"Oh come on, Bess. It's hilarious. She roared."

Maxi had told Tara all about the first time I followed the Tampax instructions. I studied them at length but still managed to stick the thing up my ass. It still hurts to think about it. I'd have given Maxi hell but I didn't want to rock the boat.

"Thanks for the bum rap. I can hardly wait to meet this woman."

"I told her you wanted to know if she was really part Cherokee. She said to tell you she was discovered at the

Agincourt Mall sweat lodge. The director is driving her crazy, by the way. He can't get his act together and is really hard on the F/X guys. I'm not supposed to quote her on that."

"She's an inspiration, Maxi, I can hear it in your voice."

"Now I understand why poets have muses. It completely helps!"

"Maxi, guess what, you were in my dream last night. We were at Toronto Golf and Tennis Court with your parents. You were sucking on their gin limes as usual."

"Oh."

"We got stuck in one of the changing rooms at the pool. We were banging and banging and no one would let us out."

"Hmm."

"Sorry, I know there's nothing more boring than someone else's dreams. I figured you could deal with this one because you were in it." I hated the way Maxi's cellphone never made it clear if we'd been cut off or not. I'd been known to unwittingly go on and on. "Are you still there?"

"Yes of course. I wouldn't mind hearing about Tara's dreams."

"I wonder if she dreams? She seems like the sort of person who wouldn't bother."

"She gave Danielle a Tag Heuer and she says she wishes she hadn't because now Danielle is obsessed with the time."

"That's the East Coast way."

"That's what I said. She said she doesn't need reminders, she remembers everything."

"That's her secret right there."

"I have to go, Babe. I need to meditate."

"You're kidding."

"Tara says it's very helpful. I'm worried I'll get a cold sore if I don't."

"Go then, thanks for calling."

"I'll call you later. I miss you! Bye."

I thought it was sweet of Maxi to miss me. First chance I got, I'd figure out what the hell she meant by that. That was the problem with Maxi: sometimes she meant nothing. I knew she'd have been staving off simplex 2 with a lion tamer's vigilance. She wouldn't have been ready to have *the talk* with Tom just yet. That could wait until she'd got the latest stats on how many people had it without even knowing it. Maxi could spin with the best of them. I was beginning to wonder if, in Maxi's mind, working up a good spin counted as generosity. After all, her mother charged big bucks for that.

Thankfully, the conclusion of the BBC detective drama was airing. I sausage-rolled inside my quilt and hopped and flopped out to my trusty armchair. I needed to find out who was killing all the little children. Turned out it was the Irish psychotic. I recalled that the cop who caught him had played Hamlet at the RSC the season before. I was glad he had recovered his get-up-and-go. I turned off the living room baseboard heater and turned up the one in the bedroom. Maxi had forgotten to warn me heat wasn't included. That was okay, it improved my powers of concentration. I could afford to warm only one room at a time, which made me reluctant to abandon my tasks at hand. I thought maybe that was why Maxi had stayed friends with me for so long: she had the gift of focus.

Hank and I ruthlessly executed tasks all week long. When Marisa checked in with us on Friday, she told us that she was close to sealing a deal on a stately farmhouse complete with pasture, creek, vegetable patch, rose garden and stables. If it happened, I had a standing invite. Maybe she'd even get me a pony. Apparently, ponies are a lot feistier than bigger horses. Feisty is as feisty does.

Hank and I plodded along at the studio, without glory but steadily. Tara had told Maxi that Evil Benefactor was the sweetest fag one could ever hope to meet. I believed it. It takes a special generosity to play villains with all due flesh and blood.

Love Is a Drug achieved a turning point. Jessica had arranged to meet Evil Benefactor's chief henchman incognito at a downbeat doughnut shop, where she was begging him, breasts first, to see the light. Obviously, he was now a marked man. I was tempted to ask to hear the dialogue, but not really. I had too many cup, saucer and spoon duties. I stuck wet paper towels in the cup to get it sounding full without slopping. Hank had brought in an extra piece of quiche for the apple pie sequence and was hoping I'd nail it in one take, which I did, since he'd ordered the blue cheese and onion. Without Marisa around, Hank's humour ran extra grim. I didn't know how I'd become one of the boys. I never asked Hank to be Mugsy to his Bugsy.

"Do him, dress like a sleaze and do him," Hank was now requesting of our heroine.

"She already screwed Evil Benefactor, silly," I told Hank. "Today's girl only gets it on with one sexually malevolent party per movie. She's got to interact with this other guy more as an urban angel, whispering fruitful truths in his ear. See how the DOP shot her with a halo?"

"Well, I'd do her."

"*Quelle surprise*."

Hank tipped himself back on his chair and squinted, a bad sign that he was forming some kind of opinion.

"Why does this chicky bug you so much? You don't usually get jealous."

"I'm not jealous! Fuck that! I may have my faults, but being jealous isn't one of them. Jealousy is an all-or-nothing principle, and you know I'm not, I'm just not."

I backed into a microphone. Hank's headphones immediately conveyed this.

"Jesus H. Christ. Okay, you're not."

"You're jealous of Homer Simpson."

"I freely admit that."

"I miss Maxi," I said after a while. "It feels like she's farther away now."

"That's dumb. You guys live even closer now, right?"

"Supposedly."

"So branch out. Call someone else."

"Nah."

Hank threw the studio in pitch darkness, another one of his tricks; he had all the controls at his fingertips. "Call another friend if you ever want to see the light of day again. You were a good-looking broad until you tripped and sliced your face open on the lawn mower that's out there somewhere. Them blades are sharp."

"All right, already. Damn."

Hank was right. I was free to hobnob with whomever else I wanted, no inviting along required. Especially not when Maxi was not only too busy to include me in her weekend plans but also too busy to tell me what they were. I thought of my old university friends, Nunci and Syl, but they were in Vegas for the weekend with Nunci's hubby, Danny, and his friendly boss. Anyone else would require a gruelling update session to and fro. I batted away the notion of calling Eddie and Elaine in Winnipeg and I refused, with the scrap of honour that was left to me, to export my disturbance to Burlington. So I called Marcus. He answered.

"Hi," I said.

"Hi Bess."

"It's Bess."

"Tell me something I don't know."

"I'm in a really bad mood."

"Excellent, so am I. But Rocks is feeling great."

"Really? Put him on the line."

"I'd rather not. He drools into the receiver."

"What are you guys up to?"

"I'm supposed to go out for a drink with Tom and Maxine."

"Oh."

"Tactfully, you're not invited, you see. Because it's common knowledge that I bug you."

"That's too bad."

"Come out with us."

"Nah."

"Just do it."

"No really, it's okay."

"Well, I'm not going out either then."

"You go!"

"Nope. You're coming over here. I'll make us popcorn with maple syrup. I want to prove how good it is."

"Are you sure?"

"Well, the kernels may get a bit soggy but I think it works."

"What are you going to tell those guys?"

"They won't care. Besides, Maxine is trying to set me up with an actress."

"Tara Dickens? You're going on a double date with Tara Dickens?"

"No. I'm staying home drinking beer with you. Tara and I want to meet but it's business, it should wait."

"If you say so."

When I hung up and then picked up the receiver there was a beep on my voice mail. Maxi had called after all. She sounded pointedly overwhelmed. It was all Tom's idea, Marcus was going to be there so obviously I wanted to give it a miss, she promised to call in the morning, she was really sorry she hadn't called earlier, could we do brunch? I careened from resentment to pity. I called Maxi's number. She was on the other line with Tom and said she'd call me right back. I phoned Marcus right back, to convince him to stick to the plan. But his line glided straight to his mailbox. I hung up. So much for my second thoughts. I figured I had better come up with third ones when my phone rang again. I was grabbing it a lot lately without my customary pause to indicate a life. It was Maxi.

"You are so right, Babe. Marcus *is* a jerk."

"How so?"

"He just called Tom to cancel on us tonight, and I've got Tara all lined up and ready to go. Bloody hell, what a mess."

Maxi punctuated this with a long, whistling inhalation of Camel smoke.

"Why don't you bring Tara to Antico? Marcello will knock off early and join you. He's cute by anyone's standards. If you say it's Tara they'll have a good booth waiting."

"That might do."

"I have half a mind to go over to Marcus's and tell him off. Do you want me to?"

"Prepare yourself because Rocks is vomiting non-stop. Tom thought it was funny."

"In what universe is that possible? Tom's, I guess."

"Trust me, I gave him hell."

"You've gotten to the giving-him-hell stage?"

"Kind of."

"Even though he dresses in Boss."

"Tom's wonderful though, really."

"He's great on paper for sure."

"Maybe that's all that counts. Lord, look at the time. I still have to do my hair and mouth."

"Sorry, go."

I got ready, too. Not even Maxi could ever figure out what to do with my hair. I rubbed some pomade into it and succeeded in something of a downward tilt. Hopefully, I wasn't really a cross between Simon and Garfunkel like I feared. I was surprised by my need to fix myself up at all. I wouldn't have thought Marcus called for a wardrobe change or a makeup job. But I had gotten the bumster Earls hemmed and they weren't the kind of jeans you debuted without lip gloss and a cute top.

The snow was gone with hardly a trace. Winter was shirking its duties. Perhaps by our senior years Ontario would be its own Florida. I strolled the whole way to Parkdale, my red jacket making me feel like a beacon of comfort when the streets ran demographically harsh. The walk was quite therapeutic. I marched to Marcus's place under sentinels of streetlights then kicked his door until it shuddered. Immediately, Rocks wanted to dance a slobbery polka. Marcus had to rush back to his corn. He was popping it in a metal cage over an open fire.

"Very Pioneer Village," I said.

"Sometimes you can get too space age for your own good. My screenplay goes better in longhand. I like to see what I've crossed out."

I finally took my turn in one of the beanbag chairs. "I know what you mean. A trail of error helps me keep my bearings. I tore out journal pages the whole way here."

"You keep a journal? I'd better be in there."

"Not really, I gave it up. I was always too vaudeville about it. I couldn't let a day go by without some kind of song and dance number."

Marcus collapsed into the chair beside mine. He handed me an outsized bottle of microbrew and placed the drizzled bowl of corn between us, then grabbed it right back out from underneath Rocks' nose.

"You take it."

What was it with all my friends and their fancy housewares? I was less and less proud of my extensive Tupperware collection, matching lids notwithstanding. This was a vast, hand-crafted disc of some sort of resinous substance that weighed a ton.

"I don't think this fits in my lap. I feel like a badly put together turtle."

I hoisted it back over Rocks' inquiring mind. Now I had to lean way over to dip into Marcus's lap. I wasn't about to play restrained, the popcorn was fantastic.

"Sorry I don't have a couch. I'm not allowed one until my script is done."

"Please, no apologies. I hate apologizing myself."

Rocks was licking up fallen kernels with pornographic yelps. We tried to nudge the blobby chairs closer together but Rocks thought this was some new game and started baying for joy. Marcus's picnic table, piled high with files in tabbed stacks, wasn't an option. It wasn't the relaxation either of us had had in mind.

"We can sit on the kitchen counter," said Marcus.

"I'll always find you in the kitchen at parties."

"Or we could go up to my bedroom? Rocks can't make it up there but he understands that. We've been through it many times."

"Sounds good to me."

What was I going to do? Get my crinolines in an uproar and gasp for my smelling salts? Rocks trotted beside us without a care in the world until he bumped up against the bottom of the ladder that led to Marcus's sleeping loft. His tail semaphored gloom. He watched me climb up behind Marcus with famine eyes then looked away as if he could no longer bear my disgrace. He slunk to his bed, disgusted.

"Wow," I said and meant it.

No hackneyed prints, no socks on the floor, no hokey sleigh bed: Marcus had a killer bedroom. A large pair of luxuriantly red, abstract oil paintings faced off against each other from two of the walls, a chest of drawers with an air of grandfather clock about it had taken over a corner and an iron bed of burnished swoops dominated the middle.

"*Bedknobs and Broomsticks* meets Gaudi, nice." I jumped aboard.

"I made it myself. It's a bit idealized but what else do you want in a bed?"

"Nothing."

There was plenty of room for me, Marcus, the big bowl and drifting music: the Flaming Lips and Stereolab. Mostly, I heard us crunching. With discreet pauses to lick at our teeth. Marcus and I had gone shimmying pretty fast up the friendship curve. The moment snapped open like a fan. I threw my head back and absentmindedly thanked the ceiling.

"You're welcome," said Marcus.

Marcus had trimmed his hair. Shorter, it made him look less devious. He was wearing a T-shirt as usual, a pink one with Chairman Mao on it smoking a cigar. He had on army-surplus pants so huge I thought they might convert to a parachute. A chain attached to his belt loop disappeared into a pocket the size of a shopping bag. He wore gold track shoes the size of egg cartons.

"From Tokyo," Marcus said, wagging them. "I shot an ad there for calling cards."

I reined in my gaze. Marcus didn't deserve to get itemized.

"What was Japan like? Sorry. Dumb question. Give me one good detail."

"They have kitty cartoons on their phone cards. Rocks would love it."

"Tell me another thing."

We were lying on our sides with our heads propped up and the bowl between us.

"Everyone was so tiny. I felt like a gentle giant. The same way I feel around you."

My gaze pinballed around. I felt a blush rising. I blew out my breath in a way that made me sound exasperated.

"You're a nice person," I said. "How'd you swing that?"

"Maturity helps."

Marcus put the bowl on the floor and reached for his beer. When you were lying like this with a guy, you couldn't help but notice his body. I saw the cords in Marcus's forearms flex. He was sinewy but it was pick-up basketball strength, not bench pressed like Tom. I had a suspicion that Marcus's skin was soft to the touch. I wanted to run a finger up his arm to feel. Instead I took another swig of beer and lay back. His bed had pillows for two.

"I'm turning thirty-five soon," I said. "Next month. In the middle of the month, actually." Really, I could shut up now.

Marcus uncharacteristically scowled. I was startled, and then startled to be startled. I wondered if he had plans, what plans?

"Frig," he said, soon enough.

"What's wrong?"

"I might be in LA. But I'll try and work around it."

"Hell, don't worry about it. I don't know why I told you. I don't do birthdays, honestly." If I didn't blush, it would be a miracle. If I did, it would be a personal inferno.

"Sometimes *I* do. It depends whose."

"If you think about it, it's not really 'Happy Birthday.' It's 'Happy One Year Closer to Death.'"

"Maybe dying isn't that bad once you get the goodbyes over with."

"Easy for you to say, men ejaculate. I wonder what women do? I guess multiples are out of the question."

"That's one of the things I like about you, Bess. You raise important issues."

"My pleasure."

I'd earned myself a couple of comfortable sips. Soon I was stretched on my side facing Marcus again. I took a closer look at his hands. Marcus's hands were outsized but somehow well meaning. He reached out and pinched one of my forehead curls then tugged, but not so hard that it hurt.

"Your hair is so great," he said. "It's really hardwired for ringlets, isn't it?"

"You be the judge, you're the one who's pulling on it."

I tried to watch Marcus's colossal fingers at work but they were so near it made my eyes cross. I checked out his face instead. Marcus's face was serious acreage. His torso was totally elongated. His leg bones were preposterously lengthy. I was a toy poodle and he was a Great Dane. I wanted to bark.

"For some reason I want to bark," I said.

"Then you should."

"Awoof!" I tried.

Downstairs from a corner below, for the first time I heard Rocks growl.

"Oh boy," said Marcus. "Rocks is really steamed."

"Why?"

"You just told him you want to kiss me."

"What did he say to that?"

"You know very well what he said."

Marcus's lips were pretty red, like he had been eating red lollipops. His nose was long and straight, like the nose of

Michelangelo's *David*. It went well with what Maxi referred to as my "Venus de Milo boobs only big." I was exciting myself with this surge of quality references. Marcus was regarding me with a mere trace of a grin. Something had to be done.

I dragged myself over to Marcus by my elbows. My face hovered smack over his. I smiled. Our smiles kept joining and reproducing. I could see there was a strand or two of grey mixed in with his black locks. It was a becoming reminder of his judiciousness. I saw Marcus had a nice jaw and hairline, the sorts of things I'd have thought I needed to be Emily Brontë to notice. Drained of attitude, I saw this was a perfectly lovely man's face. My gears did this crazy switch.

I'd intended a cheery cheek kiss but Marcus's lips drew me in. Mine landed on his like they'd been air traffic controlled. I stalled for a soft-hearted moment, then licked a bit to test for candy flavour before taking off. I resumed my lounge position on the other side of the bed. I smiled over, all satisfied and foxy. And I suddenly, violently, burped.

Marcus howled.

"Excuse me!" I cried.

Marcus got his face back under control. "Bess, you're hilarious."

"I didn't mean to, honest!"

I kept protesting while hoping it seemed like I really had meant the whole thing, because it worked better as a joke than a gaffe, but not the kind of joke I necessarily wanted to own up to. Great. Thanks to my biliousness, all would be buffoonery from now on. My wildest chance at romance in years, burped away. I took another sip of beer to regain some nonchalance. Marcus started diddling with my curls again. His expression subsided. His hand began to wander. His thumb felt out the dent between my eyebrow and my cheek bone. He gently pinched my cheek. He rubbed the hollow beneath my lower lip. He seemed to be drawing my features together into some new conclusion.

Marcus cleared his throat and said, "You're so pretty."

I froze for a moment, wanting to stay pretty forever.

"Depends who's looking at me," I said.

Marcus's T-shirt smelled of freshly mown grass. His chest felt as sturdy as country furniture. His heart sounded very reliable. He laid a hand on my back and patted me idly. If we had been in a movie the music would already have surged—the sax joining in with the strings—and now calmed to a tender hum. I focused. These were mighty circumstances and I wanted to be able to recall them for a long time after, in line-ups, in the bathtub and on public transit. I actually liked the daffy sneakers.

I wasn't sure if I could stand it if Marcus kissed me back. It would probably be lovely and yet ungainly, like watching someone play the harp. I thought I'd ducked him but I'd ignored his brawn. In an athletic instant he had me in his lap. I yipped. Marcus kept silent. How could he be so serious? How could I bear to own my face in the lamp light? What were we up to?

Marcus's kisses followed upon each other as fast and happy as a slide show. The affection went straight to my head. I was elated. I thought I could have had a chat with Voltaire, I could have sung a cameo in an opera, I could have posed as one of the putti who watched Venus crack her shell. Possibly I could even have scrawled a paragraph of my own down a margin of Alice. I tossed my arms around Marcus and spoke to his neck.

"Thank you," I said.

"Thank *you*, darling."

Pet names, holy shit. The man had no fear. *Darling* was a lovely thing to say, he was right. It was great having so many new things to notice. Marcus scooped me up again, then laid me back down; making out with him was like riding the Tilt-A-Whirl. Hemingway said that size doesn't make a difference in bed but most of Ernest's romances seemed to have gone kaput. Now I was on my back with Marcus's shaggy head over my hips, his hands covering mine. His were dry. I extracted one of mine to pet his hair. It wasn't nearly as spiky as it looked.

Marcus began to rub, right where his nose was pointing. My mind flared with worry over my underpants. Medium nice bikinis, they'd have to do. I'd recently waxed, I'd even more recently shaved and I'd showered quickly before coming over—cursory but sufficient. Maxi said a little bit of odour was good; you want to zap them in their limbic brain. Marcus was zapping me in my crotch brain. He undid my jeans and removed them with the calm of a surgeon. His other hand unbuttoned my cardigan. Meanwhile I helped him with my bra. As usual, my boobs burst on the scene without a single qualm. My nudity was glaring. Marcus seemed fascinated. I hoped it wasn't just juvenile curiosity about an orange bush, but that seemed doubtful. Marcus was pensive, not boisterous. Then I had to avoid his glance completely. You can sneak peeks but you don't want to lock gazes with a man at a time like that. Not when the pair of you are equal parts subject and object. My legs twitched; the pleasure was so mammoth as to be threatening.

Once Marcus licked me I understood why heaven and eternity are so frequently cross-referenced. I felt both weak and mighty, both empty and full, the pussy being a very paradoxical milieu. This went on for a generous stretch but then I wanted him to return his face back up to the general region of mine so that I could smile at him and fuck him big time. He chased my private parts up the bed.

"Would you like to?" I whispered.

Marcus was still completely dressed. I had on one sweater sleeve, a popped bra and pink-and-red striped socks.

"Oh yes," he said. "Definitely."

"Um, do you have thingies?"

"What, balls?"

"No, dummy. Condoms."

"I have balls *and* condoms. But I have to warn you, I also have a penis."

"I know." I was fondling it with my sock.

Marcus started to whistle. He bounded out of bed and rooted through the back of his top drawer as if he was looking for a lost bow tie. Finally, I heard rustling. Lubricated, mercifully. Marcus tossed a row of Trojans on the bed and started to strip. That I had to watch. He was lean more than thin. His hair all seemed very well planned. His belly was younger looking than his face. His thighs were textbook thighs. His dick wasn't dinky. It was definitely erect. I could only eyeball it for so long before modesty prevailed upon me to admire his kneecaps. Marcus jumped back in bed and pulled down the blankets for me to crawl in beside him. It was like Christmas Eve again already, all cosy anticipation. Downstairs, we heard Rocks give a little snuffle.

"That means he's having a good dream," Marcus said.

"Oh, I get it," I said, grabbing firmly and pulsing like an imitation heart. "He's dreaming he found the perfect bone."

We did it. We were done for. Forever we had been, at least once, carnally enjoined and mutually aroused and simultaneously carried away and screwed. Rocks seemed to sleep through it all.

"It's a good thing," said Marcus. "I forgot to feed him."

Marcus ambled downstairs to fetch us cold beers. He was one of those people who didn't seem to notice if he was naked. He was still whistling as he walked back across the bedroom floor toward the bed, his dick swinging like a metronome. He ignored his phone's several bursts into tweets, home echoed by mobile, echoed by fax, echoed by email chimes. Our shoulders rested against each other, Marcus's smooth and warm and quite Tarzan. The bed was big enough for him to slouch. Once in a while I let the covers slip. Marcus copped a few glances, which was nice of him.

We talked about the first time we had each done it.

"It sounded like he was snapping on a pair of rubber gloves," I recalled. "And then I had to show him where to put it."

"I studied my dad's *Joy of Sex* too carefully for that. I'm surprised I don't need hairy armpits to turn me on."

"I heard that in the newer edition she shaves."

"That's a shame. I mean, she could just have gone on loading on the patchouli oil and I'm sure he wouldn't have minded."

"Hot water in France costs more than Chanel No. 5."

"Let's go to Paris. Want to?"

"Sure."

"As soon as I get my script drafted and you wrap this movie, maybe?"

Marcus turned to give me a look that seemed to inquire about the finer points of our schedules, despite the larger questions to be asked, like what was Bess Grover doing having this sort of thing happen to her? Marcus seemed to plan trips to France with the same ease with which he stripped me and licked me, stripped himself and plunged in. The guy had a lot of torque.

No surprise that I did not sleep well, too few beers and too much buzz for that. I feigned steady breathing, however. I wanted to be the sort of woman who made herself comfortable in Marcus's bed. I did drowse. When I woke up the light from the skylight was a noncommittal grey. After the stunning realization of where I was and what we'd done, I wondered if Marcus would want to do it again. I hoped so. When he came back from the john I stayed curled up, eyes closed, facing the wall. Marcus slid right over, draped an arm over me and pulled me in. We did it again, stone cold sober and doggy style, before a word was spoken. I sneaked a hand of my own down into the fray. I came fast and hard, grinding my ass into Marcus's hips, terrified of missing out on a scrap of pleasure and yelping when it all hit home. I thought it was a good sign how my coming made Marcus come. Frisbee in the park was never going be the same.

After a while I sensed Marcus revving up his energies to work. His references to his script started to come quicker and more ambitiously. I thought it would be nice to get home in any case. There was no way I was going to loiter around long enough to discuss the meaning, ramifications and quality of our bonk. I'd read that females seek out predictable accountant types on one hand but live to pass along powerful, reckless, heartbreaker genes to their sons on the other. I didn't want to be talking to Marcus about that either.

"Dolphins buzz each other's genitals," I said instead as he kissed me goodbye at his door after repeated offers of breakfast. "They also indulge in flipper-to-flipper touching."

"All the smartest animals fool around."

With me in boots and Marcus in sock feet we approached a dynamic that was almost functional, height-wise. I would remember that if we ever kissed again. On my way I stopped in at a bakery I'd spied around the corner and bought two big carrot-raisin muffins that stained the bag with fat. One was for the cab ride and the other I slathered with my mom's blueberry jam when I got home. I finished off a pot of camomile then napped the sleep of the cherished before waking up and whipping off some quickie, albeit morally instructive, *Gash*.

MODERN GASH

Fashionisms—January '00

By Bess Grover

OUT	IN
Narcissism	Existentialism
Categorization	Unconditionality
Depression	Happiness
God	Scruples
Boob Cleavage	Butt Cleavage

Farting	Burping
Antico (except a booth)	Crawford Avenue
Fucking	Fucking (best done In and Out)
Cute Dogs	Ugly Dogs
Friendship	Gangs

Maxi phoned me Sunday at high noon to apologize for blowing off brunch on Saturday but with big news to make up for it.

"Babe, I've decided what I'm giving you for your birthday!"

Year in, year out, my birthday coincided with Valentine's Day—a bundle of TNT ripe for explosion that sometimes only hissed for a few weeks before it went away.

"What? Maxi, what?"

"A party! I'm having a party for you, Babe. My article will be done by then."

"You can't. I mean don't come to a decision yet. You might want to spend it with Tom."

"Oh, fuck Tom."

"My point entirely."

"My first party at my new house. You should feel honoured. I insist."

It wasn't really birthday season yet. Maxi was just bringing it on hideously early. I wasn't sure what she thought I'd done to deserve that.

"I'll help. With the prep and stuff."

"No, you won't. It's my party. Well, yours, but you know what I mean. I'm thinking an all-red theme. Cute, huh? Listen, come by. I need help painting my upstairs wainscotting.

Ralph Lauren Bimini Blue. I'll make hot chocolate with marshmallows."

I promised I'd be right over. I remembered those marshmallows all too well. They were over five years old. Years ago, Maxi had convinced me I needed camping skills. Real roughing-it-in-the-bush stuff to capitalize on the Canadiana wilderness thing. She'd learned her share at exclusive girls' camps where she'd spent the balance of every summer steering canoes. Whenever Maxi had a mania on the go I was seriously implicated. Reluctantly, I agreed to an outing at a coniferous provincial park with a low rate of grizzly bear sightings. We were told about a great swimming beach at the far end of Lake Wapamagouche, or whatever it was called. It took us over an hour to canoe there but it was very hardware-store-calendar pretty. Maxi gave me a refresher course in the breast stroke and she was right, my tits didn't really get in the way. But I still didn't improve much. We splashed around until the sun went in and a breeze picked up, so fast it was wind by the time we got paddling again. What followed was dire slapstick. No matter how fast we stroked, the shore practically stayed put. The waves were getting bigger by the minute. The wind whipped my words out of my mouth and tossed them high over Maxi's shoulder. From shore we must have looked like a stupid speck. We couldn't stop or we'd be mashed backward. If we capsized only Maxi would float. We'd forgotten about life jackets—that they even existed. It was dusk when we clunked up against the campsite dock. We cracked open beers the way men do, like it was interferon instead of Molson Dry. The cool of the bottle soothed my torn palms. My trembles dislodged extra bubbles. Maxi had told me not to be silly—of course she would never let anything happen to me.

By time I got to Crawford Street, Maxi had spiked the last of the cocoa with Amaretto. She dragged me straight upstairs for a quick house-painting lesson. She would never be able to ignore it if I got a hair stuck to the wall or let a drip dry. She was wearing new flared $89 yoga pants that I could tell were going to make regular old working-out leggings miserably obsolete. After an hour I had bright blue smudges all over my face which, in combination with my native orange, made me look like an ad for plastic tarps. Maxi had a well-timed headache.

"Twist tie the paintbrushes into baggies for me, Babe. I'll make you tea."

Maxi never just made tea: she primed the pot and steeped. I knew to sit there quietly while she bustled. Kitchen fuss was for Maxi what other people might derive from a foot rub. She set out some fresh gingersnaps. When in doubt, Maxi baked.

"So how are things with Tom? Spare no details. What gives?"

"I hope he calls again after yesterday morning. He and Tara both crashed here, can you believe it? Breakfast was quite the yuk fest. I tried to joke along but the cupboard doors kept banging so loudly and I got eggshell in the French toast batter and they had an extremely irritating marshmallow-tossing contest. They were laughing about how funny it was that they could still eat them when they fell on my floors. Tom told Tara I vacuum every day. It's just not true. DustBust, yes. Then Tara teased Tom for snoring. She could hear it from down the hall. I knew I should have put the guest room on the third floor."

"Tom snores as well?"

"No, in fact Tom doesn't snore at all, but luckily Tara is unaware of that. And why, may I ask, must men be so keen for you-know-what in the morning? A woman looks her best the night before; they should learn to respect that."

"How was that action?"

"Good."

I knew in Maxi's terms that *good* meant sex as predictable and efficient as a knock-knock joke.

"Orgasms are the closest most adults get to revisiting infancy. I guess that explains all the 'Oh babys.'"

"Only 29 percent of women always orgasm but almost half their men think they always do."

"I keep telling you, Maxi, stick a hand in and you'll come out a winner. It's no time to be a stickler."

"Catholic women are less likely to climax than Protestants. Maybe that's my problem?"

"Nah. That's just too many Catholic men begging their madonnas to be whores for a quarter of an hour while the spuds boil."

Maxi had her hair in braids. I thought it was a cute look but she refused to indulge in it outdoors. That was probably a good thing because she had a habit of grabbing the ends and scowling at them, as if a split end was an especially wounding form of betrayal.

"Tara thinks Tom is vain."

"All men are vain. It keeps them young. At least Tom is balding. That teaches a guy life skills."

"I'll try and relax until I get to six weeks. Six weeks is do or die."

Maxi was leaning as far back in her chair as one possibly could, a childhood talent of hers. Her mother historically took exception but Maxi couldn't resist the rocking motion.

"I'm becoming less convinced that anything is predictable."

"Yes, well, anything can still happen to *you*, Babe. Nothing's been cut in your stone. But you have been through a ton of men, haven't you?"

"More if you think about it. A ton is only two thousand pounds."

No, I wouldn't be telling Maxi about Marcus. No could do. Not yet. It was strange to be withholding such crucial information, but I could tell Maxi's energies were veering around too sharply. Turning them on me was her last resort against turning them on herself. Better for both of us if I was the human equivalent of ibuprofen.

"Your article must be going well, what with you getting so up close and personal."

"Tom asked Tara about her ring over breakfast, can you believe it? I could have killed him. But he got a lot out of her, thank God. It turns out she was doing some research for *Love Is a Drug* and arranged to meet this up-and-coming endocrinologist at Stanford, future Nobel material, blah blah. She thought he was so lovely, all the rest of her life made sense to her, it was all very stars uncrossed, very whirlwind. She was supposed to meet his family at Christmas, that's why she was in California over the holidays. But two days after giving her the ring—which is Canadian-mined by the way, the kind with the tiny polar bear etched into it, which I personally think was a bad omen—he got cold feet and backed out. She's devastated."

"Wow, poor Tara. Who'd have thought?"

"Professor Caleb Mortimer is his name. She warned me to leave him alone but obviously I've got to get in touch. She'll understand in the long run. No word of this to anyone, Bess. This info is all mine. I need it to condense her nature."

"Maxi, you're after the kind of mood only the Germans have a word for."

She liked that. She poured me the last of the tea and took another cookie. It was Maxi's turn for PMS. I wouldn't be reminding her of that. She took a napkin from her faux-diner dispenser. She had the whole sugar and vinegar set. Then she took an extra napkin to wipe off the finger marks she'd made reaching for the first one.

"It's the Golden Globes tonight, don't forget."

Maxi loved the concocted ebb and flow of awards-show suspense. She found it very soothing to see "It" people foiled.

"I should let you be. You probably have a lot you want to get done first."

"I do want to alphabetize my CDs, and hopefully do a hot-oil conditioning."

"Man, I'm glad I never had to play Barbies with you."

"Bess! That wasn't very nice."

"I'm sure Tom will call."

"I shouldn't have had that cigarette. Tara called me Iron Lungs. She has a thing against second-hand smoke. Now Tom's going to start complaining, too. I need my morning smoke. Quite frankly, it keeps me regular."

"The way I see it, I'm not going to try and get between a man and his sci-fi so he'd better not come between me and my Tweety Bird slippers. Although hopefully he doesn't like sci-fi."

"Hopefully you don't have Tweety Bird slippers."

"All's fair in love and wardrobe."

"Finish your tea, Babe. I want to clean up. And start thinking about party guests. I want good ones."

My Sunday evenings were never all that tranquil. Maybe I still felt guilty for skipping Sunday school, although, as little United Churchgoers, all Eddie and I ever had to do was make clothespin dolls and sing "Jesus Loves Me." Out of vague professional duty, I switched on the Globes. I was happy for Tom Cruise when he won—those marvellously stocky thighs the Hollywood Foreign Press and I would never forget. Otherwise I wasn't paying much attention to the celebrities. Not when I had Marcus to take into so much new consideration. Thinking about Marcus had suddenly become so satisfying that I could lie staring at my hand for half an hour and consider it fascinating—this hand that had stroked him, that had been held in his, that had wandered all over him. My hand, my ally, the part of me that went ahead and grabbed stuff. Who you end up with determines what cosmos you inhabit and then you take it from there. That night I was grateful to time and space for having thrown me for a curve.

I thought I'd have just one gingersnap for a midnight snack. I discovered Maxi hadn't just brown bagged cookies for me, she'd sneaked in some new *Gash* along with the napkins. Her stuff was always gorgeously spell-checked and laser printed now, which put my blotchy scribbles to shame. This item was short. And Maxi was absolutely right: the whole point of *Modern Gash* was not to be sweet. At least that was what I concluded by 3:30 a.m.

MODERN GASH ASKS
What's So Funny About Funny?
By Maxine Bishop

Yes, it's statistically evident that men like women to have a sense of humour. That can mean only one thing if you're a wise woman—laugh long and hard at *his* jokes. Cool it with your own gags if you know what's good for you. They aren't really getting you anywhere. Look around you. Who's hooked up? Who's planning a productive future with a total dreamboat? Who's stuck at home alone watching British television? It's one small step from *wit* to *witch*. Is hilarious what you really want to be? Then hang out with gay guys and get yourself a talk show because that's all you'll ever be. Amusing, isn't it, that Oscar Wilde died miserable and lonely? Congratulations on the snappy replies, Funny Lady. How is that working out for you, romance-wise? Think you might be draining people just a little? Think you're going to get all the laughs and then the last laugh, too? Remember, it takes a good friend to ask.

Week Four Acid

I worked as diligently as I could, but I was haunted by birthday party countdown. Fourteen days to go became thirteen, and then twelve. Not a lot of time to change my fundamental nature if that was what I had in mind. Otherwise, I was stuck being a chick who didn't necessarily carry off things like parties and Paris. By Wednesday Marisa was back, pleased with what I'd done so far and keen to see more. I wasn't summing up Jessica's tale quite yet but I was getting there. Soon I'd be schlock-free. Income-free as well, but there was no point worrying about that while dollars waited to be exchanged for francs to spend on Marcus and crêpes. I'd been measuring my nest egg from every angle. Finally, I decided that although I was not yet making big bucks, I had enough little bucks to finance an adventure. I dropped this thought into the hazelnut decaf I was stirring. I wouldn't be drinking crass, flavoured coffee while in Paris, that was a given. What I would wear while I drank coffee in Paris was another question. That did it. All thoughts of Paris were to be contained like Ebola.

I couldn't help but notice that Marcus hadn't brought it up when he'd called that night. Instead, he told me about the meeting with Tara that afternoon, that it had been "really productive." I said that was "good." I thought about asking Marcus if he preferred his women to look like surfer girl pin-ups or old fashioned paper boys but I refrained. The best news was that he'd be back in town by the fourteenth and of course he'd come to the party—he wanted me to live through it. But if Marcus and I were flying to Paris the next day then we had to book fast to get a discount. Unless we were using points? I didn't have any points. These logistical concerns were fascinating but deeply private. I'd have sooner talked to Marcus about my underarm hair than charter flights.

And it was better that Maxi wasn't privy to any of this just yet. I didn't have the guts to process both my disappointment and Maxi's pity if things didn't work out. I knew if Maxi had been the one invited to Paris she'd have made every necessary reservation already and locked her man into dates and an *arrondissement*. I was too honest with myself about how unpredictable everyone else was to be that resolute.

"Bess, could you give me a hand with this?" Marisa was kicking open a roll of broadloom while a sink filled.

I jumped to it. Up on screen Evil Benefactor was about to receive a mysterious delivery (elevator bell, carpet footsteps, envelope swished under the door). Chopped-out newspaper letters advised him to (rustle, rustle) seek virtue while his *mentis* was still *compos* because it wasn't going to stay that way forever, blood tests had proved it. Done in by his own DNA. He slumped into his chair (we used Hank's chair, which made him grumpy). He crumpled up the note, then smoothed it, then crumpled it again. Marisa took charge when I made it sound as if a whole monastery was palming its parchment. Then, a despairing smack of Evil Benefactor's palms against his domed brow, very Colonel Kurtz. Marisa offered it to me but I wanted it to be hers. I was so proud when her slaps, slams and thunks were featured in clips at the Oscars; Marisa provided the entire world with punctuation. Evil Benefactor ducked into his executive washroom for some panicky swashing, which got the ends of my woollen sleeves wet. After that things eased off, thanks to a violin whine while Evil B stared himself down in the mirror and gnawed at the apples of his eyes.

"No way!" moaned Hank. "The asshole is going to redeem himself."

"In the nick of time," I specified. "Before he goes B-movie crackers."

"Dear me," said Marisa. "Such hostility."

"Apologies, Marisa. Hank and I hate cautionary tales."

"Looky, looky, Jessica's gone sporty again," said Hank.

Jessica and her new sidekick, a hunky guy from the next lab over, were now infiltrating the dark labyrinth where Evil B's criminal system originated. For this Jessica obviously had to dress in belly-baring fatigues. They—and we—had a laptop, naturally, now that they'd replaced pistols as the weapon of choice; Studly probably didn't take a bite of bologna without downloading FDA ingredient regulations and then hacking into Oscar Meyer operations.

I had a brief unprofessional, unbecoming moment of wishing I could hack into Marcus's email for a look-see. Happily for my soul, I got over that. Tom's email, on the other hand, would be worth a gander. Tom *was* a gander. I knew what Maxi could see in him but I wondered what she could hear in him. The AOL–Time Warner merger had made Tom nervous enough to work over, over, overtime. In my opinion, Tom was the kind of man who made being a man seem really tiring. I thought he must have been as taxed by his showmanship as anything else: all his balls looked to be constantly up in the air. Marcus seemed to deal with Tom without noticing that he was dealing with him, which was fine. Marcus deserved to be on familiar terms with at least one player. If the worst thing about Marcus was someone else, I figured I had got off pretty easy.

"Bess, I'd like you to take a shot at this," Marisa said.

Jessica was hoisting herself up a rope in pants of nouveau nylon: creak, rustle and grunt. If Tara could climb a brick wall then I could damn well pretend to.

"Scuffle is Grover's specialty," Hank sang. He knew I detested jingles so he even made them up.

"Bess stumbles beautifully," Marisa said.

There were worthy whiffs of former tomboy detectable in Tara, I had to give her that. My respect for Tara was less grudging now that it turned out that Marcus admired her enough to do business with her. I liked knowing what Tara Dickens was up to well before anybody else did. Maxi had even made her way into a gossip column, picture and all. Hank had found it in the paper that morning and whooped his head off as if *I'd* done something wacky. I felt bad for Maxi; in the wrong light she had a bit of Don Knotts about her, even when she remembered to press her tongue against her top teeth as instructed by *Seventeen* for the perfect prom portrait. When I got Jessica in the window, then Studly to boot, Hank rewarded me with the old Ken-L Ration "My dog's bigger than yours" jingle. I countered with "Aren't you glad you use Dial, don't you wish everybody did?" Hank bitch slapped me with "There's something about an Aqua Velva man." Marisa permitted my escape.

"HELLO," boomed Marcus on my voice mail when I got home: sound the trumpets, fill the flagons, poke an apple in the hog's mouth. "Hello, hello, hello, hello," he said in several intonations, accents and octaves, then one long, falsetto gooood-byyye.

I phoned him back right away before I could start rehearsing anything.

"Paris," Marcus said instead of hello.

"*Quoi?*"

"Don't tell me you don't want to go now."

"It's just that, well, I generally like to take my vacations somewhere, damn, *un peu plus chic*."

"If you come to Paris with me I'll buy you a dress."

"If you buy me a dress, I'll buy you a tie."

"If you buy me a tie, I'll buy you dinner."

"If you feed me, I'll give you anything you want."

"I'll feed you, then I'll eat you, then I'll start over again."

My heart stopped for a second, considering this was the best thing anyone had ever said to me.

"Bess? Hello, hello? Oh no, I've done her in. The anticipation of that Frenchy pleasure was too much for her. What have

I done, oh, what have I done? Rocks, down! He's trying to lick my tears."

"Can Rocks come to Paris?"

"He'd love those little poodles, wouldn't you, boy? Oh yeah. Rocks likes the ladies. You'd have to be careful though, Rocks, my man. Some of those boy poodles over there look pretty fruity."

"Does Rocks like lap dogs with bows in their bangs?"

"He's a sucker for a watery bug-eye. I'm telling ya, Rocks loves 'em all. Even the cocker spaniels. But he's too easygoing for the cockers. They twist him around their tails. Oh, great, Rocks heard me say P-A-R-I-S and now he's gone and put on a beret. Next thing you know I'll have to play all his Charles Aznavour records and toss him French bread in the park. We're going to have to sneak off to Paree when he's not looking. Maybe the day after your party. Does that work for you?"

"Sounds good. I hate getting stuck with the cleaning up."

"We'll hire a Molly Maid for your friend Maxine. This isn't a guilt trip. Is that my line beeping or yours?"

It was his. I let him go. I was nervous how important Marcus's other calls might be, coming from LA titans or New York–based Scorsese acolytes. And I was hopped up plenty enough for one conversation. Fucking Paris. It was time to tell Maxi what I'd been up to. I had slept with her guy's friend and developments had ensued. I'd protested the Marcus set-up at first and then caved completely. The news was so juicy and pulpy that I hoped Maxi would overlook the delay in my handing it over. My guess is she would want plenty of latitude for herself in dealing with the smoothie that was Tom. And Maxi hated to be accused of hypocrisy; she liked to organize more invincible terms for herself than that.

It was blustering out. Phantasmagoric whirls of snow dashed around in a sly, biting wind as if they were doing some ultra-modern dance. I kept my hands inside my mitts inside my pockets, twiddling my fingers for warmth like I was Glenn Gould practising sonatas. For celebration's sake, I'd dug out an old beret. Too bad it was lime green. Too bad I had to pull it down over my eyebrows. Maxi's windows glowed warm. I rapped the knocker once, twice, once more for good measure, then tried the door. Surprisingly, it opened. Music was blasting from the kitchen; Maxi had a secondary stereo in there. She was getting in a late bout of cardio, her and Cyndi Lauper. I'd known for years that Maxi was more new wave than punk.

"Maxi," I called from as far away as I could. "Yo, Maxi!"

I had never seen that look of terror on Maxi's face before. It took a while for it to slide off. She'd halted, mid-jumping jack, with one hand outstretched toward her knife drawer and the other reaching for the phone.

"Oh my God, oh my God, you scared me, Bess. You really, really scared me."

"I'm so sorry. I knocked a bunch of times. But you said I'm walk-right-in, right?"

"When you call and warn me, yes."

"I tried to but you didn't pick up."

"I was talking to Tara. She called just as I was walking in the door. Anyhow, what's up?"

"I need a drink." I collapsed at her table.

"At this hour on a school night? Tsk, tsk, Babe. But I guess I can make an exception." I assumed Maxi was being ironic. In any case, she poured us a couple of stiff single malts, one cube for her, two for me. "Cheers then. To what do I owe the honour of a social call?"

"I was lonely and I felt like seeing you."

"That's nice."

Maxi got up to root for a cigarette. Her ambition to quit was almost a shame; she had such "You've come a long way, baby" flair. The sight of Maxi's tossed-back head as she pursed and exhaled should have been forbidden to impressionable teens.

"I have an idea," I said. "Let's play Either/Or."

This was a game we'd made up for ourselves way back when. It had no object as such. We just ransacked our brains to present each other with two equally intolerable alternatives and then forced each other to make a choice between them. There had been a time in our mid-twenties when we'd played Either/Or for hours on end. Maybe life seemed less threatening once we'd cranked its parameters way beyond reason. Maybe we just loved writhing. I always privately made my apologies to Kierkegaard: this wasn't what he'd meant by exercising one's subjectivity to the point of fulfilled individuality.

"Babe! We haven't done that in ages. You go first. I'm rusty."

"Okay. *Either* you tell Tara this whole profile thing has been merely a ploy to satisfy your mad lesbo passion for her and please would she go strap-on shopping with you, you don't mind who wears what. *Or* you intercept the live Channel Seven weather report by singing your phone number to the tune of "Yankee Doodle Dandy" and flashing your tits in the blizzard. Which is it?"

Maxi wore the contemplative look of a cabinet minister on a cross-fire show.

"Lordy, this is a toughie. Either or, either or . . . bare boobs, I guess."

"No point screwing up your article."

"It's disgusting the kind of bacteria that can live on a sex toy. Unless I could sterilize everything I'd be completely grossed out. Okay, my turn." Maxi shook her head back and forth the way she did when she was thinking hard, as if there were the wrong ideas caught in her hair. "Got it! *Either* you revive The Revolted for one last show and loads of people are there and right in the middle of "I Suck" you stick your hand down your panties before anyone can stop you, you start, well, you-know-what and groaning into the mic, 'I'm going to come, I'm going to come—'"

"Okay, I get the picture."

"*Or* you make love to Marcus all night long with Enya playing top blast."

"You're good, Maxi. You're very good."

"I know!"

"I wouldn't revive The Revolted on pain of death."

"Either or, Babe!"

"Marcus. I'll take Marcus."

"I was convinced you'd choose the diddle. I'm shocked."

"More shocked than you realize."

Maxi slammed down her glass like a saloon regular after a varmint had walked in. There would be no peace for either of us until I surrendered the truth.

"What do you mean?"

"I did do it. I did *it*. With Marcus."

"You what?!"

"Marcus and I slept together. It was actually quite fun. I want to do it again."

"You like him? You *like him* like him?"

"So it seems."

"This is nutty! When?"

"The other night, when you were all supposed to go out, when he bailed on you. I tried to stop him, honest."

"Oh well. Tara can find herself a man at the drop of an eyelash."

"Not like me."

"That's not what I meant. I can't believe you kept this a secret, you bad, bad girlfriend. I *told* you Marcus was a goody. Didn't I tell you Marcus was a goody?"

"Yes you did. I owe you."

I saw Maxi was appraising me. She poured us another, stiffer round. Her eyes narrowed, squeezing me in.

"I think you got the better one," she said.

"What?"

"I think between the two of them, between the two of us, you picked the better guy."

"I don't know if I'd put it that way. How's Tom? Your turn."

"Let's talk about Marcus some more. How is he in bed?"

"Good. Very good. Sorry. I'm not in a details mood."

"Oh, so it's special. Lah-di-dah. Well, since you ask, Tom's great. He's gorgeous, he's ambitious, he smells good." Maxi lit up another cigarette.

"Does he not mind you smelling of Camels?"

"What kind of a question is that?"

"Sorry, it's getting late, Maxi. I should go."

"Suit yourself. Which you seem to be doing a lot of lately."

"I'm on a journey of self-discovery," I said in a goofy voice.

"Well, I hope you don't mind if I don't come along."

The wind was sounding like distilled widows and orphans. I was guessing the snow had drifted over boot height already.

"I think Tom is a great choice for you, Maxi. I really think things are going to work out. Who knows what's going to happen between me and Marcus?"

"Well, I'm not expecting Tom down on his knees any time soon."

"Rise above the wedding industrial complex. You're better than that."

"I want the honeymoon in Paris. So shoot me."

I couldn't do it. I owed Maxi better timing than that, so I kept my mouth shut. When she air-kissed me goodbye, her cheek felt warm and smooth against mine. *I* loved her smell. Cigarettes be damned, Maxi always managed to smell predominantly of potpourri and fresh linen. She had sachets stuffed into her dresser drawers and steam-cleaned her sweaters. She'd once taught me how towels could be perked up with a rub of fabric softener.

"Bye then," I said at the door.

"Goodbye, Bess. Next time don't scare me half to death. No matter how guilty your conscience is."

My next workday was a banner one. Marisa was waiting for me at The Coffee Shoppe with two large teas and four whole-wheat raspberry scones for our breakfast.

"Bess, there's an animation job coming up," she told me, squeezing creamers into her tea then delicately twiddling her fingers dry. Marisa made low fat seem déclassé.

Damn. Paris.

"Great, Marisa," I said. "When?"

"Late February I should think, perhaps early March. In truth, Bess, I'd like to offer the job to you. It can be yours from start to finish. I'm giving you the number of the production office and inviting you to handle the whole business. I couldn't have recommended you more highly. They're very pleased and so they should be."

"Amazing, Marisa. Thank you so much. I can't believe it."

"Believe it. The time has come."

When I first started to do foley I'd had to apprentice for a year without pay. That was a lucky break; I could have waited a lot longer than that to go gainful. Film is a rich-kids business, generally. I've paid everybody back except for owing Maxi a few dozen dinners. It seemed I now had a trade once and for all and was locked, stocked and barrelling on toward solvency. When people asked me what I did, I would never again have to bury them under an avalanche of qualifiers. From now on I would be moistening my own hot-water bottles in search of the perfect tire squeal. I'd be tramping through my own cornstarch snow and stabbing my own melons.

"Hank," I said once we got to the studio. The sip of tea I took tasted extra sweet. "I need to hire you for a gig."

"Be good to me, Boss Lady, be good."

"I'll still get you coffee but a raise is out of the question."

"Better make that Irish coffee."

I could tell Hank had heard everything from Marisa already but that was fine. They were proud of me. I felt like a glutton. I had my own real parents and I had this surrogate downtown version, one of whom was a priestess and the other a dirty-minded old goat. I felt like saying something horrendously politically correct to Hank to bug him senseless, something about his special needs.

"Crap almighty, could someone get this chick a dénouement?" I begged instead as Tara started flickering up on-screen.

The sad sack who had helped out Jessica and Studly was a goner: knife to the throat. Loose-skinned oranges work well for cartilage and sploosh. Then we had to deal with the body fall. Marisa couldn't quite get the corpse to slump the way she wanted. We managed by doing it together with rolled-up phone books and a punching bag.

"Rest in peace thanks to Everlast," I said.

"I love death," Hank said cheerfully.

"Ever the peanut gallery," said Marisa.

Hank was hoping Jessica and swain would copulate in some bushes. Balled-up cassette tape worked great for roll-in-the-hay crackle. But Hank was out of luck. Jessica headed back to the lab and that's where she and Studly finally got it on, test tubes and clipboards flying. Coitus interruptus, natch. Evil Benefactor loomed in the laboratory doorway holding out a swanky handgun at a trembling arm's length. Jessica rustled herself upright. Glass tinkled. Studly caused some chalkboard rattle. Then Evil Benefactor rotated 180 degrees, morally, and pointed the Beretta at his own head. Jessica slowly creaked across the floorboards toward him. EB knocked a couple of textbooks off the desk behind him. He was shaking, he was crying, he was mad with corruption and we were done with him for the day.

I hoped Marcus might call again that night but I kept pinching my mind on the way home from work to keep it from hoping too hard. My optimism would go from fine wine to vinegar if left to sit out unrefrigerated. The night was harsh with cold; winter had gone unrelenting. The streetcar smelled of mutton and mothballs and people with the flu. When I got home there was a message waiting but it was from Maxi. She'd heard something a little strange from Tom and thought maybe we'd better talk. The gossip about Marcus and me had no doubt ranked as an excuse for her to put in a call to Tom's office line. Now she had dirt in return. I could tell from her midwife's composure.

"Don't be mad, Babe, but I have to warn you about something. Don't panic."

"Yeah?" I could manage monosyllables.

"You know Marcus is working on a screenplay?"

"The love of his life, sure."

"He was blocked for a while but it's going great guns all of a sudden."

"Good. I'm glad for him."

"He was blocked over a *sex scene*. Apparently, he's finally fixed it."

"Oh."

"I know!"

"Weird timing."

"Maybe not so weird."

"You think I'm artistic Metamucil?"

"You know how ruthless artists are. Quite frankly that's why I gravitated to a business type. With a suit, *you* get to be their creative project. They spend more on you that way."

"I don't know, Maxi."

"You said yourself he's a strange one. Don't forget that, now that you've slept with him."

"What does Tom think?"

"Oh, you know Tom. He thinks everything's funny when he's not exhausted."

"Wow."

"Just be careful, that's all I ask. I'm the one who got you into this."

"Okay. Fine. Thanks."

"Are you mad at me for saying something?"

"No. But I've got to go. I haven't taken my coat off yet. I'll talk to you later."

I sat there in my futilely cheerful jacket wondering what the lesser evil would be, a beer or two beers. I picked Marcus.

"Hi," I said. "It's me."

"Honey, you're home! How was the studio today? Enough gurgles and footsteps for you?"

"Just a little murder and sex. How'd your day go?"

"Badly. And Rocks kept trying to get me to play Yahtzee."

"Sounds like you guys need to get out of the house."

"Are you inviting?"

"Why else did I just order the giant pizza?"

"Yahoo. Rocks, get your muffler, we're outta here."

That surprised me, my sudden mad-psychologist mode, my decision to experiment minus a control group. I dialled Classy Pizza and went all out: feta, spinach, portabellos, sexy roasted red peppers and pepperoni for Rocks.

"Succulent city," I said, once Marcus and Rocks and the pie had arrived to crowd my kitchen. I was munching a wedge of pepper from off the tip of my slice. "Roasted red peppers are the closest I come to girly action."

"Try fresh figs some day."

I thanked them for coming over. Poor Rocks really was Jimmy Cagney homely. Even if Armani fashioned dog suits it wouldn't have helped. Rocks caught me looking at him and whined searchingly. Jung would have approved of Rocks' passion for the Other. I cut him another slice.

"I'm sorry your script didn't go well today," I said.

"Ah, it wasn't so bad. I'm not one for suffering. If a scene wasn't working I'd ditch it."

I liked the way Marcus was tucking in without asking. I liked how he looked in a turtleneck, very French Resistance, as if he'd pass along secret codes rolled up inside trick baguettes. I wasn't sure where he'd found velvet camouflage pants.

"Damn, satiation point already," I said, after three pieces.

This was my excuse to wipe off my chin and head to the bedroom.

"Things are lookin' good, buddy," Marcus stage whispered to Rocks.

They traipsed in after me. Marcus chucked a mottled piece of rawhide at Rocks then dove for the bed and hit his head against the wall with this hilarious boom. I'd run out of candles so I lit a flashlight and draped it in a Niagara Falls scarf.

"She's soitenly got poissonality," said Marcus. Ever since I'd told him how much I loved The Three Stooges he'd been relentless.

"Stop," I said. "I ate too much to laugh."

We did it side by side this time—the easy-access position for lady-like pleasures. Marcus took over for me. I usually waited fifty times before bothering to suggest that, by which point one party was usually winding up to dump the other. Evidently Marcus's doofus nature was a huge turn-on for me. It made sense, considering my history of romancing class clowns. The massive O was much to his credit. And it gave me the strength to "darling" him back. I was so glad Maxi had been wrong about me merely serving to jump-start Marcus's powers of description. So wrong I didn't even want to discuss it with her. Darn Rocks found one of my Tweety Bird slippers under the bed and dragged it out for a tussle.

"What on earth is that?" I asked. "I've never seen it before."

"Rocks, man, don't go bringing over your slippers until a lady invites you to."

Rocks tenderly licked Tweety upside the head.

"At least he has good company," I said. "Just like me."

"By the way, darling, I booked the flights to Paris."

"How much do I owe you?"

"Nada. Thank my points. And get your curls out of my nostrils."

On Friday morning my phone rang crazy-early. Thankfully, my father hadn't had a heart attack. It was Marisa calling to tell me to take a look outside. Snow had fallen overnight as if by bureaucratic decree and had stopped just short of a record. School was cancelled, commuting was discouraged and I had an unexpected holiday since Hank was stranded in Etobicoke. I told Marisa I was grateful but not spiritually prepared. She said she was off to see her horse, Zeus. Marisa was embarrassed to own a Range Rover but she of all people deserved one. Then she invited me to come along. As plans went, this won a prize. Marcus congratulated me over raisin toast. At my doorstep he pretended he and Rocks were off to verify polar north. Marcus had ski goggles in his knapsack, which he was glad of, he just wished he had some for Rocks, too. It was a snow-blindness kind of day. The snow was up to Rocks' neck in places. It made him sneeze. He was good about the inundation, as if it was just another of our jokes. Marcus turned around to wave five times after he said goodbye. I loved the war-bride romance of that.

Marisa came to my door to pick me up right on time as usual. I thought most people might not actually be getting their fifteen minutes of fame, but everyone deserved fifteen minutes of rendezvous leeway. Maxi appreciated that but Marisa had no need of it. Marisa generally valued her plans too much to delay herself. Despite being a good driver, Marisa, I knew, didn't talk much behind the wheel. She had Vivaldi's *Four Seasons* playing. I made her laugh by fast-forwarding to "Winter." We steadily motored our way out to Unionville, to Zeus and his gang.

The barn was full of hail-lady-well-met types: jovial, hardy females who were so used to physical courage, recalcitrant horses, sacrifice, frustration and inconvenience that everything was either amusing or temper busting but, I suspected, rarely petty. They ranged in age from twenty-two to sixty but you'd never have known from listening to them. Their equine concerns had them tightly harnessed, socially.

"Bess, this is Gladys, and Marion. Over there is Letty, that woman with the hose is Margo and here comes Tish," Marisa said.

I envied them their breeches, tall muddy boots, snug jackets and, in Marion's case, chaps. I was the only one without swagger. I loved how industrious they all were, with their clopping big beasts, saddle girths, water buckets, curry combs, and ability to nourish and medicate. This was exactly what I'd needed a shot of: high-quality stable management. I could tell the horses knew what they were up against, even Zeus with his showy prancing. After we'd had hot tea and Bourbon Cremes in the riding school office, I watched Marisa groom Zeus and put on his saddle. Everything had to be just so. That seemed like one of the major pleasures of riding to me—being thorough by necessity.

I felt bad for Zeus that he was being held in place with ropes clipped to either side of his halter. He seemed used to it, though. Zeus had nothing in common with a merry-go-round horse. He was twice the size and far less frivolous. The first thing I thought of when I looked at Zeus was horse and the second thing was health. I was convinced that Zeus was proud of himself. Marisa wasn't so sure.

"He's a herd animal. That's what's essential to remember with him," she said as she picked out dirt from his feet, which he lifted with emperor forbearance. "He wants to be guided. He doesn't want to be confused. It's a constant lesson in communication for both of us."

Zeus stared at me with equal parts apprehension and disdain as he waited to see how I'd react to this.

"What do you love about riding so much, do you think?"

"When you're with a horse it's hard for anything else to matter. You have to ride every stride. It's both challenging and relaxing."

"I guess it's a really grand tradition."

"I rode with my parents and they rode with theirs and so forth, yes." Marisa's father had been master of a Cotswolds hunt, her mother riding to hounds every bit as avidly. "When I had the measles, Mummy led my Shetland pony up the front stairs to my bedroom to wish me better."

"Marisa, that's fantastic! All I remember about chicken pox was getting to eat a lot of raspberry sherbet. I wonder why kid's ailments become dangerous when you're older?"

"I know that mumps can affect adult male testicles to the point of sterility."

"Whoa!" Zeus looked down his nose at me with the consternation of a Prada salesman the first day of the January sale. "Sorry Zeus, not you."

"As long as all parents continue to vaccinate we'll continue to stamp out the worst of things."

"You know, Marisa, I bet you would have made a good doctor."

"Thank you, Bess. That's very kind of you." Marisa could always chat and do at the same time: now she was putting on Zeus's bridle, a complicated affair with enough buckles and straps to stump a dominatrix.

"Is Zeus a virgin?"

"Yes, indeed. Zeus was gelded as a yearling."

After Marisa unclipped Zeus from his restraints, she gave me his lead rope to hold while she fetched her helmet and gloves. I wanted to touch that sooty-looking muzzle but I was afraid he'd bite. Marisa wasn't in the habit of hand feeding horses; she said it gave them conniving habits. I didn't blame Zeus for being aloof; it was taking a little something out of me, too, to share Marisa. She led Zeus into the ring. I could have done it but I didn't want to put him through anything too humiliating. I knew I was being anthropomorphic but I didn't care; Marcus and Rocks had got me in the habit. Just before Marisa mounted I sneaked in a pat. I was touching a magnificent animal, bred scientifically and tended to meticulously. It was going to be hard not to keep smelling my hand afterward: I was a sucker for *eau de cheval*.

Dressage being the art of putting horses through intricate paces versus galloping over fences, I wasn't sure exactly what exercises Marisa had planned for the day. Their trots and canters were nicely "collected," I gathered from Gladys and Letty, who took a break from mucking out to watch along with me and murmur encouragements. Letty had cracked two vertebrae in a spill in October and everyone was relieved to have her back, with a lot of Superwoman jokes ensuing. Riding again had never been a question for Letty. The others implicitly understood that. I wasn't sure I did.

"She would have missed the poop," Gladys said.

"Listen to her," said Letty. "Her horse lives cleaner than her family."

"Priorities, priorities," said Gladys.

"Bugger it," said Marisa, frustrated to have cut a corner. Zeus seemed extra prancey.

"Oh Zeus, you're a little bastard," said Letty.

"And twice the horse he was this time last year," added Gladys.

"Do you all go to competitions together?" I asked.

"We try to," said Gladys.

"We prefer to," said Letty. "At least we know we'll enjoy ourselves."

Zeus's hooves thudded out rhythms as he snorted around the ring. Marisa switched directions, with horsey pirouettes resulting. Birds gabbed in the arena rafters. Dogs snacked out by the stalls. The barn cat joined me on a dusty bleacher. I took it all in with an interest that was comfortably, indefinitely prolonged, like a car trip with excellent music. Tish brought me more tea. Marisa had packed whole-wheat chicken sandwiches and pickles wrapped in wax paper. Marisa even looked good in a helmet. All going smoothly, Marisa would be wearing her breeches most days. She'd be shipping Zeus off to Palm Beach or Holland for major competitions while I took meetings with grouchy production accountants. Somebody else would assist me.

After Marisa and Zeus had called it a day, Margo and Tish did some Herculean jumping and then a beginner class of half a dozen little girls filed into the ring. Their proud mothers clustered a few rows below me. The little girls bossed around their horses in a way that boded extremely well for their dating lives. The mothers seemed buzzed with all they had provided. Marion took every one of her students seriously. I tore myself away to find Zeus and Marisa. She was applying hoof oil.

"I love how Zeus moved while you stayed so still," I said.

"Thank you, Bess. What a lovely way to put it."

Zeus was in his cosy coat now that he'd been cooled down. He didn't look like too much of a sissy having his tail brushed.

"Zeus has it good," I said.

Zeus's ears rivalled Hank's decibel meters for sensitivity.

"Yes, he does," said Marisa. "Now let's get you back downtown."

As we left, the little girls were taking turns doing figure-eights on horses that all looked like they were dozing. This was where I would fit into the scene, if I had wanted to, but my pastures were less literal. We listened to a soprano compilation on the way home, soaring arias that expressed all the euphoria and yet melancholia to be had from being female.

"I'm happy you enjoyed yourself, Bess," Marisa said. "Any time, as you know."

"Is one of those women your best friend?" I asked.

"*Best* is one of those less useful words, in my opinion."

"Like *perfect?*"

"Quite."

Marisa drove away with a toot. I smelled my hand all the way up the stairs: acorns mixed with potting soil and honey. As odours went, it was beautifully solid. I was so glad Marisa and her friends had it to rely on. They say fresh air isn't so much a smell as air with nothing in it. The city smelled of drainage, polymers and exhaust. I must have been ovulating. Day Fourteen didn't just boost my cup size, it made me hyper-receptive. Invitations, suggestions, odours—I took everything possible in.

❧

There was a message from Maxi waiting for me when I got home, reminding me that she was taking Tom to meet her parents at Toto that night. It was a radical dating strategy but I could see how it made sense; le tout Toronto wanted to be seen there. Toto was the chef's nickname. He travelled the world in search of poignant flavours that he combined in such a way that his appetizer menu read like *haiku* and his main courses like *koans*.

His desserts looked like rare orchids. The restaurant was on King Street, right around the corner from Tom's condo. If anyone could handle Josephine it was the courtroom warrior. And if things between Maxi and Tom didn't work out, that would bother Josephine, too: the only thing curbing Maxi's ambition was her desire to exist as her mother's one failed project. I thought Maxi had to learn to stop excusing herself for her rancour, as if she was battling an evil stepmother. Hopefully, Chef Toto was going to come on strong with *les amuse-gueules*.

Maxi had told me she was flashing Code Red. I hoped she didn't have cramps. I told Maxi that when she went menopausal Advil stocks were going to plummet, and that whenever possible I treated mine with a wank—a cramp in my opinion being an orgasm's delinquent cousin that needed to get taught by example to do better. Maxi just huffed. Years before we'd both sworn off the pill. Mini or not, it didn't seem worth the hormonal disturbance now that rubbers were more than just someone else's good idea. Maxi had been sick and tired of the weight gain. We knew we could rely on ourselves to avoid abortions. We egged each other on but our mayhem had its limits. I'd long thought that was the most wonderful thing about a best friend—the same person you go crazy with is the person who keeps you sane.

When my phone rang at half past eleven it was Maxi, halfway to smashed in the back of a cab, thanking God I'd answered. Predictably, she had offered Tom some after-dinner fellatio. Not as predictably, he had declined. In a panic she'd feigned a need to go home for the night, and Tom had been too bagged to protest. He'd asked her for a "rain cheque." Now she was calling me, feeling like Courtney Love.

"Maxi, he did just fly in from Philadelphia, right?"

She made me listen to the message he'd left on the way to the airport, cordial but constrained. (For easy mutual access we had the same password: 47825 — I SUCK.)

"So what, Bess? Come on."

"You're right, you would have gladly rung his Liberty bells—what a clod."

"I am so sick and tired of 'tired.' Tired is just plain rude. I don't get tired."

"Maybe Josephine drained him?"

"She drained *me*, if anyone. She made this huge fuss over my new reading glasses. She kept calling Tom 'Tim.' She hogged the maitre d' for a quarter of an hour. She made a big to-do over paying instead of Daddy. Like the whole thing wasn't tax deductible, please!"

"Was Tom in an okay mood?"

"Yes, he won his stupid case, something stupid about gelatin moulds."

"Marcus says it has North American implications."

"Well then, fine, hooray for Tom. He fell asleep on the couch with three remotes on his lap. Wearing track pants, elasticized, you know? So I decided to sneak him a treat. Quite frankly, it should have been foolproof. What is Tom's problem?"

Maxi and I approved of Lewinsky-Clinton–sized appetites. We thought they were only to be expected in the powerful. We were pretty sure we would have had sexual relations with that man, too, given such proximity to the Oval Office. Maxi also had a thing for Rhodes scholars, although she herself could never have managed the community-service requirements.

"It's so weird sucking on a dick when it's soft, isn't it? It's like stepping on an escalator that isn't moving. You're prepared but you still kind of lurch."

"Don't tell Marcus about *any* of this, Bess, I mean, *nothing*."

"What do you take me for?"

"Tom thinks you're going to get fed up with Marcus. I said only if you get FOI."

"What's that again?"

"Fear of Intimacy."

"Do one of your yoga tapes, Maxi. You need to chill."

"At midnight?"

"Sure, why not? You're obviously in the mood to breathe deeply."

"Can we meet for brunch, Babe? I really need to."

"You pick where."

"Arrow at ten."

"You got it. Now go downward dog."

"Tom did kiss me goodbye."

"That's nice."

"I wanted to bite his nose off. God, I should hurl. Don't be late."

"I won't."

⁂

I surprised Maxi by getting to Arrow first and scoring us our favourite table—out of the draft, in view of the door, with room to sit side by side. There was a baby murmuring like Pebbles at the table beside us. As Maxi doffed her hat, scarf, gloves and coat, the baby looked up in drooling stupefaction. I nodded down at it.

"Infants stare longer at attractive faces," I said.

"Mothers pay more attention to attractive infants," she said back. "Yuck, someone burnt toast. They'd better not do that to mine. So Babe, I hear Marcus is going to LA next week. Hope that doesn't rain on your parade in any way?"

"He's getting back in time for my party."

"What party?"

"The fourteenth?"

"Oh right! Silly me."

"So tell me about Toto, the good stuff."

"The waiter looked like Jason Priestly."

"He probably has a Getty's ransom in tech stocks. Those Toto guys make a killing."

"Everyone started discussing their Napa Valley experiences, blah, blah, blah. It was obvious Tom had been there with an ex. I had no idea he went to LSE. Now Daddy's in love. You know, Babe, I bet you Tom declined the BJ because he EPD'd."

"Toto is just not an Eat-to-the-Point-of-Discomfort kind of place, is it?"

"Tell me about it—the idiot. Do you know why the male sex drive peaks at eighteen? Because they fight hard for status when they're young. Females peak in their thirties because their fertility is dwindling."

"How depressing is that?"

"But by the time a woman reaches fifty-five she's statistically much less likely to become clinically depressed. A man of that age is much more so."

"I wonder where Tom's libido will be by then?"

Maxi laughed hard and abbreviated. The baby joined in, gurgly and leg-thumpingly. It could have been in an ad promoting babies, it was that cute. Maxi ripped into a mini bran muffin; she was having a bread-basket kind of morning.

"Babe, did you know that infants can have orgasms?"

"Shh, no. What's up with that?"

"They can have hormonal buildup at birth. That's why some of them get pimples."

"Might as well learn early to take the good with the bad, I guess."

Maxi ordered frittata with salad instead of fries. That was going to calm her down. I went for the waffles with blueberry sauce. I could see from other tables that the stack was cartoon-sized.

"My mother started threatening to sell the house again. Bloody fine by me."

Off-loading the family manse had been one of Josephine's idle threats for years. Maxi's vast childhood bedroom had a turret, gas fireplace and Juliet balcony. The French provincial four-poster had long ago been disposed of, but it still housed Maxi's filed and indexed *Tiger Beat* collection, her five-hundred-plus British Invasion cassette tapes and her Siouxsie and the Banshees posters.

"But what would you do with the Maxi Museum?"

"All that junk makes me feel old. As does bloody talking to Tara. She calls me every day. I'm forced to answer because of my work ethic. Everyone wants to go into everything with me lately. It's a trial."

"How old is Tara again?"

"Going on twenty-eight. Seven lucky years younger than us. God, I hate younger people."

The baby began to cry. I hoped it wasn't due for a breast-feed; Maxi couldn't deal with those in public. Our plates were delivered: waffles for Maxi, and a bright green mound of shiny mesclun for me. I quickly switched them over while Maxi grabbed the last muffin. I was glad she'd left me all the butter. I loved melting it into all the little compartments, trying to even it out but dousing some deliciously. Maxi was now pondering whether Tom's erotic fatigue could be blamed on her breasts. She'd noticed he always made sure to uncover her boobs and then did nothing with them. It was amazing Maxi and I had ever become friends at all, what with each craving the other's cup size so badly. Maxi was brave enough to want "work" done but Josephine had said no. Maxi hadn't given up. She was just waiting to make sure bigger boobs weren't a passing fad, and until liposuction could do something about cellulite.

Maxi had been busy on the Tara job, calling up Tara's old drama teacher, cheerleader pals and former roommate in LA, who was now doing well playing a drug-addicted teen in a hospital drama. Apparently, Tara had a way with practical jokes, which had at various times involved fake body hair, an Australian accent and a California congressman. Once, she'd plucked a wandering toddler out of the way of an oncoming motorcycle on Melrose Avenue then totally played down the civic-award possibilities. She was also really good at neck rubs and she did a mean Puff Daddy imitation. So much personal force didn't seem at all natural; I couldn't imagine behaving naturally around it. At least hearing all about it gave me time to finish my waffles.

Outside the wind chill was cruel but sunshine was beaming and rebounding, so a walk home seemed largely sane. We were down on Queen Street, among hysterical boutiques, effortful galleries and steely Pilates studios, and headed up through the park. Maxi stopped to light up a sub-zero smoke. I cupped the Zippo. The Zippo and I were good friends. I was always hearing its flick and whoosh, especially on the phone, especially when I'd made a point that was worth mulling over.

"How's Marcus, by the way?"

"Good, he's good. Consistently contemplative beneath it all."

"Sounds French."

"He's got some *cahier* in his *cinéma* for sure. Actually . . ."

I had to stop short so Maxi had to halt with me.

"What?" she puffed. "Don't think I doubt the man's talents. He's definitely a next-big-thing."

"It's not that."

"Babe, please. You know I'm too stressed for suspense right now."

"Marcus is taking me to Paris."

"When?"

"Right after your party. He's got points."

"No, when did he ask you?"

"The other day. We're not going for long."

"Congratulations, Bess. Aren't you the lucky one."

"It's the kind of thing that usually only happens to other people. To you, in fact."

"Not to me."

"Venice counts. And Nevis."

Maxi's cellphone rang. If this was Tom calling in abject penitence and remorse it would be perfect timing. "Tara," she mouthed, sucking on her smoke much less perceptibly now. I wanted to keep moving to stay warm but there was no way

Maxi was going to walk and talk at the same time, not with Tara Dickens on the line. Maxi laughed, as carefree and easy as a chick in a Stayfree ad. I could hear the buzz of Tara's voice. It sounded loud. And deep. Especially compared to Maxi, who often squeaked and peeped. Eventually, I got Maxi back.

"So Tara's at the Four Seasons having lunch with the old queen who plays Svengali. She invited me to join them. Quite frankly, it sounds like just what I need."

"Do what you will."

"I'm going to grab a cab from here."

Maxi clambered up onto the dirty snow bank and surveyed her chances.

"Work hard or have fun, whichever applies," I said.

"Both, actually."

"Thanks for brunch."

"Thank Daddy."

Maxi's way with cabs sustained itself. Her arm was that bit longer than average. She flagged this one with the precise motions of a corps de ballet member pointing out the Swan Queen. We hugged quickly in the traffic. Marble, crystal, linen and silver awaited Maxi. Her mimosa would go down well. It was an outlandish indulgence but I thought I might also get a taxi to whisk me the few remaining blocks to the Maxi Pad. My feet were so cold it felt like they'd been bound by an old-fashioned granny in Szechuan. I finally got one, right before I would have arrived home if I'd walked. I kept my boots hovering over the pool of slush threatening to flood the footwell. I tried not to gag on the pine freshener. It was a good thing Maxi wasn't along, she'd have given the driver royal hell, recent Ethiopian immigrant or not.

When I got home I spent the energy I'd saved in the taxi on my stability ball. I was out of practice and wobbly at first but eventually I balanced and pivoted hard, sending top notes of Happy and Herbal Essence wafting through the air as I assumed fighting form. "Take the safety off your gun/Let's go have some combat fun/Find some enemies roamin' around/Take your aim and mow 'em down."

Saturday at 5:23 p.m., I'd synchronized watches with Marcus when he called, then met up with him shortly after at Groceteria. I spied him first through the window wearing a Peruvian knit hat of shameless pink and turquoise with the ear flaps down and the tassels dangling. And jumbo buckle galoshes. Rocks was tied up outside, receiving a wide berth from strangers. We got a range of dips from the deli counter—assorted Mediterranean goops, artichoke paste, black olive tapenade and lox cream cheese—and picked out fancy crackers studded with seeds and rosemary plus the good old giant-sized biscuit selection from Carr's. Marcus drove us back to his place in the wood-panelled station wagon he'd bought that week, more for Rocks' sake than his own, he claimed. Tom pulled up just as we got there.

At first it was just the three of us, hanging out and drinking beer. Maxi was invited, too, but running late according to Tom.

"She's coming straight from the Four Seasons," he said. "I think she's had a few."

Tom seemed proud of Maxi's dissipation. It was the same smile he'd probably resort to if she trashed her budget at

Barneys, gobbling up Miu Miu mules and Lucien Pellat-Finet cashmere. I noticed his little black cellphone was within easy reach on the kitchen counter and made a mental note to tell Maxi about this when I got a chance. It would warm the cockles of her heart to think of her man on high alert for her bulletins.

No doubt Marcus and Tom managed to make plenty of small talk when they were alone together. I hoped I wasn't making things stilted for the boys. Tom seemed more amused than anything else by the fact that Marcus and I were going to Paris. But I suspected I was getting only half his reaction. In private he was probably ribbing Marcus about the joys of simultaneously getting blown, scarfing down *pain au chocolat*, and listening to Citroëns gun their way up Haussmann's boulevards. Paris: home of the indentured BJ, flaky pastry and early urban planning. Also a good place for a girl to buy a blouse for once in her life. Something crisp but pretty I was thinking. And bright white.

"Love this French brew," said Tom, polishing off a Stella Artois. "Better get used to it, kids."

"It's Belgian, actually," I said. "The Belgians excel at beer."

Tom didn't care but Marcus laughed. I had confided my Belgian fixation to him. He knew the beer issue would be especially irritating, encroaching as it did on one of the few areas of Canadian dominance now that so many Czechs were hockey stars and the Austin Powers franchise was at its peak.

"So Bess,"Tom said. "What do you think of Tara's movie?"

"So far, so great." I knew Tom's definition of *great* had a lot of useful elasticity. "She's gorgeous in it, needless to say. And it looks like she's going to get her man and triumph over Big Pharma, all in ninety-nine minutes."

"Didn't I tell you?" Marcus said to Tom. "She's a Bond girl without a Bond. It's revolutionary."

I prayed we wouldn't now get into a conversation about who had been the best Bond. Tom would beat us to the finish by making swift declarations about the superiority of Sean Connery, and then a discussion of Bond would steer us dangerously toward the concept of action movies as a whole. At the turn of the twentieth century this must have been what poetry was like—a lot of swaggering men in black velvet capes going on and on about iambs and rhyme schemes, their Edwardian girlfriends the victims of Rimbaud, not Rambo.

"When are you leaving for LA?" I asked Marcus, heading us in a more useful direction. If I was Marcus's girlfriend then Tom would have to get used to our domestic inquiries. Now he was watching us with a cockatoo's beady inquisitiveness.

"Wednesday. Early. I have a party in Toronto to get back for on the fourteenth."

"Right," said Tom. "Max's dinner party. She wants to have a little something to shut up her parents."

"It's also Bess's birthday." Marcus mentioned.

"Maxi is a great multi-tasker," I said.

I hoped Marcus knew that I didn't really care if Maxi's party wasn't strictly in my honour. I had to believe that he knew me that well already, our sex acts having somehow conveyed pivotal information about our dispositions. Then I realized that Marcus could absolutely tell that I cared, but not in such a way as to make a scene. All this confirmed how much I detested birthdays and had since my single digits—the goody bags gossiped over at Monday recess, the tuneless singalong as the cake loomed, the crowd's groan when I failed yet again to blow out all the candles, the whole wish fuss.

Marcus's steel door thundered like a Norse god with a bad grudge. I made a mental note to ease up on my own kicks in the future. In tumbled Maxi in hilarious humour, followed by Canada's chief red-carpet consul: Tara Dickens and her endless legs. Good thing we'd got the bigger biscuit tin. Maxi and Tara squawked over the last empty coat hook then wobbled over to the granite kitchen island in their heels. I was wearing my boots, too, praise be, which improved my chances of looking like I belonged to the same species as the glamazons, or at best like their tribal mascot.

Tara was such a bright spot she left dark blotches behind her. Her hair, eyes, teeth, and smile were all bright. She was skinny like me and tall like Maxi. Her skin was supernaturally clear. Her eyebrows were arched in sustained, amiable wonder. This was beauty so resplendently smooth that everything else bounced off it: beauty that impressed first, and seduced later if it wanted to. Tara was wearing what looked to be two men's suits that had been chopped up and sewn together into one ingenious item. Ann Demeulemeester maybe, or Martin Margiela, or some other agent of Flemish know-how. I would ask as soon as it was appropriate.

"I love your outfit," I said immediately, but that was okay, I was offering up a meta-feminine greeting. We both knew it was highly unlikely I would ever snap up the same item. "Who's it by?"

"Dirk Bikkembergs," said Tara.

"Fun to wear and fun to say."

"Hey, the pronunciation's approximate. The dude's from Antwerp."

Great, a ground-breaking Belgian I hadn't even heard of.

Tara extended a hand. "Nice to meet you. I mean it. All I ever hear is Bess Bess Bess!"

I bet Tara blushed milkmaid rosy rather than my scarlet fever. Maxi rushed over to hug me so tight and bouncy I was on Jolly Jumper toes.

"This is my Bess Babe."

"Roger that, Bubbles," Tara said. "Now wouldya put the poor woman down?"

Tara hugged the boys, the same neutral hug for both. Getting edited since her youth must have taught her to sort through moments lucidly. Maxi, however, was a better editor on paper than in person, drunk. Too much alcohol with too little food dissolved the censorship lobe in Maxi's brain. Out of wine, champers, ale, shooters and vodka came her truth.

"I'm Bess's best friend in the whole world! I've been her BEST friend since she was EIGHTEEN. And soon she's going to have a BIG BIR—"

"Save it for the fourteenth, Maxi," I whispered in her ear. "It's great to finally meet you too, Tara. And meet Rocks. C'mon, boy."

Rocks had been napping. Now he was in blink mode. He growled as he rose, yelped as he stretched, and ambled over to the newcomers. After putting up with a few off-kilter pats that didn't make proper fur contact, he padded back over to me and barged head first between my legs. I knew Rocks was no Lothario, but it was nice to have the proof. I kneaded his muscle-man hips.

"Meeting Rocks is much more profound experience than meeting me," I said.

"I don't know about that," said Marcus. He booted Rocks aside and went in for a kiss. Anyone with eyes could tell he had a dashboard comfort with me; the guy could rev me at will. I saw Tara saw.

"Lilly Pulitzer here said you guys wouldn't mind me coming over," Tara said. "Hey, it was this or a night at the bath house with Roger after some serious rounds of cinnamon schnapps at Woody's."

"You're safe now," Marcus said. Tom handed her a beer. Maxi insisted on having one too.

"The more the merrier," I said, then wished I hadn't come up with such conversational deadwood. "Pull up a stool," I patted.

Tara sat and Marcus ousted me from my stool and placed me on his lap. I tried not to feel too Charlie McCarthy. I did feel a bit teddy bear. All of us did a cheers next, but then Marcus had a strict rule that you had to look everybody right in the eye when you cheers-ed them, so we had to do it all over again, with even more commotion. I hated having to look Tom in the eye. Tara's eyes were one of those splendid colours, say cerulean, which no one else's eyes get to be. Maxi's gaze was wired. Marcus's eyes were a goofy mere three inches from mine when I turned around. I stuck out my tongue at him. I hoped it was pink.

"Speaking of Woody's, I heard they're shooting the North American *Queer as Folk* here." Marcus passed me another beer. "Toronto has to pass for Pittsburgh."

"I promised myself just one thing when I got into this business and that was no American remakes of anything," said Tara.

"I'll fuck someone *not* to get into one of those. This world would be a better place if we all read more subtitles. Am I right, or am I right?"

"I make a point of doing foley in French and English," I said. "And Flemish."

Tara chuckled. Young as she was, she was past giggling. She and I clinked bottles. Tom and Maxi were whispering and canoodling. The rest of us weren't inclined to get included in their sweet-nothings circuit. Fortunately for Maxi she had worn her four-hundred-dollar Dolce & Gabbana jeans that day, engineered to make one's ass look like a piece of fruit and one's old 501's feel like paper bags sewn around one's legs. Levi's stock was going to take a tumble.

"YOU PICKED A HOTEL ALREADY!" Maxi wheeled around and pretty well yelled at me. "You should have checked with Tom first. Too late now."

"Ya gotta go Meurice or Bristol. Trust me, guys, I know Paris."

For an awful moment I thought we were on the verge of a suggestion that we go to Paris *à quatre*. But then Tara saved my vacation.

"Way to hang with the bourgeoisie, Mister Pompadour. By the way, I've listened to you order French wine and you've got a lousy accent."

Tom wagged what looked suspiciously like a manicured finger at Tara. "Max, I want it in the article that she doesn't respect her elders."

Tara saved his face by winging a paper plate at him so he could catch it all sporty-dextrous. Marcus had put a stack out for Rocks. We took turns whipping these at him now—

Rocks's version of manna. He caught every one until he almost crashed into the stereo going for Maxi's final throw. Marcus promised it wasn't her fault.

"So, love," I said to Tara when we'd settled back into party pods. "I hear it's a drug."

"I couldn't have taken a step without you."

"She's the best," said Marcus.

"Actually, my boss, Marisa, is the best. But I try," I said.

I was back in Marcus's lap. One of his arms hugged me like a seat belt while the other surfed the snack buffet. I'd inquire later if I had hummus in my hair. I knew there was no need to ask if I was getting heavy; his lap was big enough that I could sprawl. I sat proud and tried to avoid puncturing his calves with my heels. Tara and Marcus started talking weekend grosses, festival buzz and Oscar hype. I hoped that Marcus was aware he could have those conversations with me as well. Meanwhile I enjoyed listening in on his critical analysis. Tara had a good business brain. She did indeed seem lit from within. I wondered if she switched herself off in private.

Maxi was grabbing Tom's balls. Drink made her lecherous as well as blunt. There wouldn't be much journalism going on tonight; Maxi was far too slap-happy.

"Good news, by the way." Tara wagged a breadstick at Marcus. "Harry's on for Thursday. I think he might even pay for lunch."

"Righteous," said Marcus. "Nice work."

It was time for me to winch myself back into the conversation.

"Are you going to LA as well, Tara?"

"I'm about due for some atonement, yup," Tara said. "Hey, I like paying for my sins. I get more of them that way."

"Bess wants to go to LA some day," said Marcus.

"LA is Mecca," I said.

"You're welcome to crash with me." Tara slid her palm along mine, evidently the updated version of a high-five.

"Do you have a Spanish-style bungalow?"

"No, but I just bought a Richard Neutra."

"Is the pool kidney shaped?"

"Not yet. Note to self: call landscapers."

There was a thought: Tara Dickens and me, side by side on chaise longues, wearing SPF 60 and exchanging witticisms as we surveyed an arid canyon. I wondered if we would add up to more or less than the sum of our parts.

"She can't stay with me," said Marcus.

"Dude, what's that supposed to mean?" Tara said.

"I'm giving up my place," said Marcus.

I smiled at Tara as if I had known this and merely forgotten.

"Can you do that?" she asked.

"Going, going, gone. Adios, Los Feliz. I can handle everything I need to from here."

"Hey, guys, way to justify my guesthouse."

Now I was dizzy. It wasn't just that I could have broken a leg falling out of Marcus's lap. It was more of a minor swoon, like the kind brought on by a Beth Orton ballad, or an unexpected compliment, or finding one of your favourite movies playing late at night on TV. Definitely I was pleased that Marcus was settling deep into town, but it also had to do with the way latitude and longitude had been compressed to non-issues. A warning skimmed over my mind that this could be a short-lived phase where I was concerned. I hoped not. I was very much enjoying this mood, company and sphere, where glamour got brewed like coffee. It was Maxi who had brought us to this place and I knew she planned on sticking around. I jumped out of Marcus's lap to check in with her.

"Tom thinks my legs come out of my bum funny when I walk," Maxi was pouting.

"Just be glad you have a bum," I said. This was not strictly true. Maxi had pita breads more than buns.

"Max, be fair now. I said I love your walk." Positive appraisal or not, Tom was a man who took his judgments with him everywhere.

"Get Tom to play the favourite animal game," I said.

"Okay! Tom, what's your first favourite animal?"

"Panther."

"Second favourite?"

"Parrot."

"Third favourite?"

"Hamster."

Tom took too much pride in answering quickly.

"You see yourself as a panther, others see you as a parrot and you really are a HAMSTER!" Maxi thought that was cute enough to merit a kiss. She seemed to be claiming Tom with the same excitement she'd show over a front-row seat at a Galliano show.

"No hamster jokes, people," Marcus called over. Spoken like a true dog-chimp-dolphin.

There were vague ideas of heading out somewhere to eat but we all got too tipsy to move. Marcus had some upmarket instant risotto mixes in his cupboard—asparagus, saffron and porcini—which he stirred up while I tossed greens with Roquefort and walnuts. I noted Marcus's fine olive oil and vintage vinegar. I was proud for him, if dismayed for myself. Groceteria had a special on their house-brand extra virgin so I had bought the $9.99 vat, which now made me feel like a hillbilly with a jug of xxx. My excuse was how much of the stuff I went through. Olive oil was the magic elixir that was keeping me sane through my thirties as other pleasures lost their lubricity.

The main course roped us all back together as a conversational whole. We managed pretty well: no awkward silences as forks scraped the crockery or the cooking getting one compliment too many. Marcus forbade any display of dinnertime generosity toward Rocks. His digestion had gone dicey; one false move and everything was liquefying.

"I never thought it was that great a deal, being man's best friend," Tara mused. "It's got to have some serious downsides."

"I worship the dog," Marcus said. "God spelled backward."

"You're very good to him," I agreed. "It's an inspiration."

"Dogs are a lot of work," Tom grimaced.

"And they shed," said Maxi. "And stink."

Tara's godmother apparently had eight dogs. She was a Wiccan named Juno who lived outside Flesherton. She'd worn every colour of the rainbow to Tara's christening.

"I guess your parents kind of overestimated her devotion to patriarchal monotheism?" I asked.

"Hey, Juno makes some really good points." Tara was eating straight from a risotto pot; she'd fought me rock-paper-scissors for the scrapings. "That Bible God is a grouch."

"A warmonger in the right place at the right time," I said.

"Babe, Babe, shut up, shut up. We are so going to get thundered on."

"Hey, no wonder the dude is in a bad mood," Tara said. "Think about it, nothing decent to eat. Those clouds are slim pickin's."

"No getting a leg over either."

"Babe, shut UP for once in your life! If there's locusts it will be YOUR fault."

"Hey, Woodward-Bernstein," Tara intercepted, "are you sure you don't want the last of this? I don't think you got that much to eat. Anyhow, God as a broad, with child-bearing hips, a thing for whipped cream and a bunch of pain-in-the-butt boyfriends? That I can relate to."

"Not exactly in your image but I can see how it works as an alter ego." I enjoyed making Tara Dickens laugh, even if she did laugh easily.

Marcus passed around a box of Creamsicles for dessert. "God is your free will, idealized and personified," he concluded.

"If you're going to be a brainiac about it, yes." Tara winked at me.

"Marcus is God," said Maxi, drunk enough to slurp cheap ice cream.

By midnight, after cracking a lot of jokes about our incipient middle age, which none of us really believed and that Tara tactfully refrained from adding to, everyone else took their leave. Maxi had broken two wineglasses, one right after the other. Maybe now she'd believe me when I said stemware wasn't worth the trouble. Marcus's glasses had that perfect ping. They were a gift from his mother that I banned from the dishwasher and dried with special care. I asked to go along on Rocks's bedtime walk and was happy to catch his puzzled showdown with a dumpster rat. Rocks knuckled under, smart dog. Marcus was clever to have invested in Parkdale. It was scampy and trampy, but the bones of the neighbourhood were too grand to go undeveloped for longer than a Toronto decade. I stopped myself from worrying if the sidewalks were stroller friendly.

That night between the sheets I performed a certain sexual service. God forbid Marcus should find out Tom was having all the luck. I swallowed, no problem. You know you really like them when they're appetizing. Marcus was touched and made that very clear. "Darling," he said. Marcus wanted to do me next but I wasn't interested in starting up a tit-for-tat program. Oral sex is not about going Dutch in my estimation, although I'm sure the Dutch have some randy variation on the theme that they've taught to the Belgians. I was touched by Marcus's offer, especially when his brainwaves flipped over right after from beta to delta. He was so tired he fell asleep while I watched. I kept my elation quiet and still. It was a chance to develop my acquaintanceship with Marcus's space. His paintings, bureau and skylight all seemed to appreciate having me there, and eventually his bed succumbed to me, too. Unfortunately, I dreamed of a Greyhound bus with a nasty toilet but I knew I couldn't have everything.

"What's up?" Marcus was playing with my hair, his new bed toy.

We had had a nice bout of Sunday-morning sex, me on top then Marcus on top; then we lay there too glazed to move. Rocks was sleeping in, happily for us, since it was hard to stay up in the bedroom when he was down there mourning every moment that expired without us. I thought about the word *cuddle*, how it was such a stupid word for such a great thing. I couldn't mention this to Marcus, however, because that would entail saying the word out loud.

"Vanity," I said. "It's getting me down."

"You deserve to be vain. Go for it."

"I read somewhere that infatuation is a form of vanity. You think the object of your affection is wonderful, so of course this wonderful person deserves to be with someone wonderful. *Ergo*, the more wonderful they are, the more wonderful you are. But I'm not in the mood for that. I just want you to be wonderful."

"You're stuck being wonderful, I'm afraid. There's nothing you can do about it, since I insist on being wonderful myself."

"It's just that as a girl you learn to be on guard against guys who only want to get laid. Then you get a bit older and wiser and realize you also have to be careful of the ones who only want a little romance. Men can be pretty sentimental."

I was dragging us somewhere noxious, playing tourist at a sulphur mine.

"Bess, I promise this isn't puppy love."

"Supposedly puppy love is so intense because youngsters aren't distracted by survival demands. But back when I was a teen, I was obsessed with surviving. The Sex Pistols were worth it. And the guys at my school weren't. Damn, it scares me how little I've changed."

"What do you mean?"

"I've experienced so little discrepancy. You keep waiting for yourself to love jazz and hate pop music, to prefer dark to milk chocolate, to keep a tidy bedroom. And it never happens. That's the thing about inclinations, I guess. They're accurate."

"No one's going to arrest you over the rate of your development, Bess. Take it as it comes."

"I know. I'm getting to know. I want to lie here for a while and be grateful for what I know. What *we* know. Let's not joke."

"The jokes just have to do with how everything else is serious."

"Maxi must be pretty serious then, because sometimes I feel like her personal joke service."

"I'm sure Maxine would love to be taken seriously. She's your friend so I'll wish her good luck with that."

"You'll probably be getting a thank-you note for last night. Her whole family has monogrammed stationery. Maxi had to write thank-you notes to Santa when she was little. I don't see that it was worth the Easy-Bake Oven."

"Now the poor girl is probably never really grateful for anything."

"Maxi is a good friend, but she's got to get out of this bed."

"She's gone. I just saw her leave. She's still wobbling."

Marcus and I lay there for a while in the pleasant nude aftermath of pillow talk. I was proud of us. I felt like we were running a real gamut with pit stops at home truths. We lay there even though our stomachs were growling up a symphony.

"In Russia, bright red hair is the sign of a tart the same as bleached blonde is here," I said eventually. I primped my curls.

"Come here, my little Bessanova."

We did it again. I hung off the bed frame while Marcus jounced. Sex is much better for a hangover than Big Macs, which is what Marcus wanted two of for breakfast from the drive-through. He was celebrating the fact that he owned the kind of car he could slop special sauce in. I made him promise we'd return during Shamrock Shake season. Marcus finished off my fries. I'd got the large to show off. I reminded him the best frites are Belgian. He dropped me off at home, kindly turning off the car outside my door so we could make out a little, licking salt off each other's lips.

"Can I see you again before you go to LA?" I asked.

"As long as *I* can see *you* before I go to LA. Rocks will want to say goodbye."

"What are you doing with Rocks while you're gone?"

"If I let him have the run of the place he'll have his buddies over to listen to gangsta rap and do catnip. Nope. I'm going to have to stick him in the dreaded kennel."

"I can take care of him," I said.

"Do you hear that, buddy? The lady is extending her hospitality."

Rocks yawned.

"I'm serious," I said. "I want to."

"Take a chance to think it over." Marcus turned on the ignition.

I blew them kisses from the sidewalk although only Rocks was looking, with his eyes full of sorrow, wondering why I always had to be such a lone wolf.

I was so glad it was Sunday. I could not have faced work without some time to mentally flatline. I finished the Saturday papers but at daydream speed, dwelling mostly on the lifestyle columnists, who had nothing much to say about achieving monogamy in the face of ennui, surviving as the sandwich generation or how the handbag was the new shoe. Emerging sane from the paper gave me the strength I needed to get practical. The first thing I had to do was butter up Maxi, the better to get her help with Rocks. I needed her to walk him once a day while I was at work, since dogs are unwelcome at foley studios. But there was no way I was broaching anything this tricky while she was still hungover. I hoped that Tom was being prompt with the cold compresses; no one wanted that headache to last for two days. I decided some *Gash* was my best bet for openers, a novelty item I'd been promising Maxi for ages. I could deliver it early Monday morning on my way to work. I scrawled a note across the top, asking Maxi to call me right away because I really, really needed her help with something. I had a serious task up for grabs and only she would do. Honesty is definitely a good policy between friends. Not that honesty can't be helpfully exaggerated. It's the sycophant's revenge.

WHORE-O-SCOPES

Modern Gash Reveals Your Sex Self

Who's the horniest sign of all? Who screws like a bordello maven? Who's as cold as ice? It's all in the stars, Baby!

By Bess Grover

ARIES

You ram your privates in people's faces. Don't be sheepish, you were born during spring fever. Be baaaaa-aaaddd. Try doing it with wool over your eyes.

TAURUS

Don't give me your bullshit, you forced him into it, so don't complain when he sticks to you like dung. Stop plodding along: you shtup in a rut.

GEMINI

Get over all that mystical crap about finding your soulmate, it ain't going to happen. But your fickle fanny sure loves the chase.

CANCER

No wonder you're crabby! You're not getting nearly enough. Crawl out of that shell and down to the nearest sandbar to pick up a sea snake. Clamming up will get you nowhere. It's time for low tide.

LEO

So you're queen of the beasts. Take a breather, you roaring floozy. It isn't that much of a jungle out there. And keep it down—the neighbours are going deaf.

VIRGO

No one is fooled by the virginity act. Yes there's gossip, and yes, it's all about your sleazy doings. You should probably rethink the kilt and knee socks.

LIBRA

Nice work Libra: you're on top just about as often as he is. Weigh your options. Push your way up there. Just stop falling for him.

SCORPIO

Yeah, the fellows just love getting stung. Sure, they dig your claws and scales. That explains why you always have to sneak up on them, right?

SAGITTARIUS

When they fail to satisfy you let them know, half man, half horse or not. You might consider not sleeping around wherever the arrows fall. At least you've got one over on that ass, Cupid.

CAPRICORN

You'll cross any bridge that comes. Try not to head-butt the gents so much; they're more fun to rut with when they're conscious. Beware your odours. Bonus points for your beady gaze.

AQUARIUS

Harmony and understanding happen when you're horny. Your moon is in the seventh house of ill repute. You're not promiscuous, you're a humanitarian!

PISCES

Something is fishy around here and it's you. You're a very happy hooker. You've got a great eye for a rod, all right. And one hell of a thing for worms.

Week Five Poison

When Maxi called me at the foley studio as requested, Hank and Marisa said to go ahead and take it, they'd have a tea break—or in Hank's case, a Coffee Crisp break. Hank loved the vending machine, especially kicking it. Maxi was still hurting. I asked if there was anything I could do, making it a point of honour to be an even better hangover buddy than drinking buddy. What I could do was to listen to the latest with Tom. They'd had sofa sex on Sunday afternoon and Maxi had caught herself cooing like a pigeon halfway through, but I promised her Tom wouldn't have noticed. He had picked up Thai food for dinner on Sunday night and Maxi had rented *The Thomas Crown Affair*, which had seemed a better bet than *Runaway Bride*.

"Thai takeout and a video, the new Toronto classic. I'm surprised it took you guys so long to get around to it."

"Tom kept complaining because I haven't upgraded to DVD yet."

"Don't take that personally."

"God, why must weekends go so quickly?"

"I know, for a weekend to feel like a weekend it has to be long."

"I don't know why all the long weekends have to be in the summer. The summer is nice enough already. They should put a long weekend in at the end of January."

"To help people cope with the flings they started by getting smashed at New Year's."

"Tom is more than a fling. He put a pail beside the bed."

"That was very Flo Nightingale of him."

"Florence Nightingale was apparently a real shrew."

"That's how she got so much accomplished. Military wounded were treated despicably before the Lady with the Lamp forcibly came along."

"Okay, Bess, fine. No history lessons today, please."

In December I'd driven Maxi crazy obsessing over the published results of the UN inquiry into Rwanda. Maxi couldn't believe I'd gone so far as to get the Hutus and the Tutsis straight. I shouldn't have snapped at her when she congratulated me on my concern, but I knew so well that concerns like mine didn't translate into action, not unless resubscribing to the newspaper counted, or winning the odd wonksmanship contest when cocktail chatter got political. What I wanted to see happen was national public mourning over the death of peacekeeping—something I thought Canadians could consider engaging in with Belgians once we'd all come to terms with Kigali.

"No history, Maxi. Just a favour to ask."

"Go ahead, try your luck."

"The things is, I offered to take care of Rocks while Marcus is in LA and he'll need a little walk around lunchtime, which obviously I can't do. You said it makes you hyperventilate when you realize you haven't been outside all day, right? So I was hoping you might do that once a day, only on weekdays, until Marcus gets back."

"I don't know. Rocks might attack me. Believe me, I'd sue."

"Not a chance. Rocks likes everyone; he's very saintly that way."

"How long does this walk have to be?"

"Once around the block, tops. Or until he lifts his leg. Sorry, I know it's cold out. Please, Maxi? I really want to do Marcus a favour and it's hard to swing that, he's so forward-thinking."

"Well, you've really got me cornered, Bess. So I'll do it. But each walk counts as a separate favour."

"Thanks so much. I love you. Your wish is my etcetera."

"Okay, then. Firstly, my parents are coming to the party. I had to invite them to keep them out of my hair until my article is finished. I don't need my mother over here right now complaining that the kitchen cupboards look wrong. It'll be worth it, Babe. I told her about your pathetic lack of Prada. Josephine can't believe how old you're going to be. I told her you had nothing to worry about considering you're still totally cute."

"Okay."

"You also have to pick up a cellulite brush and cream system that I want from France. But you can't tell Marcus. Don't worry, I'll write it all out for you and give you the money."

“Maxi, I keep telling you, it’s got nothing to do with the fancy brushes. It’s that French chicks are so busy running around to spas and discoursing on linguistics and planning their six weeks of vacation that they don’t have time to snack.”

“They’re just lucky they have French bread to take for granted. I’m sure that calms them down.”

“True. We lack an iconic carb over here.”

“I should get going. I have to dust. That’s what I get for having Tom over so much.”

Maxi was forever haunted by the fact that dust largely came from flaked skin.

“Maybe you should do your French maid thing.”

“If I can convince him the outfit is brand new, maybe.”

“By the way, Evil Benefactor has totally lost it,” I told Maxi. “He’s holed himself up in an adobe hut not far from Jessica’s ancestral lands. The airport scene went well but now we have to do the screen-door bang.”

“Get back to work then, Bess. You need to keep Marisa on your good side.”

“Have fun with the Tara Dickens parable. Show us what fame can do to the right mind and face.”

Wednesday at 7 a.m., Marcus showed up with Rocks, a crate of Science Diet, the doggy bed, five Frisbees and French *Vogue*.

“I installed a hook on the kitchen wall so his leash will be in easy reach,” I said.

“That’s the least of your worries. Rocks brought his banjo.”

“Can he play the theme from *Deliverance*?”

"Yes, and he laughs at the 'Come here piggy, piggy' scene."

"I put out a big water bowl."

"Tell him it's Evian. He insists on it but then he never knows the difference. You're almost done with that feature, right?"

"We're nearing the dénouement, oui."

"Listen to my little French immersion vixen. You're going to be in charge in Paris."

"Then you'll have to kiss me, you fool."

"Just you wait."

I could wait, but only just. I was growing more and more fond of Marcus. And I was looking forward to having Rocks around. It would make for an interesting week and it would keep me from calendar chomping my way to Marcus's return and on to Paree. In my heart of hearts I knew that I was Maxi's handmaid so it wouldn't do to be time's as well.

"Be nice to Maxi," I begged Rocks before I left. He yawned.

Midday, Maxi called breathily from her cell on the way back to her place, pleased that Rocks hadn't pooped, which she took as a special favour.

"If and when he does, just close your eyes and think of Elvis," I said.

"You know I hate Elvis."

"So does Rocks, that whole hound-dog thing. Rocks would never put Shasta Cola in his Jell-O."

"The dog is a dog, Bess. Hopefully Marcus calls you every day to check on him."

"Nah, I want to convey more competence than that."

"Tara just called me from LA."

"All these long-distance plans. Talk is getting so cheap. We're going to lose our sense of significance."

"She was a varsity hurdler in high school. She claims to be embarrassed by that now."

"She should be proud of herself for dispensing with metaphors. Actual hurdles are a lot easier to get past. Did you find out what she and Marcus are up to in LA?"

"That's your job, Babe. I can't ask again. Tara keeps calling me Nancy Drew. I invited her to the party, by the way. She's very pleased. She says it will help with her Valentine's Stress Disorder."

"Hmm—VSD, I like it. So, did you tell Tom about how helpful you're being with Rocks?"

"Naturally. He said it was really nice of me. Now if only he'd do the nice thing and stay over on a school night for once. This weekend-only business is all on his terms. So help me God, I will break down the bachelor fourth wall this time, I really will."

"Try not to put the cart before the horse, Maxi."

"Everybody always says that but they never say which is the cart and which is the horse."

"Commitment is the cart. Tom is the horse."

"You get so self-righteous when you're in love, Babe. It's a nightmare for me, quite frankly."

"Sorry. Sorry, sorry." Three was the magic number when it came to telling Maxi you were sorry. "FYI, Jessica just got to 'Six months later.' She's busy tallying up her drug trial results. The lab is so spic and span it looks as if it was taken over by Disney. Guess who the deli delivery boy was? That other cute bartender at Antico. The one with the Slavic cheekbones."

"Poor Marcello."

"Marcello doesn't mind; he just wants to sell booze and flirt. Thanks again for helping with Rocks. I couldn't have done this without you."

"I have to say, as dogs go, he just isn't my look."

"You're on again for tomorrow, right?"

"If I said so then yes."

"Call me if you need me."

It was no wonder Maxi was getting testy, with her draft almost due. Tara really was a paradox—both a generator and a product of her era, both canny and blithe, both Californian and Canadian. Sue was going to be calling any day to find out where Maxi was at. I hoped for Maxi's sake she'd refrain from using the word *text* or referring at all to Derrida. She could easily buy herself some time now that she had everything pretty well amassed and expressed; she just had to kill some babies. Maxi said that was her favourite part, getting rid of the things that just didn't work. She liked her pages as neat as her houses.

The Maxi Pad might have been at its most untidy with Rocks around but he cleaned the place up in his own way. His contentment was restorative. It was a lesson in life to see how a dog's tail wagged down to every last nanosecond of what could be construed of as *walk*. I made a note to get a clip-on bag holder for Rocks' leash. When the timing wasn't quite in his favour, poor Rocks was a three-bag man, a lesson I learned the hard way. I rolled the offending article in snow and kicked it into the gutter. then Rocks and I made a run for it. We'd missed a call from Marcus. I let Rocks listen to the message, but he couldn't quite wrap his head around the physics of it and hunted out a Tweety slipper for socializing instead. It was great for both of us that companionship was running so abundant.

When I got home from work on Thursday, Rocks was gone. Like a fool I checked every corner and closet but he was gone. One Tweety slipper was an unidentifiable mush of chewed yellow, but his bed was empty—no woof, no sneeze, no yawn, no shake. I actually checked to see if my lock had been tampered with but it looked normal and nothing else was missing. If Maxi was hogging Rocks I was resentful. If something had happened to Rocks I'd be horrified. If something had happened to Maxi I was ruined. I called over to Crawford Street, furious with the phone for taking so long to click over. Maxi had to understand how miserably disappointing it was to walk in the door and not have Rocks there performing what looked like it might be the latest dance craze in Rio.

"Yes, the dog is here," she said.

"Maxi, I was so scared something bad had happened."

"Something bad did happen."

"What?"

"I was kind enough to take him to my place. Because, quite frankly, I didn't really have time to walk him. Sue called around noon and I had to email back and forth with her about five times until I finally got my extension. For the fourteenth, by the way. Anyhow, I decided to make brownies to celebrate."

"That sounds good."

"Nix on the brownies, I'm afraid. Your friend Rocks here ate all the chocolate."

"What?"

"I gave him a couple of nibbles, just to be nice. Then I left the kitchen for one second to see who was on *Oprah* and he ate the whole package. Don't worry, I told him off. Can you come and get him? He keeps whining."

"Fucking hell, Maxi. Chocolate kills dogs."

"Well, how was I to know?"

"What's Rocks doing right now? How does he look? Fucking tell me, Maxi."

"Panting. Pacing around. Don't blame me for this."

"Find a vet. I'll be right there."

Idiot, I sobbed, or would have sobbed if I hadn't been sprinting. I felt for my wallet. I cursed the red light and took the intersection anyway, holding cars off with my bare hands. Rocks was precious, lovable and irreplaceable, the true meaning of *pet*. Especially from Marcus's point of view. Contemplating Marcus's point of view would skin my heart raw if I did too much of it. Soon I'd be confronting Rocks' suffering face-on. I had to be the most resourceful I'd ever been in my life. I ran toward Maxi's house so fast my lungs felt shredded and I had to pretend my aching legs were someone else's.

"I called a cab, it'll be here in a sec," she said. "It's just a few blocks. They're expecting us. Calm down, Babe."

Maxi had left the front door open knowing I'd have pounded it down in fury. Rocks was leashed up in her foyer gulping water by the gallon.

"I am calm. Get the wrapper."

"What?"

"Get the fucking wrapper from the fucking chocolate so we know what kind it was and how much."

Maxi silently retreated to her kitchen. The cab pulled up and I bustled Rocks into it. It was like he had Attention Deficit Disorder all of a sudden; he wasn't so much walking as whirligigging. Maxi hated sitting in the front seat of cabs so much that she had to squeeze into the back of even this one, crowding Rocks' hindquarters. We were headed along Dundas to a clinic near Bathurst that I'd never paid much attention to before. Rocks was hyperventilating. It boded ill for his pulse.

"I just wish he'd be sick," I said. "Sir, please hurry," I told the cabbie.

"Damn it!" said Maxi.

"He's going as fast as he can," I said.

"No, the dog just peed all over me. Yuck!"

"Give him a break. His nervous system is completely under attack right now. Get the cab and I'll pay you back. Hurry. The vet's going to have some questions for you."

"Fine, Bess. Bloody hell."

There were people in the waiting room sitting with cat carriers on their laps and one woman cradling a ferret. I was very sorry but I had to go first. The receptionist was prepared for this.

"Maxine Bishop?" she asked.

"No, yes. This is Rocks."

The next thing I knew Rocks had been hoisted onto a stainless steel examination table by the receptionist, myself and a man in scrubs with cheekbones as wide as the tundra who looked like he could have been the one good *yakuza*.

"Hello, I'm Doctor Chin," he said. "I understand there's been some chocolate ingested."

"Baking," I said miserably. I knew that was the worst-case scenario.

"He's a big guy, huge in fact. That's going to work in his favour."

Maxi spilled into the room, proffering the empty packet.

"How do you do," she said. I saw her eyes light up and glance down at Doctor Chin's ring finger. *Idiot, idiot.*

"Was it the whole packet?" Doctor Chin asked her.

"Most of it. Too bad I use such high-quality stuff!"

"When was this?"

"Well, I picked him up around three."

"Three?"

"I told you, Bess. I'm having a very busy day. You're lucky I went to get him at all. I had no idea it was going to be so cold out."

"Maxine is supposed to walk him for me at lunchtime," I explained. "Down, boy. Easy. He's actually my boyfriend's dog."

"'Boyfriend'? My, my!"

Idiot, idiot, idiot.

"Here's what we're going to do, Bess, is it? I'm going to induce vomiting with a hydrogen peroxide solution, after which we'll administer an activated charcoal slurry. Then we'll start up an IV for hydration and include some anti-seizure medication. Worst-case scenario is a coma, but I think this guy is more uncomfortable than in danger. Still, we'll keep him here for observation overnight."

"Thank you so much," I said. "I'd never forgive myself if anything happened to him. He looks like a monster but he's a total sweetie. He refutes the whole first-impression thing."

"He's going to be fine, ladies. Why don't you stay a while, Bess? You seem to have a great touch with him."

Joe Chin had a great touch; he'd obviously sailed through his bedside-manner class. He looked to be the cleanest-cut man who had ever walked a city street. Maxi asked him if everybody knew that chocolate was bad for dogs, agreed with him that they didn't, thanked him profusely for the excellent service, asked him if he had a card and announced to me she'd pay the bill.

"Really, Bess. I can afford it; you can't."

"Maxi, no," I said. "Please, just go. I'll take it from here."

Maxi backed out of the room with her zombie smile on. I turned back to Rocks who had piddled again and was coiled in hangdog shame.

"Urinary incontinence," said Doctor Chin. "Not unusual in this situation."

"It isn't your fault, Rocks," I promised. "Blame the idiot," I whispered.

There were a couple of technicians with us in the room now, to mop up, give needles and bustle medically. This was the only team I could conceive of belonging to for the time being. I went crazy over Rocks' ears, giving every comforting scratch I could as he twitched his way through his ordeal. Rocks could have my Paris money, I didn't care. I attentively watched him vomit.

Two hours later, when I had been persuaded to take my leave of Dundas Animal Care, I knew I didn't want to call Maxi when I got home. For that reason I had to drop in on her. Somehow, a face-to-face would make it easier to keep things brief to the point of truncated. I thumped once and waited on her porch with my hands stuffed in my parka pockets. She answered primly and steered us toward her living room, but I slumped on her hall chair instead. She had on her post-adventure grin, as if this was something we'd have fun talking about.

"Too bad Rocks couldn't be here right now," she said. "I've read that petting an animal lowers one's blood pressure. That's why dogs get taken to visit old-age homes."

"He's going to be okay," I said. "But only because he weighs a hundred pounds. So try not to feel like an idiot, I guess."

"You try not to feel like an idiot, too, Babe, for not warning me about the chocolate thing. I'm making date squares instead, by the way. They should be ready soon if you want to wait."

"No, no thanks. I have to go home and call Marcus."

"I already talked to Tom. He said this isn't my fault, legally."

"Marcus wouldn't sue you, Maxi. Get a grip, fuck."

"Firstly, Babe, language. I know you're stressed but it's really unattractive and simply not fair. Secondly, do not tell my mother what happened. She's already goes on about what a wise soul you are. She'll jump for joy if she finds out about this."

"Why would I do that? Look Maxi, please—next time, let me know if you're too busy to help. I'd rather get someone else to do it than worry."

"I should be fine now that I've got my extension. Let me know if I can go to the vet with you again, Babe. Yum, yum."

"I doubt it."

"Martial arts are really becoming fashionable lately, don't you think? All of a sudden they're less nerdy."

"I'm wiped out, Maxi. I've got to go."

Hugging goodbye was an old habit that felt like it was all we had to go on just then. Maxi felt very plush; she had a thing for any item that looked knit by a granny. Luckily for her, so did Marc Jacobs. Sexy-prim was one of Maxi's favourite forms of irony. It seemed to me that when an economy is besotted with information, pretty well everything implies at least one other thing—baby names, ice cream flavours, shoe toes—meaning gets loaded, layered and extrapolated. An injured dog, however, is a fast track to sheer, hard reality. There is no ideal injured dog. Words fail an injured dog. Wittgenstein would have been stopped in his tracks at the sight of Rocks huddled and chastened, breathing triple time, left behind with strangers, badly done wrong.

Jessica was going gangbusters, hosting a press conference at the newly sunny drug HQ. Her posse of faithful were befriending a bunch of FDA honchos and Marisa and I had to shake on it, over and over, to get those soft, meaty sounds. I took charge of the camera handling: shutters and motor drives. When a call from Marcus blinked through in the afternoon, I played down my distress as best I could. It was part of my new life's mission to protect Marcus from as much disappointment as possible. My bright, bouncing guy was outing aspects of my femininity I'd presumed were defunct: I'd taken *nurture* down from the same shelf as *cuddle* and dusted off both. I had to be careful because, if not, I'd end up—against the odds, against my fearful judgments, against my former habits, in accordance with Barry White, Merchant Ivory movies and the headliners in the vows section—*making love*.

"What a ham that guy is," Marcus said. "I should never have let him watch *ER*. He's got a thing for nurses now. I bet you he's got them all feeding him out of their hands."

"I'll pay the vet bill," I said. "I mean it."

"Actually, Rocks has insurance. He talked me into it during his heli-ski phase. So it's covered, darling. But thanks anyway. Have a great weekend. You're good."

Marcus was obviously an all's-well-that-ends-well type. It was a wonderful quality, and I felt guilty about mistaking it for inanity before. Of course, guys don't get away with much futzing unless they're setting up your new computer. Wisely, Marcus was keeping most of his focus out in LA. He and Tara were hooking up later that day for another meeting. My guess was that Tara was urging higher-ups to attach Marcus to one of her next projects as director. Or Marcus was angling to have Tara taken on at his agency. Obviously, there was some kind of coup afoot that they didn't want to blab about, not even to me. The two of them seemed to operate fairly neck and neck in the Hollywood scheme of things, trotting up the chain of command at a similar clip. They both were quick to move out of the starting gate, eyes glued to trophies. And with Marcus by her side, Tara got to be a dark horse, a candidate for indie-film credibility. Her body language had reassured me that she didn't want to be anything more than that when I'd seen them together. Admittedly, I'd scrutinized. I was looking forward to hearing what was up when Marcus got home. Maxi said if Marcus didn't divulge all, it would be a terrible sign. Then again, Maxi had trust issues upon issues upon issues.

Jessica seemed to have borrowed Maxi's new reading glasses. It was time for her to deliver Evoke to an anxiously waiting world. Furthermore, there was to be a foundation established in Evil Benefactor's spit-upon-and-polished name, dedicated to pharmaceutical research unhampered by profit motivation, built on Jessica's native lands. Jessica finished off with a Navajo chant, an elderly uncle having been flown up to do drum duty. I managed: Marisa had collected all manner of ethnically valid musical instruments. Cut to Evil Benefactor creaking in a rocking chair, his tears dissolving into drool and cognitive malfunction. Cut to Jessica's buckskin-clad granny moaning gibberish in a pony-skin teepee with open-faced maidens crouching at her knee. The pair of them were going to be needing that Evoke damn soon. But they weren't going to get it in time for the weekend. Hank had a high school reunion to go to.

"What kind of high school has its reunion in February?" I asked.

"Hamilton Vocational Institute. At HVI we try, try, try. I'm a proud donor. There's a band saw with my name on it in the junior shop."

"Enjoy yourself," said Marisa.

"I'm afraid that will be impossible," Hank said. "Tracy is coming."

Hank had an adoring, long-suffering wife and four broad-of-beam daughters whom Marisa and I never saw very much of. They were all too busy with their own lives to take Hank's very seriously, beyond making him feel like a king when the mood hit them. Hank's dark underbelly was very Poppa Bear when you took a close look. The studio was shady enough to hide most of our irregularities. It was hard to imagine Marisa with any misdeeds up her sleeves. One day, I hoped simply to pull up a chair as well as she did.

That night, I collected Rocks from the animal clinic and we had an enjoyable night at home now that as much anxiety as possible had been swept up and dustpanned away. I'd picked up some shoe-shaped rawhide treats, figuring he'd appreciate the joke. If the ground hadn't been frozen so solid we could have gone to the park to perform burial rites on the mangled Tweety slipper. I was tempted to give Rocks the other one but that didn't seem fair to Marcus, who might then have to train him out of munching on his Converses. After a macaroni dinner for me and an extra half scoop of kibble for Rocks, I moved his blanket into my bedroom and curled up in bed with *Vogue*. As I gazed down at sprawled, snoozing, Deputy Dawg Rocks, his limbs lolling every which way, I felt honoured to belong to his pack, to have his doggy bliss back in my charge. No call from Maxi, so I figured her date with Tom had gone okay. He'd booked them side-by-side massages for His and Hers Night at the Regency Club. I suspected any advice I'd have to offer about Tom would fall on deaf ears. Maxi knew I couldn't really help with this one.

Evidently, I was incapable of truly tearing a strip off Maxi, no matter how justified. She'd probably always known that without needing the evidence. For years I'd loved how well Maxine Bishop understood me. Now I was beginning to realize that her sharp insights were something of a liability for me. My party was slithering inexorably closer. Nine days away, ten until Paris. I was anxious not to head to France with petty feelings detectable in my nature. I doubted the concierges, *vendeuses* and *garçons* would let me get away with that, in a land where people learned to argue along with sucking milk. An out-and-out peace offering wouldn't do but I thought of something that would. Happily, Maxi wouldn't know quite what to make of it.

THE ENVY FILES

Modern Gash Is Jealous of... Maxine Bishop

By Bess Grover

In our regular series on chicks whose lifestyles we want to rip from their polished fingertips, this month we feature Maxine Bishop. It all began on the Riviera where Maxine was conceived on a yacht bound for Stromboli. It is said the pope took a sudden fever that day, perhaps clairvoyantly anticipating her abundant contraception collection. Or her major crush on a Jesuit film theory instructor who put the *agog* in *pedagogical*. Certainly, this world would surely be a better place if Ms. Bishop ran things at the Vatican, where she'd have contests for the bling-iest rings and serve caviar on the wafers.

The Enviable Background

At the age of five Maxine fired the interior decorator who had been hired to "do" her bedroom. One spectacular tantrum saw little Miss Bishop vomiting into a matched set of antique Chinese vases. She broke Camp Lackwanawana records as the youngest camper of all time. Her major disappointment was never to have slain a rattlesnake. She did once scare off a grizzly with a blast of VO5. Maxine always packed a second knapsack with product.

Adolescence was a breeze for Maxine. She hired the chemistry major down the street to invent ointments specially designed for her skin tone. Her deflowering, however, was granted to Viscount Abernathy, who chose as his colonial project wining and dining our Ms. Bishop. The Viscount would certainly have continued to send Maxine fresh strawberries and clotted Devon cream if he hadn't married his cousin.

Maxine continued on to the university of her own choice, not her mother's. It was there she befriended an exceptionally short, bitter, carrot-topped émigrée from a lustreless bedroom community who can't seem to make a move without asking Maxine's advice first. Maxine's tolerance of this individual has been remarkable. Maxine has given this person the G-string off her bum. No bras have ever passed between these two, however, because Maxine does not require over-the-shoulder-boulder-holders.

Having now left her mother far behind, Maxine is scoring the choicest freelance assignments in the city, dressing like a diva, dating a total hunk, living in the loveliest house and might even be getting a car.

Earmark your Gash Cash contributions to the Maxine Bishop Foundation—pledged to provide every depressed Canadian woman with a panic kit containing Estée Lauder flight cream, a piccolo of Veuve Cliquot and an $800 Jill Sander tank top. Maxine Bishop, welcome to the *Modern Gash* Honour Roll, for your outstanding bravery when accused of pretension. WE ARE SICKENINGLY JEALOUS OF YOU!!!

On Saturday I figured that since Maxi was busy with Tom, Rocks and I might as well head out to Burlington overnight where the backyard was big and safe. My parents were coming to pick us up. They'd driven downtown to run some errands and said they'd drop by the Maxi Pad after. My mom needed special embroidery thread. In her retirement she was producing needlepoint pillows with jaunty sayings like "The Flowers of Friendship Never Fade" or "To Be Tired of Paris is to Be Tired of Life." She'd invited me to put in a request but all I could think of was "Too Drunk to Fuck." And she'd already said no to "Hell Is Other People." My father had plans to treat himself to a smoked-meat sandwich on their way over and there'd been all kinds of jovial fanfare about this, but then they discovered that his favourite Spadina Avenue deli had moved uptown to Thornhill.

"Rocks feels your pain, Dad. He loves smoked meat, too."

"Oh my," said my mother. "He's a brute all right. I'm glad you warned us."

"I warned you you'd fall in love. I know he looks like he belongs on the Doggy Most Wanted list but he's a total sweetie. He wouldn't hurt a fly."

"He might poop on the carpet though."

"Dad, have a little faith."

Rocks thumped his tail on the kitchen floor and looked up at my mother like Oliver asking for more. That did it. He would be denied nothing now.

My parents expressed admiration for all my same old junk, reconfigured. They'd never been to the apartment when it was Maxi's so the place was all mine in their eyes. They seemed to tolerate the differences between Eddie's life and mine with the same equanimity with which they had accepted one boy and one girl, one stable contributor to society and one hardscrabbler. I didn't tell them much about my latest promotion. They were too accustomed to Eddie's, which led upward in a straight line. Mine might bewilder them if the Canadian dollar went up, runaway production went down and Hollywood North went splat.

"I must give you that old sofa in the rec room," said my mother. "I keep forgetting you don't have one."

"Wow, Ma, I'd love that! Thanks."

She was referring to the old teak number from their nest-feathering days that now belonged in a mid-twentieth-century specialty shop. I appreciated the Wonderland charm of my mismatched armchairs but not enough to forgo the ruby-red, nubby Danish barge when offered. With a couch of my own, I'd come that enticing bit closer to real adulthood.

Rocks enjoyed the drive, his eyes drooping like a turtle's while my parents and I had a good gossip. I told them they were getting a taste of Rocks to prepare them for grandparenthood. Rocks perked up at his name, and when nothing came of it, he tumbled his meathead into my lap. We were progressing faster in our intimacy in some ways than Marcus and I.

"Elaine says they're going to call the baby Jack if it's a boy and Madeleine if it's a girl," my mother told me.

"No way! That's the Dylan and Chloë of the new millennium. There'll be six of each in every JK class."

"Now Bessie, not everyone has your originality." My dad had always been a master at shutting me up.

I listened obediently to golden oldies the rest of the way home. We all sang along to "The Wanderer."

When we got to Burlington, Rocks and I relaxed on the mod couch watching TV while we listened to the reassuring sounds of parental banter and dinner being made. I could smell my suppertime favourite, wafting from the kitchen: *coq au vin*. All of our favourites corresponded with my mom's exploration of seventies chic. My dad enjoyed her *boeuf bourguignon*, Eddie championed her Swedish meatballs and she herself loved *stroganoff*. CNN was reliably tumultuous: avalanche in Alaska, ethnic clashes in Kosovo, demonstrations against the new virulently right-wing coalition in Vienna and the Bush Junior camp panicking as McCain gained ground in New Hampshire. I supposed I could live with all that.

After dinner I took Rocks upstairs to my bedroom. For the first time in a long time—adding to the time-capsule flavour of the event—I decided to leaf through my memory box, an old boot box from Aldo that I had used throughout high school as a repository for letters, photos and other personal debris.

I fondled my old report cards. *Listens well, needs more confidence, excellent reader.* Phys ed marks were my only variable. I did fine during cross-country season but lost out bad during volleyball. Stamina, not power, that's Bess Grover. I leafed through my final term paper for Grade Thirteen psych about ESP, about how the cup of live yogourt reacted biologically when the plant nearby had its leaves torn off, all carefully footnoted and diagrammed. As usual I chortled at my prom photo: lookin' good in a black leather mini and fake paint-stain top. My date, Nathan Block, and I had on matching Ray Bans. Nathan was wearing a sharkskin suit and winkle pickers. We'd wanted to look menacing but got told all night long how cute we were. In anguish we headed out to the parking lot to service each other in Nathan's dad's car. "Bela Lugosi Is Dead" was playing on the tape deck. We zipped up and listened to the rest of it, not holding hands because we could only find one tissue. There had been gum in the glove compartment, though. The flavour of cinnamon Dentyne has held a certain flagrant eroticism for me ever since.

I had no idea where Nathan Block was in 2000. My old friend Sherry Foster would know. Sherry was my first best friend. She and I went all through elementary and high school together, and plotted escapes from Burlington together, although in different directions. Sherry had just moved back into the neighbourhood from BC. She'd embarked on adulthood safely countercultural and ended up the mother of twin boys, now six bouncing years old. We'd been the founding members of The Girls in Black, a clique we'd cobbled together with the few other Dead Kennedys fans at our school. I gazed deeply into a Polaroid of Sherry and me in the art room posing beside our joint creation. We'd broken a bunch of mirrors and then hot-glued the shards together into an effigy that we dubbed *Miss Take*.

Sherry and I didn't talk very often but we were always there for each other. Now she was right around the corner once more.

"Are the rodents in bed yet?"

"Bess! It is *so* good to hear from you."

"Not only that, I'm home. Can I come over? I'll steal some of my dad's beer."

"What do *you* think? I'll tell Brian. He's been begging me to do something *selfish* so that I'll stop bitching about having to be so *unselfish* all the time."

"I still cannot believe you ended up with the class president. It's almost surreal but not quite. Like the CN Tower."

"The CN Tower? What's *that*?"

"Oh, a big landmark in a little place called Toronto. You wouldn't know. You never visit."

"Get your butt over here *right* now."

"Damn, you sound like a mom."

"Don't worry, I'm *anti*-spanking."

"That's too bad. We grown-ups spank each other all the time downtown."

Sherry and Brian had decorated their family home with as many hard edges as it could take—the Edvard Munch *Scream* print in the largest size; sofas, chairs and tables on chunky wheels; a framed *Night of the Living Dead* poster above a bright red, plastic dining-room table. I thought it all looked great. Brian was upstairs bathing the kids when I got there and he shouted down a hello.

Brian O'Reilly had always been good at shouting. That was how he'd won class elections and debating tournaments and Sherry's heart. She had gone to the same university as Brian and kept hearing him from across the lecture halls and quadrangles. They had a speechwriting business now and were doing well providing provincial ministers and branch plant CEOs with addresses to strategic gatherings. Sherry was drinking a glass of something warm, spicy and red that I joined in on, although my dad had indeed given me a six-pack of Molson Golden. I sat down at the breakfast bar while Sherry puttered. I decided not to tease her about the rubber gloves and fluorescent light. She was still dying her hair red—a tasteful auburn. I appreciated the gesture but it didn't really count as solidarity.

"I was going through the old memory box tonight."

"So now you want to know what Nathan Block is up to?" Sherry teased.

"Do you have any idea?"

"He just got married to a French-Canadian gal in Montreal. Marie Josée, I think her name is. He hosts the CBC radio afternoon show and *she's* a pediatric dentist."

"Wow, good for him. I can't believe he went through with the whole wedding thing. I would never have thought he was capable of that much self-consciousness."

"You'd be surprised what you can do for your parents."

Sherry and Brian had held their wedding on a farm out in Mennonite country. The reception had included hay rides and many baked goods, and cows had wandered across the field to check out the hired fiddler. I brought Maxi as my date. She figured she had eaten two whole pies by the end of it. Maxi was a sucker for baking done from scratch.

"How's work?" Sherry asked.

"Fine. Good, actually. I get to do my own job next month. A little animation gig, but it's a start."

"I am so glad, Bess. That's wonderful. Okay then, how's your love life?"

"The radar has a blip, I'll say that much."

"You know I need to know more than that."

"I met a guy who I really like and we've been seeing a fair amount of each other. But it's early days. Marcus. You'd like him. He's one of those smart guys who pretends to be a big goof in this really smart way."

"We *loved* Buster Keaton when we were kids. Remember?"

"I remember burning the popcorn because neither of us wanted to miss the good bits. We were selfish."

"We were honest. So where are things going with this Marcus?"

"For one thing, he's taking me to Paris."

"Wonderful!"

"He's got lots of air miles. It's not like he's a big moneybags or anything. But he's done well for himself. He's a director. He's fun. I'm taking care of his dog right now while he's in LA."

"Brian thought he saw your dad with a dog. You should have brought it over."

"Aren't Cavett and Carson both allergic?"

"Fuck 'em. I'm kidding. They seem to have outgrown that. The little monsters spared me a peanut butter intolerance at least. They love the stuff, bless their hearts. Sometimes, I think peanut butter is what binds my wits together."

"You should have had girls."

"You're right, what was I thinking?"

"Oh well. Boys are probably a lot less complicated. For the mother, anyway."

"Until they date a trollop like you."

"Maybe there'll be a puritanical revolution by then. You'll have eighteen-year-old prudes."

"Speaking of mother issues, how's your friend Maxine doing?"

"How did you know she has mother issues?"

"Because she never shuts up about it. Sorry, I know she's your friend. But in my old age I have to be honest with you, the woman really bugs me."

"I'm beginning to realize she bugs everybody, the poor thing. She's more like her mother than she realizes."

"Well, she needs to stop going on about how fat and stupid she is so that we don't all have to drop what we're doing and tell her how gorgeous and smart she is."

"One day she'll get there."

"You pander to her too much, Bess."

"I'm exploring my pander options right now. I'm hoping to get down to the minimum."

"Just make sure you don't pander yourself away to nothing."

"I guess you don't have time to be self-deprecating. Not that Brian would let you get away with it."

"Did I just hear my name?"

Brian appeared in the kitchen with a munchkin under each arm. I was proud to have been able to tell the twins apart since day one. Cavett was in Jays pyjamas with the part on the left, and Carson was in Leafs gear with the slightly higher ears. They were such sweet little imps, with mini bare feet and teensy shoulders and gigantic skulls. Their hair was brushed into neat, wet helmets and they smelled of Mr. Bubble.

"Greetings, guys, I brought you some beer," I said. I made them have a burping contest for me. They let me kiss them good night but I licked their little cheeks instead to make them holler. They wouldn't bed down without Sherry's special touch so Brian and I hung out while she went upstairs to read one chapter of *Harry Potter*.

"Children's lit is in the top three spots on the *New York Times* best-seller list, Brian. What do you make of that?"

"It's a CATACLYSM!"

Brian loved discourse. As school president he had been instrumental in getting a philosophy class added to the Grade Thirteen curriculum. Sherry and I had enrolled. I still maintained it was the same boat even if every nail and board was replaced. And I continued to be impressed by all the faulty arguments: pity, force, mass approval and, most temptingly, prestige, or *verecundiam*—the very word somehow arousing. It remained a matter of debate for me whether I thought, therefore I was. And I was totally against trees falling in the forest.

"We are what we buy."

Brian opened up a second bottle of Merlot because it was Saturday night and I was enough to make a party. "You're right there. It's the privilege of the INDIVIDUAL to consume. I ask you, can personal needs get much needier? People are voluntarily flushing their colons, men order mail-order brides, DOGS ARE WEAPONS. No offence."

"None taken. Rocks only indicates menace. He's the Roland Barthes of dogs."

"DISPLAY, that's the essential cycle right there, isn't it? We load up the nuances, then we revert to blatancy and on it goes."

"I take it you'll be the first one back into a beaver hat?"

"HA!" Brian spit out some wine with a hollering laugh. I guessed the kids had learned to sleep through them.

"Sherry is trying to figure out whether she's supposed to have a suntan or not. We got LEFT BEHIND, Bess. We can't keep up with what's what."

"Go see a twelve-buck movie in an armchair. That'll help."

"Oh, I do. Sherry and I have this deal. She lets me take movie nights. I let her go out to dinner with a book. Or we stay home together and watch *The World's Grossest Dares* on Fox."

"You two have quite the marital system worked out."

"We stay out of each other's hair when it counts."

"Crazy, isn't it, how we struggle to connect and then as soon as we manage that we struggle to disconnect. Forster was an optimist. Only reconnect, he might have said."

"Thanks for reconnecting, Bess. It's been a while. I hate to say it but the man in the mirror is getting fat and it's making his KNEES ACHE."

"Apparently, men are more attuned to aches and pains. Women are more in tune with sadness."

"We envy your energy."

"We envy your management skills."

I was over at the fridge perusing photos of the recent family trip to Disney World when Sherry returned to the kitchen with the air of Bukowski ambushing a bar. We had a grand old time reminiscing through the same old list of "remember whens": there was the time Sherry and I mounted the Ionesco play that got nary a laugh; the time the yearbook literary editor published one of Sherry's erotic poems ("My Ice, Your Fire") without getting it; the time Brian ran for school president with condoms taped to his campaign posters; and then there was the class trip to Montreal when George Da Silva got suspended for nailing a whore on a dare.

Sherry walked me home along the snowy sidewalk, trying out the extra powerful new family flashlight. We were drunk enough to shine it into master bedroom windows along the way, hoping to spike UFO reports overnight. I hadn't intended to use up a February hangover in Burlington but it was worth it.

"Keep in touch," Sherry said, making the concerted kind of eye contact that I knew her for. "And I apologize for bitching about your friend. As you well know, I have plenty of flaws of my own so I should just keep my mouth shut."

"No, don't keep your mouth shut. Really, I'm starting to wonder what's in my Kool-Aid. Absolutely we'll keep in touch. I'm glad you're back."

I thought about calling Maxi when I got back to Toronto to tell her about seeing Sherry and Brian. Maxi always appreciated the evidence they provided that marriage sometimes worked. But in Sherry's honour I decided the day ought to belong to her and her only. And my stellar new couch. Rocks and I sprawled on it for a while like two taciturn *pashas*. Then I reached for a pen and pad.

MODERN GASH PRESENTS

Ask Bess

By Bess Grover

Dear Bess,

What's the sign of a good friend?

Not having to exaggerate your insecurity to the point of hilarity.

Dear Bess,

Is it good to be cute?

Not unless you're a puppy or a kitten.

Dear Bess,

Do only losers live in the suburbs?

The suburbs are impressively subversive in deed, and not just in word. They are the home of many hidden gems. We should all carry some suburb in our souls.

Dear Bess,

Why do people fear getting older?

Not because they cherish experience but because it has made them feel sullied. They pine for their less storied days. They distrust their culture. They regret their corruption.

Dear Bess,

Are you going to show this to Maxi?

No, definitely not.

Week Six Rot

Maxi snapped at me when I called from work on Monday to make sure the walk had gone okay. I'd known since the chocolate incident my days in the good books were numbered. Maxi couldn't really digest blame; eventually she had to spew it back. She was irked that I was tramping all over her office hours. She said that we'd been on an evening and weekend plan for years, that every friendship has its compartments and I should have known that. Instead she was stuck being the enforcer.

"Okay, sorry," I said. Then I said "Goodbye," into thin air because Maxi hadn't.

"Who's got PMS, you or her?" asked Hank.

"Me, asshole. And I'm extremely depressed about the fact that we might never get this movie finished thanks to my snail's pace."

Jessica had travelled down to her native lands to tie up all her loose ends with Studly along to look pretty with in the sunset. There was a lot of car-door business to finesse. Marisa wanted differentiation between sedans and pick-up trucks.

"Chin up and out," said Marisa. "For the most part you've done this whole thing on your own. It's a real achievement."

"I helped," said Hank.

"Thanks, I could never have come of age without you," I said.

Jessica arrived at her granny's teepee. A course of Evoke had revived enough of Granny's wits to allow her to offer an elder's guidance and blessings. She was wearing a coyote bone necklace. I got out the box of penne and hoped for the best. No wonder I hated jewellery.

By the time I got home there was a message waiting from Maxi. She was in apology mode. This was sometimes more scary than a spat; Maxi had very specific notions about how she liked her apologies to unfold and result. She was sorry she'd hung up on me but I had really pushed her buttons. In any case I absolutely had to come over because she'd designed the invite for the party. In case I had forgotten it was in one mere week and she had to email them out immediately to whoever was coming. Also, I found out when I called, she'd had a fight with Tom on Sunday night. He'd slicked liquid soap up her thing in the shower.

"Oh boy," I said.

"I know. I told him it's not going to be my fault if I end up with a raging yeast infection by Valentine's Day. Men have no sense of pH."

"How was the sex?"

"Good, actually. I came very close."

"Worth blowing bubbles down there for a while, I guess. Was Tom excited about you getting close?"

"Babe, please. As if I haven't been faking. Last night I went simultaneous."

"So now he thinks you're in love."

"Hopefully."

"What about 'Stimulation Simulation'?"

Modern Gash had long ago published a manifesto against faking it, which I'd thought we both adhered to faithfully. Faking it was all too easy, we knew. We thought Meg Ryan's deli orgasm in *When Harry Met Sally* was highly overrated. What woman couldn't have pulled it off? You'd have to have been ritually circumcised not to manage.

"Look, I'll handle my boyfriend, Bess, and you handle yours."

I was pretty sure Maxi was handling hers like Zamfir in a crescendo.

"Maxi, should I come over or not?"

"Yes!"

"Then I have to bring Rocks. He needs another walk."

"If you must."

By the time we got there Maxi had us set us up with a roaring fire, peanut brittle and two shots of Laphroaig. Rocks sacked out by the blaze; he found qualms hard to come by. Maxi and I faced each other on the couch. She had a pad and pen ready. I was summoning up my best behaviour. I put down my treats.

"Since your parents are coming, what about mine?" I asked.

"Parental overload, methinks."

"But if mine find out yours were invited they'll be hurt. They won't stay late, I promise."

"Fine, fine, fine. Your parents and mine, Tom and Marcus, Tara. And Marcello, I suppose, to pay him back for all the free drinks."

"Nunci and Syl, right?"

"Actually they're going to Cuba. Syl joined the Last-Minute Club. They send their love. They say they'll bring you back a passport-hungry beach boy if you want."

"No, I'm good."

"You really like Marcus, don't you?"

"What's not to like?"

"A lot, when you first met him. You thought he belonged to the Addams Family, remember?"

"That's just because he answered the door like Lurch. Did you know that the Addams Family started as a *New Yorker* cartoon? Marcus told me that. The actress who played Morticia used to be married to Aaron Spelling."

"Bess, focus. The party."

"We're up to ten. Isn't that enough?"

"No, I need to submerge my mother some more. How about those old friends of yours from Burlington, the ones who just got a big profile in the Business section?"

"Wow, yes, great."

"I can also invite Marisa if you want."

"Maxi, thanks. I'd love that. What about Hank? His wife and daughters are going discount shopping in Florida."

"He'll add to the flavour of the event, I suppose. I'm going to have to warn Tom and Tara it'll be a complete hodgepodge. Well, what can I do? It's your party."

"I'll help pay."

"No! The whole point is that *I'm* doing this. That's what I've told Tom. In any case, Daddy will subsidize. He's so relieved that it's shut up his wife for a while."

Maxi had printed up a hard copy of the invite. It was a classic; she could Photoshop with the best of them. She'd crammed in lace graphics and jagged heart shapes, opted for a Gothic font and doused the whole thing in cerise. Splashed in the middle was an old photo of us from graduation day. Maxi loved it because she looked so skinny, even in the robe. My grin was stretched a bit tight. We'd gone to the Park Plaza rooftop for lunch afterward with both sets of parents. Josephine complained about the table and temperature of the butter. My parents cracked jokes about bumping into Mordecai Richler. Maxi and I ordered a banana split to share for dessert, still young enough to be excited by the toppings. Then it was time to say goodbye for eleven weeks. I was reporting for duty at Smash Mouth Catering. Maxi was getting whisked up to a resort on Lake St. Joseph. I joined her there for a week in August. Neither of us got the hang of wind surfing. But we did give cocaine a try, and socked out by the pool getting over it. I fried from white to red and back again after a fever, the shakes and several baking soda baths. Maxi toasted gleaming shades of syrup. She was proud at the time, but that was the summer that haunted her when melanoma stats started to get touted. Another of her mother's intentions gone awry. When I got back to town I received the transfer I'd requested to the craft services department, my long days on film sets finally underway.

"Give me back that invite, Babe. I want it for my records. You're staying for dinner, right? I roasted a chicken with spuds and beets, sautéed spinach on the side and boysenberry sorbet for afters."

"I haven't fed Rocks yet. Sorry."

"You and that dog. I hope you're not doing all this just to bug me, Bess. You know I'm not a dog person."

"Maxi, don't talk crazy."

Rocks had heard his name. He sleepily stood up, stretched his front paws down low, hoisted his hindquarters up high, pushed, grunted and shuddered, then relaxed with a satisfied yelp. "Rocks, you look like one of those men who do yoga," I said. I stood up as well.

"Well, take a doggy bag at least."

"No, that's okay. Thanks anyway."

I headed to the front hall for my jacket. I always felt a bit braver coated in puff.

"Maxi, are you sure want to go through with the party? It's not too late."

"God, no! That would look so weird. Buck up, Babe. Marcus is coming back soon. You don't want him to see you looking like a sourpuss."

"Marcus says I have a nice frown."

"Well, whatever."

Maxi helped me on with my hat, scarf and mitts with the deft motions of an OR nurse. If I absolutely had to bust a move then she didn't want me lingering. We hugged goodbye. It wasn't my fault I hadn't taken goodies home with me, I was honestly too queasy to carry hot chicken in a bag, even if it did mean Maxi was liable to pig out to the point of destruction when left alone with that much food. Rocks and I headed north up Crawford to College as fast as we could go, with Rocks pulling a Sherlock at every hedge and tree trunk. I was feeling investigative, too. I was questioning my ability to be appreciative. I thought perhaps appreciation just hadn't been post-modern enough for Maxi and I to prioritize correctly. Maxi didn't bother to register it, and I'd been too weak to claim it. I wanted to rescue appreciation from the butter churn, calico, buggy ride era. I wanted to make it work for us now.

Maxi had me stuck. I was lodged between hating to hate her and hating to love her. I had to ask myself if Maxi ever loved to hate me. I hated my answer to that. Even worse, I suspected she had gone ahead and given me credit for loving to hate her, which was totally unfounded. I would never have dared.

Wednesday, Maxi dropped off a couple of gifts after her final walk with Rocks—new *Gash* for me and a size-large pleather doggy motorcycle jacket for him. I'd vaguely noticed a selection of Fluffy & Fido products for sale at the animal clinic. No doubt this had been the priciest item. Hopefully, Doctor Chin had been too busy doing his job to pay any attention. I had just convinced Rocks to try on his new look when Marcus arrived. It was insanely fun to lay eyes on him again—his face doing a Rudolph Valentino on me, his skin extra olive from LA balconies and patios, his shoulders just within reach in that happy kids, jitterbug style. He was wearing a Jughead beanie—enough said. He pretended to mistake Rocks for Harvey Keitel.

I had expected the boys to want to unwind at home on their own, but Marcus lured me over to his place with a flat violet box tied up with silver ribbons that he waved under my nose like a pie. He let me open it when we got up to his bedroom. It was precisely the kind of lacy undergarments I'd intended to invest in: filmy black with pink bows, scanty but sweet. I'd spring for stockings to complete the effect. Marcus said he'd shopped at a boutique in LA where everyone who was anyone went to treat their mistresses, and I'd actually done him a big favour by making sure he was seen going in and out of there.

"Too bad we can't have phone sex." I dangled the pretty froth from my fingers. "It won't be nearly as intense if we aren't a continent apart."

"Says who?" Marcus barrelled downstairs to grab his cellphone and call his land line. I picked up the extension. "Darling, what are you wearing?" he started.

"Give me a sec here. You went big on my bum and small on my boobs, but I forgive you."

"Tell me about those boobs," muttered Marcus into the phone.

"I honestly don't think I can wait," I whispered.

"Can't wait for what?"

"It. You."

"I'll call you later."

The moment he got back to the bedroom his pants were off thanks to some Jerry Lewis antics. I tossed my new panties onto his willy, it being horizontal. Then I decided to prolong matters. Marcus was so smooth and tasty looking: gourmet dick. I sat on the side of the bed swinging my heels while my new lingerie dangled beneath my nose. I could feel how swollen my pussy was with the knowledge of good times to come. Marcus's hips were chiselled and slim. I reached out and held on to them. I loved Marcus's body temperature; he was always just the right degree of warm.

As usual, we went at it like it was the apocalypse. And this time it was without a condom. I wasn't sure what possessed me to abandon the discipline that had prevailed in my sex life for a good dozen years or so, but when I felt Marcus's bare cock, and knew that Marcus's bare cock could feel how completely wet I was, it made it too hard to get back to health-class basics. None of the potential consequences seemed major compared to the pleasure. I felt so uninsulated. And open.

Marcus was finding my hot spot deftly, bless him. He kneeled and rubbed me with a wet thumb as he thrust, the way smart guys do. If his first wish was for me to come, I soon did. I put on a great little show: lights, camera, hollering. Then I snatched back his hand and held onto it like I was dangling fifty stories. I could tell my grip down yonder had tightened, too. Marcus grabbed two fistfuls of my bum, stared at me down there and pumped until he toppled. We lay side by side, finally. He had on his Fuck Yoga T-shirt. He was swearing a flattering blue streak. I felt him drool out of me and it turned me on all over again, but I kept a lid on that while he caught his breath. We rested, languidly, in that afterglow cherished by the lustful through the ages.

Marcus cleared his throat.

“Bess, there’s something I’ve got to tell you.”

“Oh?” I made as if to scratch my nose so I could let go of his hand.

“It’s about our trip.”

I knew it, I knew it, knew it. Bad news was bound to erupt, it was just a question of when.

“Oh, okay. What about it?”

Marcus was uncurling my curls and then letting them rebound.

“The thing is, I had an impulse to change our tickets, and I went ahead and did it. I hope that’s okay. I had to decide on the spot.”

“We aren’t leaving on Tuesday morning any more?” We had flights booked for some ungodly hour that barely merited going to bed the night before.

“We’re still leaving on Tuesday morning. It’s just that we aren’t going to Paris any more.”

“We aren’t?” Montreal, maybe. Or New York so he could fit in a meeting. I could pretend it was fine for long enough to figure out how fine it wasn’t.

“No. We’re going to Antwerp, darling. It’s time for you to face your demons, and I want to be there to watch.”

“We’re going to Belgium, where the streets are full of funky tailoring and NATO convenes?”

“We’re going where The Smurfs are. There are boutique hotels. I checked first.”

I crawled up the bed to get exactly eye to eye with this man.

“Wonderful,” I said. Paris was just not us, I could see that now. “You can witness my comeuppance.”

"Good stuff. Now let's order in rotis, squash with hot sauce and cold Ting for me. I had enough mineral water and salad in LA to feed a step class."

Marcus loved curry rotis from Patty Man, where they came packed with maximum dough. He was the only person I knew who ate more carbs than I did. It was like we belonged to some starch society. I stayed giddy from the goodness for hours. It was so nice to have Marcus home. Even with Rocks' leash gone from its hook in my kitchen. For a week there, Rocks duty had filled up the Maxi Pad better than any treasures or flowers. Marcus winced a bit when I eventually told him in more detail about the trip to the vet clinic. He took my cue and forgave Maxi, but I didn't think Rocks would be wearing his jacket again.

I stopped in at home on my way to work for a quick change, otherwise Hank would tease me pitilessly. He ordinarily wouldn't pay that much attention to what I'd been wearing, but in honour of Marcus's return I'd worn my Engrish-emblazoned hoodie from Korea Town: "Happy Hearts Make Friendship's Flavour Lasting True." I took Maxi's new *Gash* on the streetcar with me. Now that it had taken me such a strangely long time to get around to it, I was looking forward to reading it. As soon as I got a seat I took a look. My interpretive skills had been finely honed over the years but even I didn't know exactly what she'd meant by this one. Maxi had to be careful. Sometimes she was too post-modern for her own good.

SPOT THE HEATHER

Readers Tell Us When They Knew "She Was No Friend of Mine!"

By Maxine Bishop

I was pregnant with my first child. My so-called friend congratulated me. Because I "wasn't going to have to worry about men hitting on me any more." I wanted to tell that twit to kiss my fat ass. I spent a fortune on a personal trainer afterward, essentially just to get back at her. Now she keeps asking how I feel about my stretch marks. I hope her womb is barren like Nevada.

—Marilyn, 28, Wabash, Texas

Whenever we'd go shopping my good friend would tell me that any sexier item I tried on "didn't look quite right." Then she'd go out the next day and buy it for herself and twirl around in front of me asking me how she looked. I'd call her a cow if she wasn't such a bitch.

—Carla, 22, Spokane, Washington

As soon as I told her I was on a diet she started dropping off Belgian chocolates at my desk. I'd ask her not to but she'd insist: "Just one little truffle." I knew she wanted me chubby and pimpled. She's ugly as sin but skinny as a rake. I hate the woman, her and her satanic metabolism.

—Janet, 35, Missoula, Missouri

She just loved getting invited to things that I wasn't. She'd go on and on about how much she was dreading going and how lucky I was to stay at home relaxing. Then she'd call the next day and say that she'd actually had barrels of fun and the party was full of cute guys and it was too bad I didn't go. How do you spell evil?

—Fran, 31, Lafayette, Louisiana

Thursday evening I called Maxi to thank her for the treats and let her know that Marcus hadn't dumped me when he got back to town. She didn't answer. Her cell rang but she didn't pick up. I left a chirpy message, about how Rocks' coat fit and so did my new bra from Marcus. Then I made myself a Burlington-style salad—iceberg lettuce, tomato wedges, carrot peelings, radish slices, Thousand Island dressing—and a couple of gooey grilled cheddar sandwiches. Horrifyingly, I was out of ketchup. I'd noticed how much Rocks enjoyed it on his kibble and had run out sooner than expected. The night was young, so I decided to get myself what I wanted and pick up a slice of hazelnut cheesecake from Antico while I was at it.

I headed past the fruit and veg shops, and the butcher shops with hams hanging in the windows, up the hill to the tussle of competing bars and bistros. Since it was a Thursday, the College Street sidewalks were crowded with gorgeous types who also had subtlety going for them, so my walk was brisk, refreshing and full of style cues. Antico was summoning itself up for the night when I got there, the bar filling up with men in flat-front pants and women whose legs reached from the top of the stools to the floor. Women such as Tara Dickens. I didn't mean to intercept the attention Tara was getting from Mike and Pete, or perhaps Zack and Jake, in any case a pair of happening, toned guys who'd pulled their stools over to Tara as if starting up a game of cards. Right away Tara was all over me. She and Marcus had definitely bonded over something and I was definitely included in the goodwill and definitely I had to be cool about playing things warm. Tara made that ridiculously easy.

"Bess, your Excellency! I'm so glad you came."

"Came to what?"

"Happy hour. Maxine promised she'd invite you."

"Oh, okay. I'm actually just here to grab a piece of cake."

"So stay. In fact come to Toto for dinner. Rick and Joe just invited us."

I sneaked a look at the Titans. They were the sort of men who ruled over women and bartenders both. Now they were supervising the shaking of their round-two martinis. Marcello wasn't on duty. I was wishing my little red jacket was black. And that I had some adrenaline to spare.

"I can't go to Toto looking like the Artful Dodger."

"Hey, pity me. I did a spa day today, yowch."

Now that she mentioned it, I thought Tara smelled of lavender. "Good work. Grooming is becoming a competitive sport lately. It's the female equivalent of golf."

"I'm, like, sea salted." Tara was completing her look with beach hair.

"Don't, whatever you do, pay for anything. According to the laws of romantic economy you get to ride for free if you're freshly buffed, arched and waxed."

"Interesting theory, John Kenneth Bess. You look fetching as usual. You are so lucky you don't have to blow-dry. Is it possible that blow-drying kills brain cells?"

"I hope not for Maxi's sake. She never stood a chance."

"She doesn't stand a chance with that Tom Fool, not that any woman does. Is it my imagination or could Tom be a bit of a jerk? Wait, is it possible to be a bit of a jerk?"

"Nowadays, sure. Diminution is the flip side of super-sizing. You can be a little freaked out, a tad drunk, somewhat depressed and sort of weird. But Tom is just a jerk."

"Someone has to tell Little Lord Fauntlelaw to stop bringing up his ex-girlfriends and how beautiful they all are. One beautiful ex counts for five. Oops, I'd better zip it. Here comes Hedda Hopper."

"Bess?"

"Maxi, hi. Surprise."

She was trying not to look stern but she couldn't help it. I wasn't stupid. I knew whatever else was going on that evening, Maxi had plans to get to the rock bottom of Tara's feelings about rejection, or commercial status versus lack of edge, or what it's like to trump your high-school enemies. I doubted she'd get much work done, however. The night was already looking too trippy, dazzling, busy and dumb. After pretending to sock Maxi in the chops, leading with her left, Tara slipped back over to the slickers, who obviously felt like they'd struck oil. I had to leave soon if I wanted to avoid an introduction. Maxi was right to take the spare stool. I didn't need it. I didn't even need to get a bartender's attention now that cheesecake would taste like clay. Maxi was wearing her Marni top, the one with the gauze panels and purposefully ravaged neck line.

"Babe, I just tried to call you. No wonder there was no answer."

"Don't worry, I'm not staying."

"Tom's been sick as a dog by the way. I had to bring him grapes and ginger ale last night and fetch his vaporizer from his storage locker."

"You finally got a school night out of him. Be careful what you wish for, I guess."

"What a drag, Babe, let me tell you. He was all scruffy and croaky. I was petrified he was going to infect me. Candy-Striping is just not my thing. He's fine today, the big baby, the fever broke of course. Lord, I'm having one hell of a week. Grey Goose martini, lemon, double, excuse me, *excuse* me! Double."

"Funny how vodka is fermented potatoes. Fermentation is really something to appreciate, isn't it? Like gravity, or photo-synthesis. Or what Tom Ford's done for Gucci."

"Who are those men Tara is talking to? They look so hedge fund."

"Head's up, Maxi, you're about to get Toto-ed. I can't deal with sea urchin–shiitake fricassee or durian flan with crème fraiche and loganberries so I'm going to sneak away."

"Well, suit yourself. Wish me luck."

"Hey, Miss Marple." Eagle-ears Tara had wheeled around. "You've got to make a path for luck, haven't I taught you anything? Bess, dude, where do you think you're going?"

"*Flemish for Dummies* awaits. Happy abalone parfait. Don't be mad if I split."

"Not without this you're not."

It was an Antico takeout container. I could tell from its heft that Tara had correctly guessed the cheesecake.

"Wow, thanks."

"Hey, you've gotta love a running tab."

Rick and Joe were bored of their drinks and interested in pair bonding. The easiest thing was to say a generic goodbye, waving the showy, energetic sort of adieu that clowns do before exiting centre ring. I knew men and women had always exchanged flirtatious energies—Homer, Cressida, Jefferson, the Mitford sisters and every Prince of Wales—but I had never been much good at the admiration game. Under pressure, I always forgot my number. The trek home was chillier, and I was too cold to stop for a keg of Heinz. My sandwiches were tepid and gummy but I ate them anyway, chomp after chomp, a zombie with residual nutritional awareness.

Friday it was high times in the foley studio because we were wrapping *Love Is a Drug*. There was one last moody showdown to be had as Jessica and Studly headed to Evil Benefactor's hole in the desert—weather vane (rusty door hinge), snapping clothesline (the Canadian flag) and mangy, airborne hawks (flapped feather dusters). Hippocrates would have been proud to see Jessica place a couple of bright yellow pills into the mindlessly cupped palm of her former tormentor. Studly poured him half a glass of water from a pitcher, hurray. I could not have coped with the outdoor hand pump again, which had taken me hinges and a hose and half an hour the first time. Jessica watched Evil Benefactor gulp down the dose of Evoke, then said, "Remember me," and headed for the rosy horizon. The wind was a strictly visual effect. And it was over. Marisa, Hank and I were gloriously free of the pharmaceutical thriller.

Marisa got out the Pimm's while I fetched ice and sliced up a cucumber. Hank opened a tin of smoked oysters and a box of Ritz crackers. This was standard fare for our closing ceremonies, but since I was embarking on my own project next it felt more like the end of an era than the finishing of a job. In honour of this, Hank let me hog most of the crackers and Marisa poured us extra Pimm's. Her rustic move was almost complete. Hank was heading out to her new place that weekend to help chop wood and check the wiring, and then they were coming back into town on Monday evening for the party.

"Please don't scare my mom," I begged Hank. Hank had tried to convince her that I regularly made him cry.

"Duh. I'll be too busy scaring your new boyfriend."

Marcus was my boyfriend for sure and I liked the sound of it. He was my boyfriend whom I had sex with, definitely, not my *partner* with whom I *made love*.

"I'll thank you to respect my partner with whom I make love."

Hank gestured at Marisa for another refill.

Marisa started making out invoices. I put microphones and shoes away in the supply closet and stacked tavern chairs, upside-down bicycles and galvanized steel panels up against the walls. It was thrilling to think of how far away Marcus and I would be before I had to kiss my wrist again to foley an onscreen seduction. Marisa and Hank had loved my news about the Belgium twist.

"Belgium is as far north as James Bay," I mentioned.

"Pack your mukluks," said Hank.

"Bring lots of water on the plane, Bess. Better not to dry out and catch a bug."

"If you think about it, catching a cold isn't something that happens to us, we're something that happens to the common cold. Rhinovirus existed for millions of years before humans came along."

"Influenza derives from Asian pigs and birds," said Marisa. "It seems the extreme animal–human proximity in that part of the world is the cause."

"That's it, I'm out of here, you sick, sick women," said Hank.

We knew Hank was going only as far as The Badger's Nose around the corner, one of those pubs that seemed to have imported its carpet and coasters authentically soiled from Manchester. Marisa insisted I would be doing plenty of paperwork myself in good time, that she was fine, no need to help with hers. I left with no small amount of joy.

When I'd called to tell Marcus I was on my way he told me that Tom had invited us to see *The Beach* with him and Maxi. Marcus told him he'd already caught it at a private screening in LA but really he just wanted to get me back in bed.

"Are vaginas hard to tell apart?"

We'd retreated to Marcus's bedroom halfway through making dinner, where dusk had immobilized us for a while.

"Come again?"

"Do you think you could ID me down there blindfolded with no voice cues or anything?"

"Yes, but don't ever make me try."

"I'd know you too. Your pace and depth."

"I had a girlfriend who preferred her vibrator over me,"

Marcus mused. I was curious to learn more, but Marcus didn't elaborate.

"Most sex-toys are bought by women in their thirties," I said. "College educated, white and married."

"Whatever keeps people together, I guess."

"Only 75 percent of people polled have experienced oral sex. I mean, what is with the other 25 percent? Maybe some municipalities rule against it."

"That's got to suck."

"I suck."

Marcus pretended to be dumbfounded, but the phone rang before I could demonstrate. Someone on the other end was going on. I might have jumped up and got dressed if it had been Tara but I could hear it was a male voice. I guessed it was Marcus's brother, Will. The boys were close. They'd shared a bedroom growing up even though the house was a large one. I figured a shrink would write down some pretty positive notes about that. I'd been fast with the Do Not Enter sign on my bedroom door, developmentally. Will had a wife, two girls and a Chevy dealership in Guelph.

"I'll tell you later," Marcus said, then signed off.

"So how was LA?" I asked. My discretion had been needled and harassed for so long that now it had slunk away. "You haven't said anything but you must know I'm dying to find out. What were you guys up to?"

"There's good news but I promised Dickens I'd wait until it was final before I said anything."

"Oh. Okay."

"A promise is a promise, right? A few things still need to fall into place. I'll tell you as soon as I can."

"For sure, no problem."

I got dressed again. I was glad to be wearing army pants. They made me feel tough. I went downstairs and put on a Red House Painters CD. I wanted to conceal my lowered spirits behind some maudlin tunes. I set the table while Marcus served up the smoked chicken rigatoni. It seemed I'd arrived at a dicey point in my life: pessimism felt cowardly and optimism felt stupid. To hear this, some people would steer me to the self-help section; I made a mental note to pick up more Russian novels.

Saturday morning, whatever it was that Marcus had accomplished in LA didn't bring his work to a halt. As soon as breakfast was done he eased his way back into his piles of notes and collection of drafts. Without any preliminary announcements this time, so I wasn't politely chauffeured home. I liked to watch Marcus's expression as he concentrated. Exasperation flickered, then sorrow flashed, then triumph sneaked its way in. I'd been perched at the kitchen island with the Saturday paper spread before me. Now I headed to a beanbag chair. What with all the sex, I hadn't got much sleep the night before and my breakfast rush was subsiding. Rocks was crashed out after a hard morning gnawing tennis balls. Somehow, everything was adding up to permission to nap.

I dreamed of being the first one to spy the rent sign above Antonetta Clothing during one of those cruel mid-nineties summers when Toronto was taking global warming way too seriously. Maxi had air conditioners poking out of every one of her Bathurst Street windows but the attic was a furnace. I dreamed of being the first one to make friends with zaftig Antonetta and talk price. The rent was more than I could afford, but Granny Grover had croaked the year before, after a decade of mistaking my dad for her husband, and left me a small bundle. I knew it was weird for Maxi to think of me leaving Bathurst Street and even weirder for her to think of me leaving first. Then she invited me out to dinner, cheap Chinese on Spadina, just the way I liked it. Basically, she'd signed the lease already so hopefully I didn't mind but if I did she could hire a lawyer to break it, no apartment was ever going to be worth our friendship. I couldn't really afford it so she was actually doing me a favour.

It was a weird feeling to awake from a dream that was essentially true. Marcus was on the phone again. Whatever he had to discuss was obviously top secret; he was deep into undertones. His loft went from being the most comfortable place in the world to substantially less so. I got on my coat so that by the time his call was over I was ready to go.

"I'm out of here," I said. "Obviously, I'm in the way."

"No, what makes you say that?"

"The way you have to whisper your business calls, maybe?"

"You were asleep."

"Initially, but not during the part where I was walking around."

"I guess I was letting you do your own thing. I guess I thought it would be okay if I did mine. I guess I thought we would be good at that."

"You're doing a lot of guesswork all of a sudden."

Rocks had picked up right away on the new scent in the air. Now he looked over at Marcus, then hopefully back at me, like a kid with sweet intentions in a divorce movie. "Am I supposed to be on probation now, is that it? I bet Tara never has to go on probation."

"You know what, Bess, I don't have the time for this. Maybe you should go home and try to relax. I'll get you a cab."

I was out the door immediately, thinking it would serve Marcus right if I was raped in his alley before I reached the street. I thought I heard Rocks woof after me but it might have been wishful thinking. Who had I been kidding with the connubial bliss routine? I'd woken up in Pyongyang. I made a cab pull a U-turn then gave Maxi's address. Maxi was my only possible source of sanity. Seeing Maxi was a matter of life or straitjacket. I had never needed anyone more than her and I had never needed her more. When I got to Crawford Street she and Tom were just leaving.

"Hi there, Babe. *The Beach* was great, you should have come. Tom and I are going to St. Lawrence Market."

The party was approaching in such a blurry rush it was already time to buy the produce. Maxi preferred orderly St. Lawrence to raggedy Kensington with its blaring reggae and piles of hairy coconuts.

"Hi there, Bess." Tom saw the madness in my eyes. "Excuse me, ladies, while I warm up the Jeep. It's another cold one, Christ."

"Maxi, I really need to talk. I just had a huge fight with Marcus."

"Oh no! What about the party?"

"I don't know about the party. I don't know a fucking thing right now."

"Wait there, Babe. Don't move, I'll be right back."

After a quick briefing, Tom drove off like a rally driver late for Khartoum. Maxi headed back my way full of industrial-strength sympathy for rapid results, I could see it in her glint and stride. "Come inside, I'll make you tea," she said.

I knew better than to take off my jacket.

"So what happened?"

"I woke up from a nap and the next thing I knew I was yelling at him."

"Bess! You know you shouldn't nap."

"He was refusing to tell me anything that went on in LA. He and Tara have got some code of *omertà* going or something. I don't know what gives."

"You don't seriously think that Tara is interested in Marcus romantically, do you, Bess? That would be ridiculous."

"No, it's not that. It's just—why doesn't he trust me?"

"Listen, Babe. It's sweet of you to try and find out what you can, but I can always squeeze something important into my rewrite. So go back to Marcus and make up. The party is on no matter what, I'm warning you."

I had thought I was going to get a chance to cry and be reminded I'd be fine on my own but I guessed not. We hurried up to College Street. Maxi figured we'd gain a minute or two that way. I let her grab the first taxi. I was scared Marcus wouldn't answer his door, just leave me pounding outside in the winter glare. Soon I would be seeing either Marcus or my stupid self, dully reflected. For preliminary punishment I gave the cabbie all my change.

Marcus didn't answer his door. I tried several bangs and a kick. I could dash to St. Lawrence Market to find Maxi and drag her to a bar but I doubted I was that kind of drinker. I could beg to use the bakery phone. I could carefully toss gravel at Marcus's expensive windows. I could die of exposure on his doorstep. I'd already left his place once that day. It was going to be hard to leave twice.

"ROCKS," I screamed.

Rocks would not let pride go before affection.

"ROCKS!" I yowled from my inner recesses.

Rocks came careening around the corner completely enthusiastic about the day and not at all confused by the way matters had played out. Marcus soon followed.

"Hello Bess," he said in a freighted tone, like he was telling me ten things at once.

"Marcus, I'm so sorry for disappointing you. I was being really unreasonable. You're so right, we each have our own things to do. I respect that, I promise you. Holy fuck."

He was having a hard time putting me down.

"You don't disappoint me, Bess, not at all. I'm sorry that I have to be secretive."

It was a marvel to get back indoors. I felt like a political exile returned home for a UN–sponsored election. Rocks was twining around our legs like they were an obstacle course he'd been ordered through by a West Point sergeant. When we bent down to pat him, he hit the ground pronto, fumbling for a bit of beta-dog humility. I gaily slapped the doggy pecs.

"I love you Rocks, I really do!" I made the mistake of beaming at Marcus right after this.

We ran for cover, to bed. It felt like we were kissing down there as well. The kind of sex where funk plays in your head—"Atomic Dog" to be specific—loudly. We both apologized more in depth afterward, me explaining that I was PMS City, not that that was any excuse for jealousy. Marcus said he hoped this was the last time he'd keep me out of the loop. A lot of it had to do with Maxi's article and the temptation I'd feel, understandably, to tell her whatever I could.

"She's a plunderer, that Maxine," Marcus said.

"She's got the guts for it."

"Don't you mean the shamelessness?"

"I'll get back to you on that."

After Marcus woke up from his nap—we were a regular kindergarten class—we went out for Korean. He insisted on treating, so to make him happy I ordered as much as I could. When he dropped me off outside the Maxi Pad we said goodbye with as much awkwardness suppressed as possible. I'd wanted to get home in any case, having required a feminine hygiene product by the time we made our way from the kimchee to the hot pot. Also, I wanted to start packing for Belgium. I fished out my duffel bag and dropped anything in there that could pass for charming. Audrey Hepburn was born in Belgium and in honour of that I wanted every element of gamine going. I was beginning to realize what a good thing it was that I was getting away for a while. Some of my reflexes badly needed resetting.

Maxi called Sunday afternoon with good news and bad. The good news was that she had just victoriously emailed off her article: 347 words over her word count but Sue could deal with that. The bad news was that Tara had showed up at Boost Zone to join in the Sunday afternoon Boot Camp class. Maxi didn't like to deprive herself of the after-class Zen state but hated doing the funky chicken warm-up to get there and found it hard not to grunt during the burpees. Worse, she had a zit stewing—her own private Vesuvius, festering beneath the skin of her right cheek. It was the first time I thought I'd heard tears in Maxi's voice.

"Turn the other cheek, maybe?"

"Honestly, Babe, it's so big it's giving me a headache."

"Can you ice it?"

"Oh God, I suppose so. Why me? And I don't think Tom is getting me a Valentine's gift. He called just now to say see you tomorrow and then as a mere afterthought wished me Happy Valentine's as if he was, I don't know . . ."

"Wishing you luck getting a dryer at the laundromat?"

"Precisely."

"What a tool. What did you get him?"

"I couldn't decide between silk boxers and a massage or champagne at a jazz bar."

The February magazines would have been unstinting in their suggestions. Maxi would have bought her annual *Cosmo*.

"How about chocolate mousse served off your torso?"

"I ended up going for sex dice and a feminist porno."

"Very thoughtful."

"Plus I made him a certificate for a you-know-what."

"Wow, you went all out. All I got Marcus is an *I Love My Human* water bowl for Rocks."

"Babe, just so you know, I didn't get you a birthday present. On top of the party, I mean."

"No fucking kidding. Don't scare me. And don't look now, it's snowing."

"Bloody hell, hell, hell, I already worked my upper body to death in Boot Camp. God, what a pain."

I sympathized. Boot Camp was so tough that completing it felt like getting over the flu.

"It's supposed to trail off by evening."

"Well, there's no way I'm shovelling, not today. I don't care who trips and breaks what."

I could hear CBC radio horns joyfully, complicatedly tooting; Maxi appreciated classical music for the prefab grace. I could also hear her inhaling. Together she and Vivaldi had earned her a smoke.

"Tell you what, Maxi. I'll shovel for you. I won't even come in because I know you're busy."

"Are you serious?"

"Sure. Now that I don't have Rocks around I lack activity."

"Well, the shovel is round the side of the house. Babe, guess what?"

"Tom is really a robot?"

"No. In three years we will have been friends for exactly half our lives."

"You're definitely my better half."

"Okay, go."

"Okay, bye."

I went over at twilight after the snow stopped and the sky had cleared to indigo, as bright as dark could get. I thought this might be my favourite part of the day, the obvious giving way to the subtle. I kept my promise to Maxi and didn't disrupt her party prep. I knew there'd be "To Do" lists lined up for her attention like nervy whippets. Marcus had promised to help me however he could in getting through the thing. He knew that in the plainest way possible, all I wanted was to be thirty-five. I stuck a little something in Maxi's mailbox to help us both get in the party mood and stay there.

A MODERN GASH HONESTY CHALLENGE

Tip-top Tips for a Killer Bash

By Bess Grover

1. **The best thing about a party is:**
   A) All the attention.
   B) Getting your social payback taken care of.
   C) The party post-mortem—dissecting it afterward for juicy moments of disgrace. Preferably that of your guests, but don't get left out unnecessarily.

2. **The best thing you can do for your guests is to:**
   A) Suck up to all comers, enemies included.
   B) Ensure a glassware shortage to bring out their primitive instincts.
   C) Crowd 'em in—no matter how uncomfortable it gets, you're Queen Bee.

3. **The sign of a successful bash is:**
   A) Dancing to your old Blondie records—you've got the moves of a veteran peeler and a heart of glass.
   B) Meeting your neighbours and that adorable police officer. Disturbing the peace? You certainly hope so!
   C) A cat fight.

4. **The ideal party guest is:**
   A) Booze laden.
   B) Willing to clean up.
   C) Good looking, rich and male; now you know why you bothered.

5. **Your basic party motto:**
   A) Drink up, you wussies!
   B) Tell me I'm great!
   C) If I don't get laid out of this, never again!

Toxic

Marcus called at the crack of dawn on February 14 to wish me a happy birthday. He was totally groggy himself but he wanted both of us get up early so as to make the most of the day. He told me what my present was. The first chance we got we were off to Antwerp's trendy beat, where I got to pick out anything I wanted from any boutique I wanted as long as it was something I couldn't get anywhere else and everyone would ask me where I got it. Dries van Noten, I was thinking immediately. Something ingeniously ethnic inflected.

"Wow," I said. "Something to do and something to keep. It's the best gift ever."

"You owe Rocks for that. I wanted to get you rubber gloves and spark plugs."

"Happy Valentine's Day to you."

"Pity the poor fools who have only that to think about."

"Speaking of, Tom is getting a BJ certificate."

"Serves him right. Remind me never to become the man who has everything."

Marcus's brother, Will, was driving in after work to pick up Rocks and take him back to Guelph. Marcus and I were flying into Brussels on Tuesday and staying for a day to soak up some NATO atmosphere. Marcus agreed that if the mood hit us we could zip over to The Hague to take in a tour of the International Criminal Court. He reminded me that we'd only postponed our trip to Paris; one day we would definitely hang out at UNESCO. Marcus was bringing his "vintage" Burberry trench coat to Europe. He apologized in advance for the aroma.

Funnily enough, I had a rubber-glove purchase high on my birthday agenda. I'd decided that in honour of Maxi's hospitality that evening I would have a Maxi-style day at home, cleaning house beyond the cursory: washing baseboards, wiping light fixtures, scouring the burner pans as well as the stove top. It was hard to believe I had been in the Maxi Pad for six weeks already. I thought this must be how parents feel when their newborn graduates to infant in a spasm. Maxi had borrowed the latest family maid to clean up after her so there actually wasn't that much to disinfect. Happily, neither was there a slew of exhausting birthday phone calls to get through, the party's major saving grace. Not even word from Maxi. I knew she'd be busy ordering herself around her kitchen like a hot-headed French chef—she could take the heat—then scenting her powder room with Windex and going over her carpets with her top-of-the-line cordless. I had promised to get over there nice and early. Maxi was going to be busy passing around blood-orange screwdrivers, so I had to meet and greet. Marcus was going to connect with me there.

After some contemplative Alice Munro in the afternoon—a bit of *The Love of a Good Woman*, a bit of *Something I've Been Meaning to Tell You*, which were so engrossing in their just gestures that I got an inactivity chill—I popped into a hot shower and thought about being halfway to seventy. I wondered if I'd still be able to sit cross-legged. I wondered if my hair would curl as much if it was grey. I wondered if I'd have learned how to make casseroles, nip people in their buds and declare myself bluntly instead of resorting to hyper rigmaroles. I wondered if Maxi and I would swap stories about our estrogen-therapy treatments and watercolour classes. Towelling off, I wondered if she would approve of my outfit for that night. For the first time in a decade and a half I had composed an important one without bugging her for advice. I'd picked up a pair of red satin hiphuggers at a teen store in the Dufferin Mall and paired them with a black tank top, a red bra underneath, matching thong included. Maxi had been trying to convince me that thongs were more, not less, comfortable. I'd see. So would Marcus. My butt looked like wind cheeks on an old-fashioned map. It had lost a little rotundity, but exclusive Brussels chocolatiers could soon remedy that. Marcus and I planned to gorge on the kinds of truffles that were misshapen in their handcraftedness. And we were going to track down some local sprouts, ideally caramelized.

Maxi gave me the all-clear at five-thirty and I headed over right away. The snow had picked up again mid-afternoon. It seemed to be falling with tact rather than malice, but it was steady. I did a quick sweep of Maxi's walk and steps before I went in. Her zit wasn't nearly as bad as she'd said. At least that was my first reaction. In the wrong light you could glean its heft. Maxi had on hostess-privilege strappy sandals, red fishnets overtop black, and a slinky, black silk Costume National apron dress that showed off her stern carriage. Crawford Street smelled deliciously of roasted red peppers. Maxi did just as good a job handling food as handling penises, if she did say so herself. Now she was performing her final touches, tending to a percussion section's worth of pots and pans with the practised rhythms of an orchestra conductor. She'd crafted beet risotto, tomato-sausage fusilli and tandoori chicken glowing with cayenne and paprika.

"Red feast or what, Maxi—this looks wonderful."

"Come check out the dining room. The apps are ready to go."

I thought maybe we should have invited Sweeney Todd to dinner. The discs of white bocconcini interspersed with hothouse tomato slices for the Caprese salad looked a bit like chopped bones amidst evisceration. This was merely awaiting a douse of Balsamic reduction. A plate of rosy carpaccio nestled beside a platter of oily smoked salmon. "Surf 'n turf, I love it."

"I was afraid someone was going to say that."

"What can I do to help?"

"Nothing. Put out some red cocktail napkins beside the kalamata olives."

"Pink pistachios, nice. And I love the apple bowl."

"That's just for décor. I'll make Tom a crumble before they go soft. Oh, and you can put on a CD."

"Any requests?"

"Everything But the Girl, greatest hits."

I appreciated Maxi's diligence. Her bare scapula bones were fluttering as she fussed with candles, table settings and final spicings. Without Maxi around to take things so seriously I'd never have been able to entertain so casually. I knew what my job was. I had to strike a balance between playing things up and playing things down.

"Maxi, this is going to be a blast. I think the fun thing to do would be to start the drinking. What do you say?"

"Sorry, I beat you to it. Let me pour you one. Happy birthday, Babe."

"Happy orgasm, Maxi. I just know tonight's the night. This house, that dress, you and Tom doing battle against Josephine together—you can't lose."

"What do the French call orgasms again?"

"*La petite mort*."

"Death?"

"Of-the-ego kind of thing. What gives? You look stunned."

"I'm trying to cut down on my facial expressions. They've classified eighteen different kinds of smiles and only the crow's foot kind produces pleasant feelings."

"Maxi, you missed your calling. You should have been autistic."

"Do you mind sitting on the bathroom stool, Babe? I put a cushion on it. You'll be tall, not short."

"No problem. Put Sherry and Brian side by side. That way they can make the most of their baby-sitting expenses."

"I'm usually so good at doing table placement but I couldn't figure out what I wanted this time. My mother as far away as possible, naturally. Don't be mad, Babe, I took one end of the table and gave her the other one."

The door knocker pounded like a high-court judgment. That was it. For the rest of the evening Maxi and I were no longer alone in the way we were capable of being alone, in the way that only females can be alone—midwife alone, menstrual-hut alone, bastard-done-me-wrong alone. Assuming it was Tom, Maxi led the way. Too late. Josephine barged in, in a full-length mink and a cloud of Chanel No. 5. Bernard Bishop followed, with a tap on the open door. He was wearing an Astrakhan hat he might have filched from Solzhenitsyn.

"So this is the mysterious house," said Josephine.

"Welcome, welcome," said Bernard.

"Hello, Daddy, come in."

Maxi passed me the parental pelts. I shoved them as far back in the closet as they would go. Josephine had brought pumps in a shoe bag and Bernard was wearing rubbers, so there was some fractious lining up for the front hall chair going on when Tom arrived, carrying a gigantic bouquet of ferns, baby's breath and uniformly white flowers plus a medium-sized box from Godiva.

"Happy Valentine's Day, everybody. Here you go, Max."

"Tim, how lovely," said Josephine.

"Marvellous," said Bernard.

"Shit," said Maxi.

"Really now, Max, you know better than that. Excuse her, Tim."

"It's just that I've used up all my vases. I'm not sure what to put these in."

"I'll help you figure it out," I said.

"Right! Bess and I will nip into the kitchen and then we'll be right back, everybody. Here, Babe, you take them."

I could barely walk without a machete. “Two bills at least,” I said as soon we were out of earshot.

“Don’t, don’t even try. My God, I am so humiliated. White flowers? White! That’s it. My night is ruined.”

“Maybe Tom has a cunning linguistics voucher tucked away in his jacket pocket?”

“Spare me the cracks, Bess, please. If you can’t be supportive then leave me alone.”

“Sorry, sorry. Tom can be such a jerk. But you know that, right?”

“I’m always putting up with such bollocks from people. What is it about me? Do they think I’m made of steel?”

Maxi hacked at the stems with her largest carving knife, battlefield-amputation style, then shoved the bouquet into a red metal fireman’s bucket she had under her sink and which I’d filled with cold water. The blooms were using up half an acre of counter space. Obviously Maxi had to get them out of the way. What with the high Crawford Street ceilings, there was room on top of the fridge. I did my best to help hoist. Maxi didn’t want to be entering any wet party-dress contest with fathers around.

“So these are the famous new kitchen cupboards,” said Josephine. “I’m sure they absolutely had to be changed!” There was no stopping her.

“A good investment I’m sure,” said Bernard.

“Sound thinking, sir,” said Tom.

“You were all supposed to wait and let me bring the drinks tray out to the living room,” Maxi said.

“No citrus on an empty stomach for me,” said Josephine. “Should we have brought wine?”

"Out, out, out of the kitchen, now!"

I opened a bottle of Turning Leaf while Maxi added more hooch to the punch. The door knocker again. My parents this time plus Sherry and Brian in a cheerful convoy. Sherry and my mom had on red dresses and Brian and my dad had on red ties, for which they all received immediate congratulations. Sherry handed me a hard, red-wrapped rectangle which I was pretty sure was the new Ondaatje. My parents had already promised me a waffle iron, which I'd pick out at the Burlington Home Depot the next time I was home. Everyone's hair was dusted with sparkles of snow. The highway had been slow going.

"Ask Maxi for a tour," I whispered to my mother.

I was scared Josephine wouldn't do the same no matter how much she wanted one. She greeted my mom with arms outstretched. My mother's placidity tended to bring out even more drama in Josephine, as if she got to be the ornery regent with a demure lady-in-waiting in a Stratford production of a cone-headed history play. My mother took a fast gulp. Tom was still cheek by jowl with Bernard Bishop, the two of them looking like capitalist versions of Soviet statues. Brian was looking sharp in a suit, too, a rare occurrence for a man with a home office. Sherry was admiringly stroking Maxi's couch and putting up with my dad's teasing. I was ready for a refill, the hit of vodka now so strong as to seem medicinal. Maxi and I clinked fresh tumblers. Her eyes had gone extra glassy. I hoped we wouldn't find her slack-jawed in a bright red bath before dessert. I also hoped she hadn't overheard the bit about Josephine's suspicions, confided to my mother, that Maxi's English pram had taught her early how to grandstand. My mother was amused to hear that I was the one with the common sense.

The door knocker reported again. I jumped to it. Marisa was under the porch light. Hank stood beside her, licking his chops to see Tara in the flesh making her way up the walk. The snow was acting like it had been invited to the party, coming on stronger, muscling in the door. "Come in one, come in all," I said.

"Many happy returns."

"Thanks, Marisa. I'm glad you got here safely."

"Ready for menopause, fogey?"

"Gee, Hank, thanks for asking. Actually, I could do with a hot flash if you don't close that door. Tara, meet my team."

Tara had invested in the Gucci Fall '96 red velvet pantsuit. As soon as she could, Marisa pried Hank away, who'd wanted to know whether Tara could score him some Evoke. Tara handed me a red envelope. She didn't have a gift coordinator, she had a selection of sponsored charities. I'd gratefully chosen Engineers Without Borders and insisted I didn't need a receipt, but it looked like I'd gotten one anyway. Maxi had gotten a little Tiffany's something.

"Key chain for the new house," Tara told me. "Obvious, but good obvious, right?"

"Totally."

"It's a thanks-for-the-attention gift. Even though she did call my ex. He didn't talk but I hear his buddy did. Isn't it nice to know that I played with all the kids at the Stanford Biosciences Christmas party? Hey there, Hostess Mostest, this is for you. Thanks for everything."

"Oh my God. I've been so busy with the party I honestly never expected—"

As soon as she could, Maxi would counter with a thank-you present for the thank-you present.

"Stop right there, Melanie Wilkes, because you know I don't give a damn. Hey, look who's here."

Marcello strode in, looking like a lad Caravaggio would have immortalized for his brawn. We ladies all got kissed and Maxi got a bottle of Amarone. From now on Marcello could hoist the drinks tray. Hank looked like he wanted Tara to do the two-step. Sherry was shaking her head no at Josephine, to which Josephine nodded yes. Tom and Bernard were still talking about grabbing the ministry boys by the nuts. Marisa and my mother were laughing as they passed each other the pistachios. Brian was scrutinizing Maxi's gorgeous Ed Burtynsky photo of densified scrap metal.

"Rust can be gorgeous," I said.

"Bess, I tell you, I'm PROUD of our patina."

It was time to start missing Marcus. I hoped he hadn't had last-minute thoughts about getting me a Valentine's gift. I'd made him promise the trip would be it. It was five to eight. Soon Maxi would want to start the shepherding to the dining room, the giving of powder room directions and the double-checking of boy–girl alternations. I forced myself to the centre of the party scrum.

"I got laser eye surgery done last year," Tom was saying.

"Now do you think that was wise, Tim? I heard it causes glaring."

Maxi glared, at Josephine. She was right; her mother was possibly the Kissinger of public relations. I saw Tara wink at Maxi. That might help, or not.

"There's been a lot of progress with the technique," said Tom.

"Bess thinks progress is a myth. Don't you, Babe?"

"One of the nicer ones, yeah. It's up there with karma."

"You two are so cynical. I don't know how you go on living." Josephine's wine glass was running dangerously low.

"Go ahead and dream of progress if you want to, Mother. No one's stopping you."

"Apparently, everyone you dream of is yourself," I mused.

"How embarrassing is that?" said Tara.

"Well, I think it makes sense," Maxi said. I knew she thought of dreams as shampoo. She only noticed them when she didn't have them.

"The self obsessed do seem to get the bonus points in this life," I said.

"I wish everyone was a little more self-obsessed," said Tara. "It would give Courtney Cox and Jennifer Aniston a break."

"So what's it like to be *famous*, Tara?" Sherry wanted to know.

"Not erotic."

"That's too bad!" Hank had caught that one. He could sniff out spicy in a Las Vegas second.

Eight on the dot. If Marcus didn't get there soon I was definitely in trouble. Maxi poured my mother a refill with the last drips of the cocktail pitcher. The party chatter was lively to the point of too loud; I could barely hear Everything But the Girl trilling about apron strings. I suspected Marcello had enjoyed a few preliminary drinks before arriving. Tom's grin was fully functioning but I thought he'd probably be glad when Marcus got there, too. My parents had helpfully commandeered Maxi's parents for a two-on-two. Josephine was claiming to be jealous of my mom's impending grandmotherhood. Then, majestically, the door knocker sounded one last time. Finally, we were going from thirteen to the full fourteen.

Fifteen, actually. Rocks was sitting on the front porch wearing a big red bow around his neck that interfered badly with his ear droop. He looked like a junior varsity wrestler dressed up for the prom. In honour of the occasion, Marcus had wiped his eyes free of gunk, but there was still a spittle situation. Marcus had on tuxedo pants and wet red Converses that must have been cold in the snow.

"The highway out of Guelph is closed," Marcus said. Then he had to kiss me before saying anything else, a warm, sweet one like a raspberry tart fresh from the oven. "Will is driving in once they plow. Rocks and I talked it over and he wouldn't hear of missing the party. He wanted to bring you a bone but I told him never to regift."

No worries about wet paws—Marcus had brought four little red booties.

"It won't be a party if someone doesn't make a fool of themselves," I said. "Nice of Rocks to volunteer."

"What's going on?" asked Maxi.

Marcus started to explain but Rocks was already on the loose among the mothers. Josephine admired anyone with bark and bite.

"Fine. But I'm warning you, Babe, now this party is going to be all about the dog."

"That's okay," I said, trying to sound like I didn't mean it as much as I did.

With her system of claps, pats and announcements, Maxi soon got everyone seated, dished up and wine poured. And in her case poured again. As a birthday benevolence I was allowed to sit beside my guy. Bernard, to my right, kept giving me his specialty sideways hugs. Tara was across from me. Josephine was safely bunkered in between Marisa and my dad. Maxi was flanked by Brian and Hank.

"Whoa, who put a gel on the lens?" Marcus ogled his red plateful. His T-shirt said "The Devil Made Me Do It" in black flocking.

"Nice to see you shaved for the occasion," sniped Tom, enthroned between Tara and Marisa. "Jesus, what a slob!"

Marcus knew I didn't mind rubbing up rough against his cheek; it was extra proof that he was there.

"An average man shaves eight metres off his face per lifetime," I said.

That got everybody talking. Then Josephine made an announcement to the effect that she was dumping her tech stocks; it was a big bubble, she was divesting it all. That brought up living-off-the-land fantasies. I knew right away I wanted a goat farm to save money on cheese. Tara offered to start up an apple orchard next door. Marcus went for a sugar bush. Hank was going to pick olives in Greece. Marisa was happy with her stables. My mom went along with my dad's trout farm. Sherry and Brian wanted to grow organic herbs. Josephine insisted on an oil patch; Bernard agreed to golf nearby. Maxi simply couldn't play along, she was a city girl through and through, so Marcus gave her a Club Med to run in Aruba.

When I offered to help collect the appetizer plates, Maxi snapped at me to sit down, then quickly thanked me for offering but said definitely not, Tara neither. Marcus had had seconds of the first course. Tom had forgotten to put his knife and fork in the "done" position but Maxi did it for him. He was too busy imitating a Québécois judge to notice. Tom didn't have quite the way with accents that he hoped. Josephine had not cleaned her plate—an old dieting strategy. Bernard whispered to his daughter about how delicious everything was.

While Hank told a loud joke about nuns and fish, Maxi rotated her main courses around the table wearing red oven mitts and a Food Network smile. When she sat down, Josephine raised her a glass. Maxi cautiously returned the gesture, like a leader of the former Eastern Bloc nation saluting Brezhnev on a state visit. Just then, Rocks made a move. He'd been snoozing at one end of the table and now he made his way to the other—under, over and past everyone's legs—a stadium wave in subtext.

"No scraps, please," Marcus said. "He's already gorged on olives."

"Nonsense," said Josephine. She'd probably lured Rocks her way with a chunk of chorizo. "It's Valentine's Day, have a heart."

Then Marcus had to whip out his harmonica. Rocks howled along, nose aloft. My dad got up to get his camera. Then we all needed to settle down and compliment Maxi meaningfully.

"What a wonderful eye you have, Maxine," my mom said. "This house could be in *Chatelaine*."

I knew Maxi would have sooner posed knees-wide for *Hustler* but she did her best. "Thanks, Mrs. Grover. I'm counting on your help with the garden. I'm really looking forward to doing some pruning."

"Prunes, dear? No thank you."

Forty years of raucous kindergarten classes had interfered badly with my mother's hearing. But Maxi wasn't taking the bait, so no one else did either. Marcus saved the day by tapping on his glass and calling us to order. I had pretty well known there were going to be toasts and I was ready with fulsome stuff. I was determined to do justice to everyone's efforts. I knew dinner party magic was hard won.

"To Bess, everyone," said Marcus. "And to her first feature-film job of her very own."

"Hear, hear," said Bernard Bishop. "Marvellous."

"Thanks, everyone, but that would be a cartoon. My first animation job. Not that I'm not grateful. And I won't be on my own, Hank will be there."

"With a big box of Kleenex," Hank said to my mom, who batted her napkin at him, flicking a blob of red garlic butter into his moustache.

"Congratulations on that gig, Bess, absolutely. You gotta love the NFB." I could tell Tara was excited for more than just me. "But when Marcus said 'feature' he meant it."

She looked back over at Marcus. He was being an utter ham, thoughtfully twirling his wine inside his glass, slowly clearing his throat. Then he looked up.

"Tara is producing my feature. I'm directing. We got the green light last week in LA. We haven't got all the money together yet but things are looking good. We're hoping to shoot next fall. A co-production with an up-and-coming Canadian foley artist, if she agrees."

"Enough about me, here's to you guys. Wow!"

Applause burst surprisingly plentiful from a dozen pairs of hands, mine especially. Rocks woofed, loving the consensus. I took an early moment out of the ruckus to hug Marcus, an embrace of "The End"–style magnitude. Then Tom reached across the table to pump his buddy's hand. Whatever I saw in Tara's eyes impelled me to jump from my chair. Tara jumped up too. We intercepted each other right behind Josephine, both of us up for schoolgirl hops and squeals. When we let each other go I noticed my parents' happy glances at each other. Hank clinked glasses with them again. Sherry couldn't stop hooting. Brian and Marcello were still clapping. Maxi was either amazed or still vetoing excessive facial expression.

"Well earned," said Marisa, when I sat back down.

"Now can I find out what this thing is about?" asked Tom. "Christ!"

"It's an Academy Awards caper, my friend. A slimy producer arranges a sting operation to dick with procedures so the Oscar vote comes in in his favour and he can make millions off his crappy thriller."

"Don't believe the hype," I gathered.

"We're hoping to get Hugh Grant," said Tara. "He's keen to do more evil."

Now Maxi's eyes clouded over. The last person she wanted hanging around Toronto was Elizabeth Hurley. Oscar's virtue was to be restored by a sassy, kick-boxing FBI operative posing as an ICM agent. Cate Blanchett was their first choice.

"I'm just embarrassed by how badly I want a blonde," Tara confided to the table. Tara's only on-camera role was going to be the movie within the movie, for which they were hoping a lot of A-list Canadians would volunteer.

"May I ask what this thrilling film is to be called?" asked Josephine.

"*Hollywood Gold*," said Marcus.

"GENIUS!" I couldn't help yelling it.

That night there was no other place for me to be. Maxi's dining room held it all—a perfect junction of my past and my plans. It was my first taste of a truly ripe moment. Spring and fall had got it on and made a brand new season for me, mixing up cherry blossoms with golden wheat. Now I understood full-fledged happiness. From then on, whenever I could, I'd take a little culmination, add some momentum and stop my whining. I had only ever whined deep inside my head or to Maxi. I could hardly wait to tell her those days were over. But she was three people away, with Bernard, my mother and Hank between us. Then she was rising uneasily to her feet. Maxi was by no means timid but she still hated to address a group.

"Hello everyone, thank you for coming to my home. My new home, as most of you do know. The thing is, it's Bess's birthday. My best friend, Bess. Hi Babe! Isn't she the lucky one? Pretty sneaky with the luck there, Bess. I should have known yours would explode one day. I guess I'll just have to try harder with mine. Well, I thought it would be a nice idea, because Bess hates birthday cakes—"

"Not *hate*, exactly," I said to my mom.

Maxi shrugged. Josephine hated shrugs.

"Okay, she doesn't hate them. Pardon me for living but the graveyard's full! What *I* thought of doing, to be nice, was to place thirty-five red candles all over my house. In honour, quite frankly, of lucky Bess and her lucky night." Maxi stepped over to pull on an unfortunately sticky sideboard drawer. "Here are some lighters and some matches. Knock yourselves out, everybody. We'll meet back here for red fruit salad with grenadine cream."

"Quite the dramatic gesture," said Josephine.

"I think it's a lovely idea," said Marisa.

"Although it breaks my heart to leave this table," said Tara. "Nice going, Michelin Star."

"Maxi, this is an amazing party, thank you so much," I said, squeezing a stack of dirty plates onto the kitchen counter. I'd gone where nobody else dared: the kitchen mêlée. "You really outdid yourself this time. The food is delicious, the house looks lovely. And your mother is even kind of behaving herself."

"She made fun of your pants."

"She's right, they are ridiculous. And to think I almost wasn't going to take them to Europe."

We scraped a couple of plates but the garbage was full to the brim. Even Maxi was temporarily defeated.

"Leave these for now. Come out back with me while I have a smoke."

"Party hooky. Long time no play."

Josephine already knew Maxi smoked but would tease her loudly about wrinkles if she caught her. Maxi had Camels and matches stashed in a jacket pocket and snow boots by her back kitchen door. I got to wear her navy cashmere, as pliant as a bathrobe. Maxi finally got her cigarette lit after five scowling tries. The snow had tapered off but the sky was still cottoned over with sodden, orange-tinted grey that looked like the underside of an elevated hell. The shivering trees lifted their arms as if any warmth would do. Candles were starting to flicker in Maxi's windows.

"It's a great party," I began again.

"Yes, well."

"Tom does look good."

"I went upstairs and ripped up the you-know-what. The gift equilibrium was just ruined. What is he, on auto-boyfriend? Bloody quite frankly hell."

Maxi was in the kind of mood where she found the lit end of her cigarette the only thing worth looking at. When she dragged on it, it was if she wanted to suck as much of herself inside herself as possible.

"Maybe he thought you were too busy with the party to get him anything and he didn't want to put you on the spot?"

"Bess, I really don't want to be humoured right now if you don't mind. Especially not by someone so pleased with herself."

"So what?"

"You heard me."

"I just didn't understand you."

"I love the way you pressured me into having a big birthday party for you—"

"Maxi, you know I didn't really—"

"—Only to rub my nose in all your fabulous achievements right in front of my parents."

"You should be happy I'm finally doing better." I wasn't even thinking in terms of Maxi's moral duty; I just wanted her to be glad I'd pay for more of our cabs and dinners. "My doing better doesn't have anything to do with you."

"Oh great, thanks a lot."

I felt like Maxi's cigarette—flung in the snow and ground under her heel.

"Maxi, that's not what I meant. What I meant was that you shouldn't drive yourself crazy making it about you. It's just about me. You still get to be about you. You know how great you are."

Her reply was the bang of the kitchen door behind her. I supposed I should have been grateful that I hadn't been locked out. I sidled back in and shuffled out of the coat. Maxi's coat was off but she'd forgotten her snow boots were still on. She was standing hands on hips, surveying her counters, which were strewn with debris that was all my fault.

"Maxi, you have to relax. You're doing so well. Cover story, Tom, new house—"

"I HATE EVERYTHING!"

"Wow, okay. You'll feel better when we've cleaned up. Here, let me help." I grabbed the designer dish-scrubber I'd got from the art gallery gift shop for one of Maxi's Christmas gag gifts. It had funny little feet and a bright yellow brush sprouting from its head.

"Drop it, Bess. I SAID DROP IT."

She really meant it. To reinforce her point she'd grabbed the brutally massive Solingen that was still lying there from the bouquet hacking. I knew it was worth a fortune, that Maxi wanted it hand washed and out of the way early, that there was nothing truly personal in the way she was waving it at me.

"No, Maxine, you drop it," said Marcus.

He'd been lured in by Maxi's uproar and, to his credit, stayed calm at the sight of his girlfriend being threatened with a butchering by her best friend. Maxi, however, was startled. She whipped around to protest to Marcus. He leaped backwards, knocked into the fridge and struggled to regain his footing while the massive bucket containing Tom's blooms and several of gallons of water tip, tip, tipped, then fell bang onto his head. The next thing Maxi and I knew, Marcus was sprawled unconscious in a puddle of high-end foliage, his forehead leaking fresh red blood all over the clean white lilies. The violent beauty of it was biblical. The smash of it brought others running.

"Check his breathing," said Tara. "I'm just going to tip his head back. He's okay, he's going to be okay. Give him some air. Good work, Bess."

I'd raided the dishtowel drawer and was gently applying pressure. I was also trying to elbow Rocks out of the way. Rocks thought this was fantastic fun. It was no surprise to Rocks when Marcus shortly came to. The sigh that arose was the closest I'd ever experienced to collective. Marcus had a lump truly the size of an egg on his brow, and a dripping cut that definitely needed stitches.

"Nine-one-one says to take him straight to Emerg," Tom informed us, snapping shut his clamshell.

Everyone's pulses were racing except perhaps for Maxi's: she was still standing in the middle of her kitchen holding on tightly to the carving knife. Josephine pulled it out of her hand and tossed it in a drawer. Marisa passed me a bag of peas she'd found in the freezer. I gingerly positioned it on Marcus's forehead.

"I don't eat frozen peas, those were for a twisted ankle," Maxi said.

"Well, well," said Bernard, as if the party was proceeding exactly as it was supposed to.

"Max, I'll call you later, I'm taking Marcus to the hospital," Tom said.

Marcello suddenly remembered some important late-night plans and skedaddled. My parents and Sherry and Brian were going to chance the trip back to Burlington now that the snow had relented. Everyone's farewells were tactful and swift. Everyone's except mine. I let Rocks's enthusiasm for a walk drag me right out Maxi's door without another word. Maxi owed me an explanation, but I owed her time to come up with it. I'd barely been able to look at her, let alone talk to her. The smartest thing to do was go.

"The freak flag is flying high tonight," Tara said as we climbed into the wagon.

"Poor Maxi," I said as I got behind the wheel. "She's wasted."

I assumed Maxi would forgive me that the party had come to a crashing halt. It turned out she couldn't do that. She preferred to bring our friendship to a crashing halt. She couldn't even stay three blocks away. That night, after her mother had seen to it that every candle was blown out, they had gone back to Rosedale, back to where she had another stab at being eighteen. I guessed she wanted to start over without me. At warp speed I'd gone from a supporting role with all the punchlines to an extra with no lines whatsoever.

Seeing Maxi at Glen Road was like visiting her in a sanitorium. She'd drag herself downstairs, deny being depressed and barely invite me to take a seat. She'd have this weird, distant, aggrieved expression on her face, like the Queen listening to everybody around her sing for God to save her. Eventually, I had to stop going.

Then she called out of the blue one day and asked me to drop by.

I knew without asking that she meant Crawford Street. She was there to finish emptying it out. Her parents had rented it to a young family and their au pair. It was her parents' house really, from a financial point of view. I couldn't stand to use the knocker. Maxi opened the door to me like I was a census taker. She did offer to unpack the kettle but I insisted there was no need. Josephine was taking her to an eco lodge in Costa Rica for a few weeks and they were leaving the next day.

"I'm really going to miss you," I said.

The fact was, I already missed her. I knew by then she'd left more than just the neighbourhood. I thought she was desperate. I thought she was cruel. I thought she was terribly sad. But I had never got the hang of telling Maxi exactly how I felt about her.

"I have something for you," she said.

"Are you serious?"

She handed over her *Modern Gash* collection—everything I had ever cooked up, drafted and delivered. The first several years were pasted neatly into a scrapbook. All the rest—whatever had survived—was randomly stuffed between pages in the back.

"You don't want it?"

"No, not really. I should hurry. My mother will be here any moment."

There are all kinds of traditional ways to rupture when it comes to matrimony and business, but no one has ever explained how to go about breaking up with your best friend. Maxi and I were weirdly, shamefully, completely over. In her honour I didn't cry. With the loyalty I had left, I went back to the Maxi Pad instead of Marcus's. I climbed out the kitchen fire escape up onto the gravel roof and waited until I knew she was gone, something I felt in my bones rather than witnessed. I waited for my panic to pass and then sat there a while longer, alone and alive.

The last I heard, Maxi had been accepted into the master's in journalism program at Columbia. I thought she'd make a great mature student. I imagine the New York habits of honking, wanting and wanton ambition are suiting her just fine.

Marcus and I are busy. It's summer 2001—*Hollywood Gold* is finally going into production. He loves when people ask about his scar. He tells them he got it hang-gliding with Rocks.

Looking back, I can see how anything could have happened to Maxi and me. Everything was so loose except for the tightness between us. I hope Maxi escapes herself. I think I've escaped Maxi. To her credit, it wasn't easy. Not all friends are for keeping. I understood that once I understood what I was going to do without her.

Acknowledgements

Thanks to my dream team: my upstanding agent, Samantha Haywood, and my down-and-dirty editor, Janie Yoon—without them it was twice the word count and half the book. Key Porter is in fact full of cool chicks: thanks to Marnie Ferguson, Kendra Michael and Marijke Friesen. Marie-Lynn Hammond was my unstintingly inventive copyeditor. Furthermore, thank you, Jordan Fenn.

Thanks to the editors who have hired me to write for them: Viia Beaumanis, Suzanne Boyd, Leanne Delap, Christine Faulhaber of fabulous Faulhaber PR, Gary MacDougall, Ceri Marsh, Sheree-Lee Olson, Tracy Picha, Lisa Tant and especially Kim Izzo, soul sister extraordinaire.

Thanks to masterful foley artist Andy Malcolm for the fact check. And Lori Waters for the further fact check, just in case he'd gone too easy on me.

Thanks to Rebecca Eckler for being the first person to whom I could show the first draft of this novel because that's the kind of friend she is—reassuring to the point of genius and beautifully speedy with her help.

Thanks to the painter Michael Adamson for the shelter.

Thanks to the poet Morley Nirenberg for the solidarity.

Thanks to Kingi Carpenter for always being wise beyond her years.

Thanks to Angela Grossmann for her kindness, smarts and hilariousness.

Thanks to Louise Hooley for her inveterate delving.

Thanks to Carole McAfee, who is tried and true.

Thanks to Sheila "Lady" McCombe for the many cute tops off her back.

Thanks to Susie Shepherd for answering all my questions.

Thanks to Judy Blumstock, Penelope Buitenhuis, Lisa Cameron, Michele Conroy, Patti Cuccia, Jamie Dolinko, Susan Fancy, Mary Frymire, Sylvene Gilchrist, Leeta Harding, Shelley Harris, Ann Marie Keating, Deirdre Kelly, Leslie Morrison, Jennifer Morton, Sita Power, Laura Repo, Marion Robinson, Sue Steele, Carrie Silverman, Susanne Ballhausen and Nadine Woo, because we chicks go way back.

Thanks to early readers Tony Keller, Cynthia Macdonald, and William Morrasutti for their generous comments.

Thanks to my mother, Margaret McCormack; my father, Anthony Sosnkowski; my brother, Andrew Sosnkowski, and his wife, Rebecca, for all the support and free storage, sometimes of myself. Thanks also to three of my cousins, Terry Kawaja, Maureen McLaughlin and Sandra Strain, for their flowing hospitality.

Thanks to Level V gym, especially Sarah Robichaud, for consistently being my best excuse not to write.

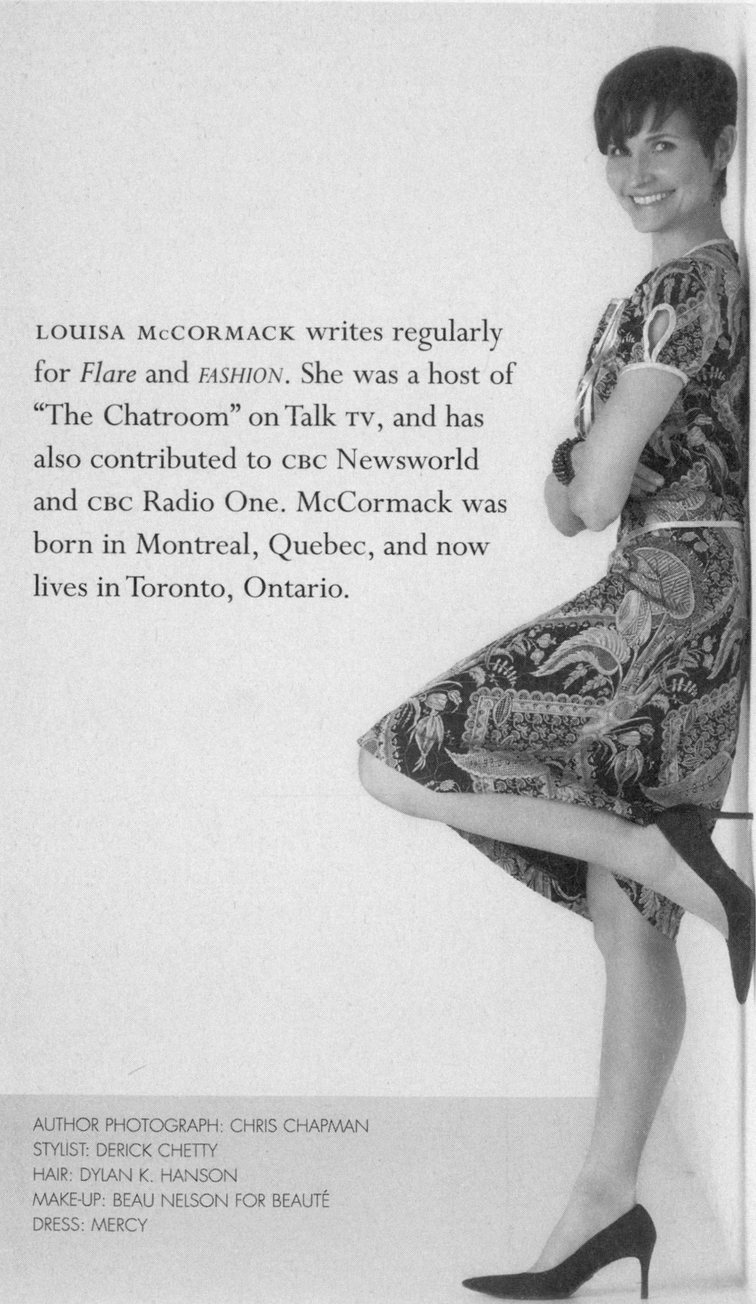

LOUISA McCORMACK writes regularly for *Flare* and *FASHION*. She was a host of "The Chatroom" on Talk TV, and has also contributed to CBC Newsworld and CBC Radio One. McCormack was born in Montreal, Quebec, and now lives in Toronto, Ontario.

AUTHOR PHOTOGRAPH: CHRIS CHAPMAN
STYLIST: DERICK CHETTY
HAIR: DYLAN K. HANSON
MAKE-UP: BEAU NELSON FOR BEAUTÉ
DRESS: MERCY